G000271067

BOOK ONE OF THE YEW TREE CHRONICLES

A RACE THROUGH TIME

BARNABY CREW

Copyright © 2021 by Barnaby Crew

Printed in the United Kingdom

The right of Barnaby Crew to be identified of the author of
this work has been asserted by Barnaby Crew in accordance
with the Copyright, Designs and Patents Act 1988.

All rights reserved. No part of this book may be reproduced
or transmitted in any form or by any means, electronic or
mechanical, including photocopying or recording without the
permission of the author.

Cover Design by www.spiffingcovers.com

ISBN: 9781916299900

First published in Great Britain in 2021 by
goldwingpress.com

CHAPTER ONE

'Spike?'

Spike looked down at his brother. 'Yeah?'

'What d'you think about Mr Price? Really, I mean? D'you think something's happened to him?'

Spike shook his head. 'No, I'm sure he's fine, Bill. Probably just gone off on one of those trips of his. Gran would tell us if there was anything to worry about.'

'Yeah.' Billy nodded. 'Yeah, guess so. She would, wouldn't she?'

'Course.' Spike smiled at him. 'Hello, what's Ed got? Ed? What's that, boy? What have you got there?'

They watched as their dog trotted towards them through the snow, carrying a long, thin object. With a soft flump, Ed dropped his new find onto the snow in front of them.

'Looks like a bone,' said Billy.

'A bone?' Spike picked it up, and turned it over in his hands. 'It's a bit long to be a bone,' he said. 'Look at the size of it.'

He stood the strange object in the snow. 'Could be some sort of oar, I suppose.'

'That's not an oar.' Billy pulled off his glove and ran a hand along the object's surface. 'No way is that an oar,' he said. 'Feel it. It's too smooth. And it's icy cold.'

'Well it would be, wouldn't it? It's been laying in the snow.'

'How d'you know? Ed could have got it from anywhere.'

Spike shrugged. 'That's true. But look at it. If that's a bone, it must be from some sort of animal mustn't it? Can't be a human bone. Not that big, it'd be a giant.'

Billy took the object and sniffed it.

'Anything?'

'Nope. Maybe Ed could find some more,' said Billy. 'He's a good tracker.'

'He's a brilliant tracker.' Spike glanced up at the sky and sniffed. 'But not today. There's more snow coming. We'd better get home, Bill, it won't be light for much longer. We can always come back.'

Billy looked disappointed. 'S'pose. Let's take it back with us, we can show Gran.'

'No, not yet.' Spike shook his head. 'We will take it, but let's keep it to ourselves for now. I want to show the others first.'

Spike pushed the mysterious object under his coat and together with Billy, set off through the shadowy outlines of Gullivan's land.

Billy turned. 'Ed! Come on!'

Ed looked up from where he was snuffling in the snow, and trotted past them. In the icy air, a few stray snowflakes fluttered in the breeze.

'Looks like you were right about the snow, Spike.'

'Good,' said Spike. 'It'll cover our tracks.'

Dipping a hand into his pocket, he pulled out his phone.

'What you doing?'

'Sending a message to the others,' Spike said. 'I want to show them this bone thing tomorrow, see what they make of it.'

Spike sat at the breakfast table, thinking. For the third time that week, something had woken him in the early hours. He'd got out of bed and wandered down onto the landing below, where he'd passed Gran's bedroom door. It was slightly open, and he'd peeped in, surprised to find the room empty and her bed neatly turned down.

He'd checked the bathroom, and then wandered downstairs and checked in the kitchen, but there was still no sign of Gran. He'd been on his way back upstairs when he'd looked through the banister to see a purple light move slowly beneath Gran's now closed bedroom door. The same door he'd left open. Where had she been? He knew elderly people sometimes slept downstairs in a chair, but she hadn't been downstairs either. And what was the purple light under her door? And then there was the disappearance of Mr Price. Could the two things be connected?

Now it was the following morning, and as Spike spread butter slowly on his toast, he looked up at her. 'Sleep all right last night, Gran?'

Gran turned around to pass them some more toast. She didn't look like someone who'd had no sleep. She was neatly dressed, her hair gleaming as usual, fastened at the back with a clip. The brown eyes that looked back into his were clear, and sparkling, like two glistening raisins in a bun.

'Wonderfully, thank you, dear,' she said. 'Slept all night long.'

No, you didn't, Spike thought, you weren't in bed at all, but how could he say that to the wonderful gran he loved so much? The gran who'd adopted them both when they were tiny and cared for them ever since?

Something odd was going on, and somehow, he was going to find out.

'What are you boys up to, this morning?'

Spike looked up with a start. 'What d'you mean, Gran?'

Gran looked at him for a moment, then smiled. 'Well, it's the school holidays, isn't it? You've got two weeks off. I thought you might be seeing your friends.'

'We are,' said Billy. 'We're going to Meatball's. We want to show them something.'

Spike gave him a kick under the table. 'Yes, yes, we found something yesterday, Gran. In the snow.'

'Really? What did you find?'

'Oh, it's nothing,' said Spike. 'Just a bit of old wood. Duke's making another one of them models of his and we thought maybe he could use it, you know.'

5

'Well, I'm sure he'll be very grateful,' said Gran. 'I have to pop out this morning, boys. Maybe you could get yourselves a bite to eat if you need it. You'll be taking Ed with you?'

Spike glanced across at the huge Irish Wolfhound laying by the fire, snoring. 'Course.'

Billy got up from the table, stacked the dishes in the sink and turned on the tap.

'Me and Billy will do these, Gran, if you want to get off,' Spike said, grabbing a cloth. 'We'll probably have something to eat at Meatballs.'

Gran walked across and gave them both a squeeze. 'Thank you, dears,' she said. 'I'll just get my hat and coat. And don't forget you're going to Jake's today, Billy. Your bag's all done, I'll be back to take you this afternoon.'

'Thanks, Gran.'

Spike watched as Gran left the room, then turned on Billy. 'What d'you want to open your mouth about the bone, for?'

Billy looked down at the soapy water. 'Sorry, I didn't think.'

Spike shrugged. 'Doesn't matter. Least you never said it was a bone.'

'If it is a bone.'

'Yeah. If it is. Maybe Doc will know.'

He ran a hand through his spiked hair. 'Let's finish these, then we'll get over to Meatball's.'

CHAPTER TWO

Stepping through the door of Meatballs' basement, Spike and Billy shut out the snow that had been blowing in their faces all through the village.

Inside, it felt warm and cosy. Leaning the large bag against the wall, Spike unclipped Ed's lead and watched him settle in front of the fire.

Meatball looked up from his computer. 'Hi, guys, what's up?'

'We found something!' said Billy, pulling off his gloves.

'Hope it's biscuits,' said Duke, staring into an empty tin. 'Have you scoffed them all again, Meatball?'

Meatball grinned.

Terri handed Spike and Billy cups of hot chocolate. 'What is it, then? The thing you found?'

'Don't know,' Spike said, vaguely.

He looked up to see Terri watching him. They were close, and she'd know if there was something wrong, but he wasn't telling anyone about Gran and the purple light, not even her. Hopefully, she'd think he was just worried about Mr Price.

'Here, Bill,' he said. 'Grab that bone thing for Doc to have a look at.'

Doc looked up from her book. She was small, and sitting in the armchair, her long, dark hair falling across her shoulders, she almost disappeared from view. At the mention of the bone, Spike saw her eyes gleam with excitement.

'What bone?'

'We thought you'd gone to sleep,' said Duke.

'Wish I could,' said Spike.

Terri gave him another glance.

'Ed found it, yesterday,' Billy said, excitedly, 'when we were taking him for a walk. We think it's a bone.' He slid it onto the table. 'Only it's a bit big -'

Duke stared at it. 'A bone? This big? It can't be.'

'Could be a horse bone, I suppose.'

'A horse?' Terri bent over to gaze at it, tucking her springy brown hair behind her ears. 'How big d'you think horses are, Meatball?'

Doc pulled a magnifying glass from her pocket. 'It's not a horse,' she said, quietly.

'So what is it, then?'

'Well I don't know till I've had a look at it, do I?'

'What about an elephant?' said Duke.

Billy sniggered. 'An *elephant*?'

'One might have escaped from somewhere,' Duke said. 'They have them in zoos and that.'

'Course it's not an elephant,' Terri said. 'Get real.'

'Maybe it's a mammoth,' said Spike.

Doc sighed. 'It'd be a whole lot easier to look at this if you lot shut up for a minute.'

'Perhaps it is a mammoth.'

'No, Billy, it is *not* a mammoth,' Doc said.

'How d'you know?'

'Because, I did a whole project on it last year and I went to see mammoth bones and looked on the net. And I'm telling you, this is not a mammoth.'

Spike shrugged. 'Whatever. So, what is it, then?'

'I don't know yet, but it looks like a human leg bone.'

Terri pulled a face. 'Come on, Doc, it can't be human, even I know that. It's too big.'

'It'd have to be some sort of giant if it was human,' said Duke.

'Well, if that's a human leg bone,' Meatball murmured, 'it must've been about eight or nine feet tall. Look at it!'

He picked up the bone and held it up against his own leg. With the exception of Billy, they were all thirteen, but Meatball was the biggest, tall and broad and muscular. The

8

bone stretched the whole length of his leg, and up past his waist.

Laying the bone back on the table, Meatball wiped his hands on his jeans. 'You really think it's human?'

Doc nodded. 'It's possible. I need to do a bit more research, of course. Anyone mind if I take it home?'

'No,' said Spike. 'Go for it.'

'Where did you say you found the bone, Spike?'

Spike looked across at Terri. She had that look on her face that said she wasn't giving up until he told her everything. He'd tell her about the bone, but not about Gran.

'On Gullivan's land,' Billy said. 'We went there yesterday and Ed found it.'

Terri's eyes opened wide. 'For goodness sake, Spike, Gullivan's dangerous. If he finds you on his land ... and you took Billy with you?'

'I was all right,' said Billy, defensively.

'Yeah, but you might not have been if Gullivan had spotted you,' said Duke. 'You know what he's like with that shotgun of his.'

'You took a bit of a risk,' said Meatball, frowning. 'He could've blown your head off.'

Doc pushed the bone into the bag. 'You are an idiot at times, Spike.'

'Well, we went, all right?' Spike snapped. 'You wouldn't have had this bone if we hadn't.'

Duke gave him a glance. 'You ok, mate?'

Spike shrugged. 'Yeah ... yeah, I'm ok. Just ... oh, I don't know.'

'Whereabouts did Ed find it, then?' Terri asked.

'Don't know,' said Billy. 'Not really. Ed was having a pee and you know when he goes, he takes ages and when we turned around, he was trotting up to us with this thing. Spike thinks it could've come from the old cowshed, don't you, Spike?'

'It could've done. I've seen Gullivan going in there before.'

9

'He could just be putting stuff away,' said Meatball.

'No, he's not,' Spike said. 'Gullivan's up to something. Definite.'

'We don't know that, do we?' Terri said. 'Just because you hate him doesn't mean he's up to something.'

'We all hate him,' said Duke.

Doc nodded. 'I wouldn't like to meet him on a dark night.'

'Yeah, but Terri's right,' said Meatball. 'I mean, just because we hate him doesn't mean he's up to something.'

'Oh, he *is*,' said Spike. 'And I'm finding out what that is, as well.'

'As well as what?'

Spike thought quickly. 'Mr Price.'

'Yeah, don't forget Gullivan threatened Mr Price,' said Billy.

Duke shrugged. 'I know he did, Bill, and he shouldn't have done that, but Mr Price was trespassing on Gullivan's land.'

'It's a public right of way,' said Spike. 'He had no right.'

Inside, Spike felt like screaming. Why weren't they listening? Gullivan was scum and he hated him. And now Mr Price had disappeared.

Mr Price was kind, and clever, the nearest thing to a grandad they had, and he loved him. Yeah, he sometimes went off on trips, but he always told them first, and he always told them when he'd be back, and now suddenly, he disappears, just after Gullivan threatens him with that shotgun of his? Why, thought Spike, am I the only one who can see the obvious? Gullivan's *killed* him.

'Your Gran doesn't seem worried,' Terri said.

'Yeah, well, maybe she isn't,' said Spike. 'But I am.'

'And me,' said Billy.

Duke drained the last of his chocolate. 'If that bone thing is human, perhaps we ought to do something about it.'

'Like what?'

'Well, tell someone. You know, report it.'

'What for?' Spike protested. 'It's our bone. You know what'll happen, the police will take it and that'll be that.'

'He's got a point,' said Terri. 'And that's if they believe us. They'll probably just think it's a bit of old wood, or something.'

'Which it still could be,' said Meatball. 'We'd look right idiots, then.'

'Let me have a closer look at it, first,' Doc said.

Duke nodded in agreement. 'I was really thinking more about Gullivan, anyway. It was on his land, wasn't it? What if ... well, you know -'

'Wouldn't put it past him,' said Meatball, yawning. 'He shoots at anything.'

Spike watched him. It looked like he wasn't the only one losing sleep. 'You still having that dream, Meatball?'

Meatball nodded.

'What d'you say it was about again?'

Meatball huffed, irritably. 'I told you,' he said, 'I'm in a cave. It's pitch black, damp and musty, like there's no air. And outside there's all these terrifying noises, bellowing or rumbling or something, then I'm walking and the ground kind of splits open. It's horrible. I don't want to think about it.'

'That's not a dream,' said Doc. 'That's a nightmare.'

'Tell me about it.'

Leaning forward, Duke spread his hands on the table. His blond hair fell across his eye. 'I reckon if Ed found this by the cowshed, it's worth a closer look.'

'Exactly what I think,' Spike said. 'We could go this afternoon. It'll take Doc ages to look at the bone.'

Doc glared at him. 'Well, sor-*ry*,' she said, crossly. 'It'll take as long as it takes. D'you want to do it?'

'It's probably just an animal bone anyway,' Terri said.

'Maybe,' said Duke. 'But we don't know anything for sure. Let's watch Gullivan for a day or so, see what he does.'

Spike chewed his lip. You do what you like, he thought. And I'll do what I like.

11

'In the meantime, we stay away from Gullivan's land,' Duke said, giving Spike a look. 'It could be dangerous. Agreed?'

Doc gave a shiver. 'You don't have to tell me twice.'

Stretching his long arms, Meatball looked at his watch. 'Anyone want to watch the match on our new telly upstairs? It's massive.'

'Yeah, I will,' Duke said.

Picking up the bag with the bone, Doc tried to push it inside her coat. A large portion of the bone stuck up over her shoulder. 'I'll pass,' she said, 'I need to get started on this.'

'Spike?'

Spike shook his head. 'No, I'll walk home with Bill, he's going to his mate's.'

'I'll come with you,' Terri said.

'What you going to do now, Spike?' Billy asked. He kicked at one of the huge snowdrifts that had been whipped up by the wind.

They stopped while Ed watered yet another tree.

'He's not going to do anything,' said Terri. 'Are you, Spike?'

'Someone has got to look in that cowshed,' Spike said. 'and if we leave it, it'll give him time to get rid of the rest of the bones, won't it?'

'But we agreed,' said Terri. 'It's safer if we all go together.'

Billy turned. 'You're not going yet, are you, Spike? I've got to go to Jake's this afternoon. I'll miss it.'

'What's that for, Bill?' Terri asked. 'A pizza or something?'

Billy nodded. 'It's Jake's birthday. I'm staying over his.'

Terri smiled at him. 'That'll be good, won't it?'

'I guess.'

'You won't miss anything, Bill.' She gave Spike a look. 'He won't, will he Spike?'

'No,' he said. 'No, you won't miss anything.'

Bending down, he picked up a stick and threw it, watching as Ed charged off through the snow.

'Grab him, Bill,' Spike said, handing him the lead. 'We need to get you back in time.'

'You're going to go, anyway, aren't you?' Terri hissed, as Billy stomped off to fetch Ed.

'Someone's got to,' Spike whispered. 'Doc could be ages mucking about with that bone. What Billy doesn't know, he won't worry about.'

Terri heaved a sigh. 'Suppose I'd better come along, hadn't I?'

'If you want,' Spike muttered.

He glanced at her, and smiled. 'Pick you up about two,' he whispered.

CHAPTER THREE

In the echoing gloom of the hay barn, Cornelius Gullivan stared down into a gaping hole. His heart pounded, thudding in his throat, and making him feel nauseous. After weeks of snow and plummeting temperatures, even here in the shelter of the barn, the ground was hard as iron, and digging that hole had nearly broken his back.

Lifting a bony arm, he wiped the sweat from his forehead with a filthy sleeve. He was getting too old for this game. He closed his eyes. No good, it had to be finished. Reaching across for a sack, he tipped it over the hole and watched as the contents tumbled in, and then crouched down to pick up the skull that had rolled to one side, turning it slowly over in his hands.

'Not so clever now, are you?'

Opening his fingers, he let the skull roll over the tips and tumble into the blackness below. It cracked loudly against the other bones and rolled toward a corner where it rested, gazing up at him through hollow sockets.

Gullivan gazed back at it without emotion, and then reaching across, closed his aching fingers around the handle of a spade, yanked it free, and shovelled the earth onto the bones until they were completely covered. Finished.

Straightening his aching back, he stood up. One thing less to worry about: leaving those bones hanging around any longer could have been risky.

Smoothing the earth with his boot, Gullivan leaned across to stand the spade against the wall. Time to go in. The freezing wind was whistling past him, whipping like a cold blade across his neck. He peered outside and looked at the stone-grey sky. There was a load more up there yet. God Almighty, he was sick of this weather. Would it ever stop? The first new flakes began to drift on the air. This damned cold, how he hated it. He pulled his jacket tightly across his chest, tugged fiercely at his collar, and then set off across the icy yard towards the house.

After a couple of steps, he stopped. What was that?

Pausing for a second to peer through the flakes, he stepped off the path and made his way towards a large spiked bush. In the snow before it, edges softened by the icy wind, were a few faint prints. He squatted close to the ground, and began tracing the outline with a finger. Paw prints. A fox? No, too big.

He spread his hand against the width of the prints. A dog. He nodded to himself. Definitely a dog, and a large one at that. His eyes narrowed. There was only one dog around that fitted that description, that mutt from the old girl's place, but how?

Glancing up, Gullivan stared at the hedge that surrounded his property. Tall and thick, it was an impenetrable mass of thorns, broken only by the occasional towering trunk of a tree. There was no way that dog could have got through there, it must have come through the gate.

Whirling around, he plodded off towards the iron gates at the end of the drive. They were bitterly cold, delicately draped in snow, and firmly closed.

Gullivan's mouth set in a line. Digging. That damned mutt must be digging its way in. He'd have to get out here at some point and have a look. He'd take a torch and search every foot of that hedge until he found where, and next time that dog came calling, he'd be waiting with his gun.

In the treetops behind him, rooks began to caw.

Gullivan smiled to himself. He'd practise on a few of those later, damned row they made.

15

Back in the kitchen he filled the kettle, spooned three coffees into an old mug, and then walked across to where his shotgun stood against the wall.

He slid two cartridges carefully into the barrel. If that kid's dog came onto his land again, he'd show it the business end of old Bessie. It would be an accident, of course, but this time that pest would be history. A leer curled his lip. Plenty of room for one more in the hay barn.

Gullivan grinned. Resting his shotgun on the table, he picked up the remains of lunch and took a large bite, then leaned across to press the button on the radio. The dull drone of the newsreader's voice faded in and out with the chewing and he barely listened, until one particular item tugged at his attention.

In mid-chew, he spun around, and gave the volume control a sharp twist. The voice of the newsreader burst out.

'We go now to our reporter, Malcolm Haskins, on the steps of the Old Bailey.'

'The trial of Toby and Molly McKendrick ended today. Toby McKendrick was sentenced to thirty years for the murder of Timothy Forsyth, a Hatton Garden diamond merchant, whose body was identified from dental records.

'Molly McKendrick was acquitted on a charge of manslaughter and walked free from the Court.

'It was revealed during the trial that acting on an anonymous tip-off, police were able to unearth new evidence in the case.'

Over on the stove, the kettle boiled furiously.

Molly McKendrick walked free? How could that have happened?

Gullivan's sandwich went down in a lump. It shouldn't have happened. Surely, he'd given the police enough.

Sweat pricked on his forehead. Molly McKendrick was out and it was only a matter of time before she came looking for him. He knew the McKendricks very well and it wasn't Toby that had the vicious streak. Molly McKendrick's hobbies were the stuff of nightmares.

Dropping the crusts onto his plate, he stood up.

Molly McKendrick ... if she ever found him ...

He kicked back his chair and began to pace the floor. Perhaps she wouldn't find him. He was out in the middle of nowhere, wasn't he? She'd never find him here.

With shaking hands, he poured the water into his coffee, laced it with rum, and stirred. Then he took a long swig from the bottle, letting the fiery liquid sear his throat.

'She can't find me. She mustn't find me.'

With a dreadful certainty, he knew it was only a matter of time. And all because of a few damned diamonds.

Gullivan stopped. *Diamonds!* Of course!

Lighting a cigarette, he inhaled deeply and felt the fear ebb away. Molly McKendrick wouldn't find him where he was going.

Grasping the chair, he sat back down and relaxed. His eyelids so wanted to close ... maybe just a few minutes ...

The noise that disturbed him came from the sitting room, and he realised he'd forgotten his guest. Best do something about him first.

CHAPTER FOUR

'This is the deepest snow ever,' Spike said, as he and Terri stepped over the stile and into the field. 'Gran said it was going to be a bad winter.'

It was just gone two o'clock, but a bank of dense cloud was already restricting the light. Snow engulfed the countryside like a heavy quilt, muffling the land into an ear-splitting silence.

Terri nodded. 'Your gran was right,' she said. She looked apprehensively up at the sky. 'You don't think it might be better to wait till the morning?'

'No. I want to know what's up there.'

Together, they trudged forward, pressing their boots gingerly onto the crisp surface, before sinking with a jolt into the snow.

'It's this way,' he said.

Terri nodded, and tucking her hands deep into her pockets, set off with Spike across the vast expanse of white in the direction of Gullivan's land.

'Thought you might've brought Ed again,' she said.

Spike peered at her, his eyes screwed tight against the glare. 'I couldn't,' he said. 'He's gone with Billy to Jake's, they love him over there. I couldn't say anything, or Bill would've guessed we were going.'

'Everyone loves dear old Ed.'

Spike nodded. 'Yeah, he's the best. He'll be back with Gran later.'

Slowly, they plodded on up the curve of the hill. In the far distance beyond the field, Hawketts Wood was just visible, standing like a fortress, shrouded in snow.

At the top of the hill, Terri paused, hands on hips, and gasped. 'Is it much further, Spike? My legs ache.'

'Not far,' he said. 'But it's no good, I'll have to empty these boots. They're getting too heavy.'

He put a hand on Terri's shoulder, reached down, and pulled off his boots.

A heap of snow tumbled out. Shivering slightly, he replaced them and they continued silently on their way, until they reached the thick hedging that surrounded Gullivan's property.

Terri stamped her feet, trying to keep warm. 'This hedge is massive.'

'I know,' Spike said. 'And he's planted a load of firethorn on the inside. It's got huge thorns on it. Anything to keep people out.'

'He's horrible,' said Terri, shivering. 'He's the most horrible person I've ever met.'

'He's evil,' Spike said. 'There's a reason he lives on his own in that farm. He shoots at anything.'

Terri sank her hands even deeper into her pockets. 'He keeps people out all right,' she murmured, 'and anything else living.'

Spike peered out from under his hood. 'Yeah, well Billy and me know something he doesn't. This way, it's just along here.'

He set off along the hedgerow until they came to an enormous tree. It looked out over the valley, tall and proud, its twisted branches reaching up as if to hold up the sky.

Spike stepped across to the trunk and patted it like an old friend.

'This is Solomon,' he said. 'Older than this hedging, older than this field even, he's been here hundreds and hundreds of years.'

Terri looked at him. 'Really? A tree? How's this going to help us?'

Spike grasped a branch with both hands, and then moved it forward and sideways, then he eased his fingers under a huge section of bark, pulled it, and lifted it to one side.

Terri's eyes widened. 'Wow!'

'And look at this … see?'

Dipping into his pocket, Spike pulled out a small torch and shone it into the depths of the trunk. Through the opening, the beam revealed a narrow passageway.

'It's hollow,' she said.

He nodded. 'Lightning struck it years ago. Burnt the guts right out. Come on, it's this way!'

They left the snow and the daylight behind and stepped into the eerie gloom of the blackened, crumbling trunk, where the air was stale and musty. As they moved through, it hung around their faces like a suffocating cloud.

'Don't touch the sides,' Spike hissed. 'It's crawling with stuff.'

Terri shuddered, and pulled her scarf tightly around her neck. 'So, where's the way out, then?'

'It's coming up.'

A few steps further on, Spike reached across, and grasped two handles in the side of the trunk. Another panel of bark lifted clear and in a blaze of light, there was Gullivan's field, crisp and white and, after the night's new fall of snow, smooth as a millpond.

Terri shielded her eyes. 'So,' she said, quietly. 'This is how you got into Gullivan's field.'

Spike glanced up at the grey sky. 'There's a load of snow up there, I can smell it. We'd better get a move on. We want to get there and back before that lot comes down so it hides our tracks. We don't want Gullivan to know how we got in.'

They set off again, forcing their weary legs onwards. The temperature was already falling, forming a crisp crust on the snow, and every step shattered the smooth surface. Halfway across, the ground dipped into a slope and turning sideways, they slid down onto level ground.

Spike pointed to an old building. It was a dilapidated wreck, wearing a thick hat of snow. 'This is it,' he whispered. 'It's in here.'

'This place? You sure?' Terri peered around the edge of the door into the darkness. 'Doesn't look like it's been used for years.'

'Well, he's using it, I've seen him. He's stashing stuff somewhere in here. Might even be a body. Ed could've got that bone thing from here, we don't know.' He passed her the torch. 'Here, hold this a minute.'

He pulled hard on the wooden panels of the door and it creaked open just wide enough to slip through and brace himself against it, so Terri could squeeze through the narrow gap.

'Put the torch on!'

Terri turned the torch over in her hands and flicked the switch. A weak beam cut through the darkness, lighting up the edges of old farming tools strewn about the floor. They picked their way across the cowshed, stepping with care over rusted blades and wheels. Slivers of daylight seeping through cracks in the walls flickered across them as they moved, throwing ghostly images onto the floor.

'We'd better be quick,' Terri said, fiddling with the torch. 'There's not much life left in this thing.'

'Yes, all right.' Spike peered through the gloom. 'There's a box here somewhere, a sort of large trunk thing.'

'How d'you know?'

'I peered through one day when he was in here. I saw him putting things in it.'

'You crazy?'

'Never mind that,' Spike said. 'I bet that's where everything is. Come on, let's have a look.'

The back of the cowshed was like an obstacle course, littered with bits of furniture, sinks, an old fridge and various motor tyres and seats. Spike eased his way through, Terri stumbling behind, until they came to a large mound in the corner.

'This'll be it,' he said. 'I'm sure he went this way. It's probably under this lot.'

Pushing away some old tyres, they pulled aside a heavy tarpaulin. Beneath, lay a battered wooden trunk.

'What did I tell you?'

Kneeling down, Spike gripped the lid firmly, and heaved it open.

'Spike … whatever's in there isn't ours,' said Terri, as she watched Spike peer inside. 'We shouldn't be touching it. We shouldn't even be here.'

Spike straightened up and looked her squarely in the face.

'And who's says it's Gullivan's?' he said. 'I've seen him, Terri. He's getting it from somewhere over the hill there. Look, I know no one believes me, but Gullivan's up to something and I'm going to prove it. Just give me a hand with this, will you?'

Terri sighed. Together, they worked slowly through the trunk, Spike passing items to Terri who laid them out neatly on the tarpaulin.

There were two goblets, wrapped in newspaper, and a large tankard with a crest on it. Next came a small bag, made of leather. Terri slid her fingers inside and eased open the strings. It was full of watches and rings. She gazed at them, watching them sparkle as she turned them in the light of the torch. Then she dropped them back into the bag, yanked on the strings, and laid them down.

Almost immediately, Spike passed her two large items wrapped in a cloth, which slipped sideways as she held them, revealing two ornate candlesticks.

'These look like silver, Spike!'

Spike looked up and nodded. 'Stolen, I bet.'

He turned back to the trunk. 'Hang on,' he whispered. 'What have we got here?'

'What? What is it?'

'I don't know -'

The heavy object lay wrapped in an oily rag. Gently, Spike lifted it clear of the trunk, laid it on his knees, and peeled away the cloth.

Terri gripped his arm. 'Watch it with that Spike, it's dangerous.'

Spike gazed at the thing in wonder. 'It's a *gun*.'

Taking it in his gloved hand, he slipped his fingers around the handle and felt the weight of it.

'I know what it is,' hissed Terri. 'Put it back.'

Spike continued to stare at it.

'Spike!'

'All *right*.'

He looked at it one more time, then re-wrapped it and placed it cautiously back in the trunk.

Terri leaned over his shoulder. 'Anything else? What's that? That's not silver. That looks like gold.'

Reaching in, Spike grasped the new thing and handed it to her. It was a plain golden band set in the centre with a large stone.

'Looks like some sort of tiara,' she murmured.

'I reckon we should take it.'

'You can't go helping yourself to stuff, it's not ours.'

'Only this,' Spike said. 'Doc can find out what it is.'

Terri shivered. 'All right, but just this. And somehow, we've got to bring it back. Now put these others back, Spike and let's get out of here, before he sees us.'

'Hang on, there's something else here.'

Spike's voice echoed deep within the box.

Terri tugged violently at his sleeve. 'Spike! Come on! It's freezing and Gullivan might be around with his shotgun!'

'Yes, all right, I'm coming, I'm coming. Look at this, we've got to take it.'

Slowly, he raised his cupped hands into the air. Sitting in his palms was a large, gleaming silver ball.

Terri stared. 'What's that?'

'Dunno,' Spike said, looking at it from every angle. 'It's got to be something though, hasn't it?'

'Well bring it then, but *please* hurry up!' Terri jumped to her feet, shoving him hard. 'Look, it's snowing already, we've got to get back.'

With a sigh of impatience, Spike lowered the lid of the trunk and flicked the catches shut. She was right and he knew it. Heaving the tarpaulin back into place, he draped and tucked it as well as he could and dragged back the tyres.

They'd barely taken a step, when a thunderous explosion blasted their ears, rocking the icy stillness.

There was no mistaking the sound: they'd heard it too often. It was the echoing report of a shotgun, and it was very near.

Terri opened her mouth to cry out but Spike covered it with his hand and put a finger to his lips.

Desperately, she clawed at his fingers. '*Gullivan ...*'

Seconds later, the wall of the cowshed erupted toward them with an enormous blast that ripped through the old timbers, filling the air with a mass of choking dust, splinters and ricocheting pellets. Spike's knees hit the stone floor with an agonising crunch and he and Terri crumpled into a heap, dragging their coats over their heads as debris rained down.

They sat, waiting, rigid with fear, ears ringing in the suffocating gloom. Spike's heart pounded so loudly in his ears, he covered them with his hands, terrified that somehow Gullivan would hear it.

Minutes passed.

Huddled together, chests heaving, they listened. The echoes of the noise gave way to an eerie silence.

Stiffly, Spike eased back his hood and lifted his head.

'He knows we're here,' Terri whispered.

A third shot. It spooked them for a moment, but it was quieter this time, and a little more distant.

'No, it's all right,' Spike said. 'He's just shooting rooks again. And it sounds like he's moving away.'

They knelt in silence, welded together, listening. Gradually, the shots grew fainter until they faded into the distance.

With some effort, Spike clambered to his feet.

'Now!' he hissed. 'Let's move. Before he comes back.'

Grabbing Terri's hand and pulling her upright, he bent to retrieve the silver ball and tucked it into his coat, then they picked their way carefully back across the cowshed, through the steady dust-filled silence. Ahead of them, a gaping hole in the wall revealed the blanket of snow and darkness of the winter evening closing in.

Spike stepped close to the edge of the hole and peered outside. Gullivan was out there somewhere, but where?

He felt Terri gripping his hand, the squeeze of her glove confirming what he already knew. Now wasn't the time to take risks. If they had to stay in this freezing wreck until darkness fell, then that's what they'd do.

Carefully, Spike looked around. Gullivan didn't seem to be about, but he had to be sure. A sudden gleam caught his eye. Somewhere in the direction of the house, someone had switched on a light.

'He's gone in. Come on, let's chance it.'

He tugged on Terri's glove and they stepped outside and slid through the shadows back across the yard.

Spike barely remembered struggling up the slope to the top. As they set off again across the field, the snow was tumbling in dense flakes.

Snow coated Spike's face, his feet felt heavy, and somewhere in the back of his mind, he realised his boots must be full of snow, but there was no time to empty them.

'We have to get to Solomon,' he gasped. 'Gullivan won't see us in there.'

Terri did her best to nod through the swirling flakes, and pulled her hood tightly about her head.

Stomping along beside her, Spike thought about the things they'd found in the trunk. Things he'd expected to find, and, if he was honest, one or two that he hadn't. He whistled softly. All that loot. He'd always known Gullivan was a thief and right there before their eyes, was the proof.

Beneath his scarf, Spike's mouth set in a grim line. He knew Gullivan was a murderer too, even if no one else did and, one way or another, he was going to prove it. He glanced back over his shoulder for any sight of the man he'd grown to hate, but the whirling flakes were fast becoming a blizzard, hiding everything and everyone.

'Spike!'

Spike looked at Terri, struggling to look back at him through snow-laden lashes.

'What?'

'The torch! We need the torch. We're nearly at the tree.'

'The torch? Oh, the torch, right.'

With difficulty, he plunged a hand into his pocket. Then his other pocket. Then his coat. Then his bag.

'Oh,' he said.

Terri spun around, incredulous. 'You haven't.'

He nodded. Chunks of soft snow slipped from his head like huge flakes of dandruff and fell to the ground. 'I have.'

'You idiot, how d'you manage it?'

'It won't matter. He won't see it.'

'Of course he'll see it,' she snapped. She glanced at him. 'It hasn't got your name on it, has it?'

Spike looked at her. 'Well, no ...'

'Thank goodness.'

'It's got Billy's name on it,' he said.

'Billy's?'

'Well, I couldn't find mine, so I borrowed his.'

Terri let out a long groan. 'D'you know what?' she said. 'I don't believe you at times, Spike, I really don't.'

Spike looked at her. 'Well, we can't go back *now*.'

'Well, duh,' she said, pulling at the panel. 'I know that. We'll just have to pray Gullivan doesn't find it, won't we?'

CHAPTER FIVE

Spike stood at the window of Doc's conservatory. It was the following morning and they'd arranged to meet at nine. Doc was often in there when she was working on something, and peering in, he could see her dozing, feet tucked up on the settee. Spike rapped loudly on the window and she sat up with a start, squinting at the snow-dusted windowpane.

Pushing herself out of the settee, she walked across and threw back the bolts. A gust of icy air buffeted her face as the door opened.

'Can't you just tap like anyone else?' she asked. 'You frightened the life out of me!'

'Sorry.'

Doc sighed, tucking her hair behind her ears. 'It's all right,' she said. 'You caught me by surprise, that's all. I must've fallen asleep studying that bone of yours. Come on in.'

Spike stepped into the warmth, hung his coat on the hook, and looked around. Doc's conservatory always fascinated him. It was so full of interesting stuff. There were bookshelves stacked from floor to ceiling, a large desk littered with various papers, and scientific instruments everywhere. An enormous glass-fronted cabinet stood in the corner, teeming with bones and creepy specimens of all kinds.

Slowly, he put out a hand.

'Don't touch anything, Spike, you know how Dad is with his things.'

'It must be brilliant if your mum and dad are doctors,' he said.

'It's ok,' Doc said. She glanced at him. 'Isn't Terri with you?'

Picking up a bottle from the table to examine it, Spike squinted at the words on the label. 'She'll be here in a minute,' he said, vaguely. 'She's had to baby-sit her brother.'

'Oh.'

He put the bottle back down and then wandered casually over to the desk to stare at the bone. 'Good job I got to that before Ed chewed it. We'd have had it if he'd started crunching it.'

Doc stifled a yawn. 'D'you know, it's odd ...'

She paused. 'Get the door, Spike. It's Terri.'

Spike walked across and opened it. 'Okay?'

Terri nodded, giving him a look that said she hadn't forgotten scrambling for her life across a snowy field. Pulling a rucksack from her back, she let it slide to the floor and then dropped into a large sofa and made herself comfortable.

'Least it's warm in here,' she said. 'Okay, Doc? What you doing?'

'I was just going to tell Spike about this.' Doc pointed at the bone. 'D'you know, I've looked online and everything and I can't find anything like it.'

'What, nothing at all?'

'Nope. There's something weird about it, as well, but I can't think what it is. I wondered if it might be worth filming.'

Spike reached for his phone. 'I'll do it,' he said. 'Why are we filming it, though?'

'Well, in case it's evidence,' Doc said. 'You know.'

Spike's eyes opened wide. 'Evidence ...'

'Evidence?' Terri stared. 'What ... police-type evidence, you mean?'

'Well, we don't know, do we?'

Another hammering at the glass made them look up. Two more faces were outside peering in.

Duke and Meatball almost fell in through the door as Spike opened it, bringing with them a blast of bitterly cold air. They hurried across to the radiator to press their backsides firmly against the hot metal.

'Oh, that's better.' Meatball sighed. 'My bum's frozen solid. Got any grub, Doc?'

'Only crisps.'

'That'll do.'

Pulling a large bag from the drawer, Doc grabbed a couple of packets and threw them at him.

'You weren't working in here all last night, were you?' Duke asked. 'It must've been freezing.'

Doc shook her head. 'Only till about ten. I had my sleeping bag and a hot water bottle. Not that it did me much good, I'm still no nearer.'

'You don't know what it is, then?'

Doc sighed. 'Not really,' she said. 'But I'm positive it's not human.'

Meatball crunched on a mouthful of crisps. 'Which means what?'

'Means it comes from a big bird, I expect,' Spike said. 'Like an ostrich.'

Doc shook her head firmly. 'No,' she said. 'It's not a bird, or a fish, or any amphibian that I can find. It could be a reptile.'

Spike almost choked. 'A reptile?' he spluttered. 'With a leg that size?'

'A reptile?' Duke gasped.

'There's something else as well,' Doc said. 'It's new. Not more than three or four days, I'd say.'

'Okay, that can't be right,' Spike said. 'I mean, if it was that new, it'd have all flesh n'that on it. And it'd stink.'

Duke looked thoughtful. 'You're right, it would,' he said, slowly, 'unless …'

'Exactly,' said Doc. 'That's what I was thinking. Someone's cleaned it.'

Terri picked up the bone. 'Why would anyone bother cleaning it? And what kind of reptile is going to have a leg bone like that?'

'Beats me,' said Meatball. He turned to Spike. 'So, come on then, what else did you find at Gullivan's place yesterday?'

'We know you went up there,' Duke said, 'you and Terri.'

There was a tense silence. 'Not much,' Spike muttered. 'Few bits …'

Terri leaned forward, aghast. 'A few bits? A few bits, he says, when we nearly got our heads blown off.'

'You *didn't* …'

'It was a close thing,' Spike said. 'Gullivan was blasting off with his shotgun again, shooting rooks.'

'We didn't hang around to find out what else he was shooting,' Terri said.

'We heard a gun going off,' Meatball said, 'but we couldn't see over that hedge.'

'You are idiots,' said Duke. 'You shouldn't have gone on your own.'

'Well, they did,' Doc snapped. She leaned in closer. 'Come on then, what did you get? Show us.'

'Well …'

Terri leaned forward, stealing a sideways glance at Spike. 'There's this trunk,' she whispered. 'And it's full of stuff.'

'What you whispering for?'

'Don't know,' said Terri.

'Never mind that,' said Meatball. 'What sort of stuff?'

'Well, we reckon it's stolen, because it's silver and gold 'n' that,' Terri went on. 'Candlesticks and goblets and watches.'

'And a gun,' said Spike.

'What, another shotgun?'

'No, it was a little one, you know, like you see on the telly.'

Duke frowned. 'A handgun? What's he need that for?'

'Burglaries,' Terri said. 'That's what we reckon.'

'I don't suppose you found any more bones, did you?' Doc asked, hopefully.

'Nope,' said Terri. She leaned across to grab the rucksack. 'But wait till you see what we *did* find.'

'Yeah.' Spike leaped to his feet. 'Show them that ball thing.'

Terry unzipped the top of the rucksack, produced the shining ball, and handed it to Spike.

'Wow,' said Doc. 'Would you look at that? What is it?'

'Don't know,' Spike said. 'But I nearly missed it. It was right at the bottom of the trunk.'

Duke stared at the shimmering surface of the ball, watching it reflect the light. 'Funny sort of ball,' he said. 'Looks like one of those mirror balls.'

'Let's have a look.' Meatball stared closely at the surface. 'It looks like silver, but it's all swirling, like liquid. Reminds me of one of those crystal ball things my cousin Rosa used to use.'

'That's an idea.' Duke took it from Meatball's hands and held it high in the air, straining to see beneath. 'There's no marks on it. Wouldn't it say if it was silver? Suppose it could be a bed knob. You know, like in that film.'

He passed it across to Terri, who shook her head.

'Too big for a bed knob,' she said. 'Anyway, what would Gullivan want with a bed knob? I suppose it isn't some kind of bowling ball?'

'Shouldn't think so.' Spike took it back and turned it over. 'There's no holes in it for your fingers.'

Doc slipped on her glasses. 'Would you mind leaving it with me, Spike? I'd like a closer look at it.'

He shrugged. 'If you want. It's not much use as it is.'

Doc took it from him and placed it on the bookcase.

'Look out, it's rolling!'

'In the desk, there, Terri!' Doc cried, making a grab for it. 'There's some sticky stuff!'

Terri took a large lump of sticky tack from the drawer and stuck it under the ball. 'There,' she said. 'That'll stop it rolling off.'

'Here, Terri, show them the other thing,' Spike said. 'That thing with the big jewel in it.'

The golden band was passed around for inspection.

'Look at that stone,' Duke whispered. 'Must be worth a fortune.'

'If it's real.' Meatball held it up to the light. 'It's probably imitation. It's not likely to be a pearl or anything, not this size.'

'It's probably some sort of tiara.' Taking it in her hand, Terri ran a finger softly across the crystal. 'It's beautiful. Look at the way it catches the light.'

Slowly, she lifted it into the air and slid it onto her head. 'Okay you lot, kneel,' she commanded, picking up a pencil, 'one wishes to make you knights of the square table. Unless one slips and then one will be chopping off your heads.'

'Perhaps we shouldn't muck about with it,' Duke said. 'We might damage it.'

He stopped and looked across at Meatball, who was staring over their shoulders at the shimmering ball on the bookcase.

'Never mind the band,' he said. 'What's going on with *that*?'

'What?'

'It's moving!' Terri spun around, grasping Spike's arm so hard, he cried out. 'It's moving!' she squealed. 'Look at it! It's *moving*!'

They stared at the ball, completely stunned. Somehow, it was moving on its own.

Around the top, where the outer surface began, the casing of the ball had broken away and was now oozing down the outside in a thick silver wave. The wave folded over and over until it came to rest at the base in a large gleaming ring, where it sat like a fat silver doughnut, shimmering gently in the light.

'What's going on?' Duke padded quietly towards the ball and craned his neck to see round the other side. The ring of silver was unbroken, but had now stopped moving and seemed to have set into a solid lump.

'It's solid,' he said. 'But it can't be. It was moving. We just saw it.'

'Must be some sort of new tech,' laughed Meatball, nervously. 'Electronic, or something.'

Doc crept a little closer. 'It's brilliant,' she breathed. 'How cool is that? What d'you reckon it is?'

'Don't get too near it,' Terri said. 'It could be dangerous.'

'She's right,' said Duke. 'Better not touch it, you never know.'

Eyes wide with excitement, Spike looked on. The ball had moved completely on its own, but how was that possible? Things didn't move on their own, did they? Course, there were drones, but they were noisy, and this thing was totally silent.

He found himself looking around as if by some freak chance someone, somewhere was controlling it. Idiot, he told himself, there's no-one else here.

'Whatever it was doing, it's stopped now,' he said. 'Perhaps we should poke it, or something.'

'*You* poke it, if you're so clever,' said Terri.

'All right,' Spike said. 'I'll do it. I don't care.'

He did really, but he wasn't going to say so. Slowly he put out his hand, and prayed he wouldn't get some kind of a shock. With a shaking finger, he pressed gently against the silver ring. It was cold. And rock hard.

'It is solid,' he said. He tapped it. 'It's like tapping a big ball bearing … aagh!'

Spike jerked his hand away just in time. The ring was on the move again. It rippled a couple of times, and then in a flash of silver, it was sucked beneath the ball, like water down a plughole.

'What's happening now?' Duke cried.

Meatball dropped to his knees to look under it. 'Where'd it go? It can't just vanish!'

Doc gazed at the ball with absolute joy. 'No good saying it can't,' she said, a look of wonder on her face. 'It just has. It can quite clearly do anything it wants.'

'It can,' sighed Terri. 'And look at what's left. How beautiful is that?'

The outer protection was gone, and now the inner layer of the ball was clearly visible. Spike looked at it. Terri was right, it was beautiful. The layer was smooth and almost translucent, the surface swirling and rippling with undulating waves of flowing colour, as though someone had just dripped oil onto its watery surface.

'It's like a huge soap bubble, isn't it?'

'Better get away a bit,' said Duke. 'It's starting to move again.'

Joggling and wriggling, the ball tugged at the sticky tack that held it fast to the cabinet, stretching it into weird and wonderful shapes.

Spike watched, mesmerised. 'What's it doing?'

'Don't know,' hissed Terri. 'But it doesn't seem to like being held down, does it?'

The ball continued to pull at the sticky tack, twisting it into long filaments like a spider's web, and then with one enormous heave, it tore itself free, leaving the sticky tack to recoil into a shivering blob.

Freed from its bonds, the ball floated gracefully up into the air to settle just above their heads.

They gazed at it, following the ball with their eyes as it hovered, suspended above them. For several minutes it hung in the air, and then it seemed to wake up and floated past them all to where Terri stood. As it drew level with the golden band on her head, it stopped again, and there it remained, glistening in the air like a full moon.

'Oh *heck*.' Terri backed away in alarm. 'What's it doing?'

She took another step backward. The ball followed. She moved sideways, crouched down low, stretched up again, but everywhere she went, the ball was with her.

'Ok … now it's freaking me out … go away! Go away! Do something, get it away from me. Get it away!'

'It's the band!' Doc cried. She pointed to Terri's head. 'The band on your head! That's what's doing it!'

Duke gawped in amazement. 'Something's happening to the stone! It's glowing!'

Yelling in alarm, Terri made a grab for the tiara, but it was too late. The gemstone in the centre was now pulsing with a regular beat. Without warning, an intense beam of light burst from the centre of the stone and hit the ball, splaying across its surface, encasing it in a rich purple coat.

Bathed in the light of the beam, the ball itself now began to open into eight gleaming segments of pulsing crystal.

They opened like the petals of an exotic flower, each segment clicking into place, a line of luminescent purple quivering along the edges. Bathed in the purple light, the crystal segments glistened like an expensive chandelier.

'Oh, look at it, it's *gorgeous*,' Doc breathed.

'Shut up!' Terri gasped with fear. 'I'm under this thing, remember?'

Breathlessly, they waited.

Then, as though someone had flicked a switch, the light went out. The ball remained in the air for a moment and to their relief, the whole thing floated gently down onto Terri's lap, where it sat, like an enormous glass water lily.

No one moved. No one even dared to speak until Terri's abrupt scream broke the silence. 'Well, get it off, then! Don't just stand there! Get it off me!'

Leaning across, Spike picked it up, staring hard into its centre. 'Wow!' he said. He ran a hand over the outside. 'It's not even warm.'

'Don't drop it,' Duke said, warily. 'Just don't drop it. Put it back on the cabinet. There's no knowing what it'll do next. If we break it …'

Meatball snorted. 'Break it? We don't even know how it works. I mean, how was it moving on its own? I couldn't hear anything, could you?'

Doc shook her head. 'And what about that band thing? Where did that light come from?'

'I … I don't know what happened,' Terri burbled, sliding the band from her head with trembling fingers and pushing it quickly onto the chair. 'All I could see was this purple light. It must have been this.'

Doc walked across to where Spike had replaced the opened ball gently on the bookcase and peered into the centre. 'That was amazing!' she sighed. 'D'you reckon it's finished? D'you think there's any more?'

Almost as she spoke, one individual segment detached itself from the rest and opened without sound, into a flattened egg shape.

'Oh no,' Terri wailed. 'What's it doing now?'

Her question was almost drowned by the sound of a plastic door crashing open. Leo, Doc's cat, had launched itself from the window ledge and was now squeezing out through the cat flap as fast as its large belly would allow.

Meatball watched through the window as Leo galloped off and pushed his bulk into a gap far too small beneath the shed. 'Whatever it's doing,' he said. 'the cat doesn't like it.'

'Something's spooked him.'

Back on the cabinet, the egg-shaped segment had folded up and returned to its original position.

'It got to be something to do with the ball,' said Duke.

A second segment moved, clicked into place, and opened.

'It's got to be,' Doc murmured. 'It has to be giving out some kind of sound.'

'Well, I can't hear anything.'

'Neither can I, Spike, but Leo seemed to be able to. I think it must be out of our range.'

'You mean like one of them whistles?'

Doc nodded. 'Must be. Only what the sound is and what it means, I don't know.'

Terri walked over to the ball, bending her head to look at it from every angle. Segments six and seven were now opening into flat shapes.

The eighth segment followed, and then whatever it had been doing, it seemed to be complete, because moments later, it started to close. The segments lifted and locked into place, and once again, the outer layer crept up the sides, and the whole thing was back where it started.

Terri puffed out a long breath. 'I'm guessing that's it, then,' she said.

Spike shrugged. 'Looks like it, doesn't it?'

'Leo must've heard something we can't,' said Meatball. 'Maybe we could listen to it again. We know how it works.'

'Do we?'

'Well, it was when Terri put on the band, wasn't it? She puts it on her head and off it goes. All we've got to do …'

Terri crossed her arms. 'I know what you're going to say,' she said. 'No way. One of you lot do it.'

'All right, I'll do it,' Spike said. He slipped the band onto his head. Nothing happened. He concentrated as hard as he could for some moments, but it was useless.

'Can you see it? The purple light?'

Spike shook his head. 'Nothing happening,' he said. 'You try.'

Duke tried. Meatball slipped it on and passed it to Doc, but it was no use. Slowly, they turned to look at Terri.

She huffed. 'Oh, all right,' she said. 'But I'm only doing it once more.'

'If we can record it,' said Meatball. 'We can bring the frequency down.'

'Good thinking,' said Duke. 'Might be able to find out what it is.'

'I did tell you there was something going on,' said Spike. 'We found this lot in Gullivan's shed, didn't we? I told you he was behind it.'

'You could be right, Spike,' said Meatball. 'He is up to something. Me and Duke saw him as well.'

'Where? What was he doing?'

'We saw him crossing the field, and shortly after he disappeared around the corner, we saw this kind of glow in the sky. Just for a second. Dunno what it was.'

'Could it have been the railway?' Doc asked. 'Sometimes you get a brilliant blue light from that.'

Meatball shook his head. 'No, I know what that looks like. This had more of a purplish tinge to it. Didn't hear any trains, either.'

'So, what was it then?'

Meatball pulled a face. 'Pass.'

Spike's eyes narrowed.

'Whatever's happening, Gullivan's behind it.'

CHAPTER SIX

In the dimly lit kitchen, Gullivan stood, frowning, turning a small red and blue torch repeatedly in his hand and squinting at the letters scratched on the casing.

Billy.

Who was Billy? One of them spiky-haired brats from the cottage? That girl who hung around with them? No, her name wasn't Billy. Something like it, but not Billy.

Gullivan chewed on the inside of his cheek. Whoever it was had made a big mistake. A very big mistake. Cursing, he walked across to the drawer and, yanking it open, selected a long, thin knife, spat on the blade and rubbed at a dark stain with his finger.

It was one of them kids all right, he'd stake his life on it. If he ever caught them on his land ...

He stepped out of the kitchen, through the hallway and into the sitting room.

Gripping the tip of the blade, he hurled the knife through the air. It landed with a dull thud in the rotting wood of the door. A large splinter detached itself and fell onto the head of the body propped below.

Gullivan marched across to stare at Joseph Price. 'What's the matter Joey, boy? Cat got your tongue?'

Seated on the hard floor, silver tape across his mouth, Joseph Price watched.

'Oh no, course, I forgot!' Gullivan sneered. 'You don't have quite so much to say these days, do you? I warned you, didn't I, about coming onto my land. When I say a right of way is closed, it's *closed*, got it?'

Gullivan leaned across and wrenched the knife from the door. He pressed it tight against Joseph's throat. The stench of Gullivan's breath almost choked him.

'Thought you could just stroll across my land, did you? Gullivan spat in his face. 'Well you know different now, don't you, old man. I'll deal with you later, I've got things to do now, see? Places to go. And I've got the perfect place to stash you in the meantime.'

Half an hour later, Gullivan dragged Joseph Price into a small room, lifted the hatch in the floor, and pushed him down. Gullivan leaned against the wall for a moment to catch his breath. How come that old guy weighed so much?

'I'll bring you some grub later,' he snapped. He looked down at the old man lying hunched on the floor. 'And then again,' he hissed, leering at him, 'maybe I won't.'

Some time later, Gullivan collapsed with a groan onto his bed. That old guy had been damned heavy to lug about, a dead weight. He laughed to himself. Yeah … a *dead* weight.

Gullivan kicked off his filthy boots, which clattered to the floor, showering the wooden boards with soil. Then for the first time in hours, he let himself relax. Relief flooded his body and within seconds, he was asleep.

CHAPTER SEVEN

In their cosy attic bedroom in Gran's cottage, Spike looked at his phone, and opened the first of two messages. It was from Billy.

Went go-karting. Brilliant. Jake got loads of computer games, lending me Alien World 2. Is Gran ok?

Spike frowned. They both adored Gran, but it wasn't the sort of thing Billy normally put in a message, he'd only seen her yesterday.

Spike sent a reply. *Yeah, Gran's fine. Why?*

An answer pinged straight back.

Just wondered. Gran seems a bit odd. Tell you when I get home.

Spike was even more puzzled. Gran seemed a bit odd? What did he mean?

He thought about the other night, when he'd got out of bed to find Gran missing and a strange purple light beneath her door. Could Billy have seen that, too? Did it have something to do with Mr Price?

He shook the idea out of his head. Gran and Mr Price were inseparable, like an old married couple. Together, they were he and Billy's family. They weren't blood, of course, Gran had adopted them both after the accident had taken their mum and dad, but they'd always called her Gran and loved her every bit as much.

Spike glanced across at the picture frame on the beside cabinet. It was the photograph he'd taken at the village fair. There was Gran, in jeans and a silver top, hair shining. Mr Price was beside her, impeccably dressed in blazer and old school tie. Standing between them was Billy, pulling a silly face as usual. The three of them were laughing and giggling.

A lump formed in Spike's throat. His family. And now one of them was missing. Why hadn't Gran said anything? Perhaps she didn't know Mr Price was missing, perhaps she thought he'd gone away on one of those little jaunts of his. Spike chewed his lip. Should he say something? No, not yet, it might upset her.

A large, hairy body plonked on the bed beside him, sending the phone flying.

'Oh cheers, Ed, thanks.'

Spike stooped to pick up the phone. There was another message, this time from Duke.

Urgent. Bernie's been asking about Mr Price. Meet at Meatballs. 10.30.

Spike sat up. Bernie? The milkman was asking about Mr Price? Why? The hairs on Spike's neck prickled. Something was wrong, he knew it. Something had happened.

Quickly, he sent an answer, and then leaping off his bed, reached down to put on his boots. He glanced at the clock. Just gone ten. Better get a move on.

At the foot of the stairs, Ed began to bark. Was that a knock? Slipping the phone into his pocket, Spike walked out of his bedroom onto the landing.

Downstairs, the knock sounded again, louder this time, and more impatient.

'Yes, all *right*,' he called. 'I'm coming.'

He swung onto the spiral bannister, whizzed down, and then jumped off into the brightly lit hallway. Ed was crouched low, growling at the letterbox.

'You're too late, Ed, Frank's already been!'

With a sigh, Spike walked up to the door and reached out for the handle.

He stopped. That shadow wasn't the postman. Spike wasn't sure who it was, but for some reason he felt uneasy.

'Steady, boy.'

Grabbing hold of Ed's collar, Spike grasped the handle firmly and clicked the door open just a little.

A tall, gaunt man in a shabby jacket stood on the doorstep, a long case slung over one shoulder. Spike looked up into the sharp, bony features of Cornelius Gullivan.

His heart skipped a beat. *Gullivan.* What was he doing here, on his doorstep? Spike's brain worked like lightning. He's found the torch. *He's found the torch.*

'What d'you want?'

Gullivan's dark eyes narrowed. The slight smile on his face showed his brown teeth.

'Mrs Makepeace in?'

His voice was low and rasping. Even from a few feet away, Spike could smell the overpowering odour of his foul breath.

His grip on Ed's collar tightened. Ed started to snarl, his lips slipping back beyond his teeth, but Gullivan didn't seem to notice or care.

'Gran's busy,' Spike said.

'Is she?' Gullivan's dark menacing eyes roved over Spike's shoulder and down the hallway.

'Well, when she's stopped being busy, you tell her Mr Gullivan called. I'd be interested in buying this place.'

Spike pulled the door a little closer. 'Gran doesn't want to sell.'

'You just mention I called.'

'I'll mention it.'

Gullivan attempted one more look over Spike's shoulder and then turned to go.

'You do that,' he said. He took two steps into the snow, then stopped and spun around. 'Oh, by the way,' he added. 'Nice dog.'

He glared down at Ed, with a look that raised goose bumps on Spike's arms.

A slow, menacing growl rumbled in Ed's throat.

'A *very* nice dog,' Gullivan continued. 'You should look after him: some people leave all *sorts* of rubbish lying about. Anything could happen.'

He lingered, staring down at Ed for a second or two longer, then walked away.

Gripping the doorframe with trembling fingers, Spike watched Gullivan crunch his way down the path and out through the gate, where he stopped again. With a glance back at them both, he pulled the long case slowly into an upright position and leaned it against his shoulder.

By Spike's side, Ed's growl erupted into a warning bark. Swiftly, Spike yanked him in and then slammed the door behind them, bolting it top and bottom. That case had hit Gullivan's shoulder with a thud. Spike had a pretty good idea what was inside and he wasn't ready to be his next victim. Surely, even Gullivan wouldn't risk that? Not in broad daylight.

Spike watched through the window as Gullivan's shape disappeared into the distance, and then, methodically, he went around the house, checking the locks were secure. He wouldn't put it past Gullivan to sneak back the minute they were gone and have a nose around.

Satisfied that everything was done, he stood a note for Gran on the mantelpiece, wrapped a thick blue scarf around his neck, then stepped out and locked the door behind him, rattling the doorknob twice for good measure. With Ed trotting by his side, he turned and left for the meeting.

Snow was starting to fall again as he made his way down the lane. Stomping along, Spike had plenty to think about. Gullivan hadn't come all the way to Gran's cottage to offer to buy it: he'd come to threaten them. All of them. And that could mean only one thing. They were on the right track.

Spike headed down by the hedgerow, Ed lumbering through the snow beside him. The wind was getting up again and it tugged and pulled at him, throwing spiralling snowflakes into their eyes and mouths.

Reaching the stile, he stepped over and jumped down with a crunch into Thicketts Lane, then meandered along, smashing one or two of the frozen puddles, until he came to the junction with the road.

He slowed, as something bright caught his attention. Reflected in the roof of the church opposite, he saw an arc of purple light.

It flickered for a second, blazing against the white of the snow, and then it was gone. Spike stood, wondering. A trick of the light? The glare of the snow? He'd seen it all right, he was sure of that, but what was it?

The chill wind nipped his fingers and he sank his hands deeper into his pockets as he turned off past the church and up the road. Whatever it was, it'd have to wait. Meatball's house lay straight ahead. The sight cheered him. Meatball was bound to have some toast on the go.

'All right, Meatball?'

Meatball swung the door wide open. 'You're early, Spike,' he said, standing aside as Ed charged in.

A rush of warm air engulfed Spike as he stepped through the doorway, melting the snow on his coat into glistening droplets. Ed shook himself from head to tail, showering them both.

'Thought I was going to be late,' Spike said. 'I had a visitor.'

He followed Meatball into the basement, which was bursting with equipment, and humming with the sound of computer fans and the faint smell of hot circuitry. Wandering over to the fire, Ed settled himself down and soon his fur was steaming.

Spike parked himself on the corner of the desk. 'They're late, aren't they? Must be gone half ten by now.'

Meatball picked up a slice of bread and slid it onto a toasting fork. 'It's ten past. Must be something wrong with your watch.'

Mystified, Spike looked down at his watch and then at the clock above the mantelpiece. The clock said ten minutes past ten. His watch said the same. Ten minutes past? That couldn't be right, surely. It was gone ten before Gullivan called.

'Hold this a minute, will you?' Meatball held out the toasting fork. 'I need to finish connecting this lot.'

'Hmm?' Still deep in thought, Spike grasped the fork and pushed it near the flames.

'Watch it! Not that close!'

Spike jumped. 'Eh? Oh!'

A flame licked the underside of his toast as he pulled it clear.

'Sorry,' he said, blowing frantically on it. 'I was thinking about something. How long d'you reckon it takes to walk from my house to yours?'

'Bout ten minutes, bit longer in this weather.' Meatball grinned. 'Bit longer than that if you have to wait for Ed.'

'And smash puddles,' Spike murmured. 'And stop to look at stuff …'

'Guess. What d'you mean?'

Spike shook his head. 'Nothing,' he said. 'Doesn't matter. Here, Meatball, have you heard anything else about Mr Price?'

'No, only what Duke put in that message. I expect he'll tell us the rest when he gets here.'

Spike nodded, thoughtfully. 'Yeah … yeah, you're probably right.'

From under the table, Meatball's head reappeared. 'Did you say you had a visitor?'

Spike pulled in the fork, turned the toast, and pushed it back near the fire. 'Yes, there was this knock at the door.'

'Who was it? Frank?'

'No, Frank had already been with the post.'

'So, who was at the door, then?'

Spike scraped butter onto the not-so-burnt side of his toast. 'You're never going to believe this,' he said. 'It was Gullivan.'

A screwdriver hit the floor with a clatter. Meatball jerked up, narrowly missing his head. 'What did *he* want?'

'You tell me,' Spike said, between mouthfuls of toast. 'He gave me some rubbish about buying Gran's house.'

'Like she'd ever sell Yew Tree Cottage. What did he really want?'

'He didn't say.' Spike pulled a second slice of toast from the fire. 'But he threatened Ed.'

'He's lucky Ed never had his hand off.'

'He would have done if I'd let him go, but Gullivan had this long case with him and I didn't want to chance it.'

'Case? What sort of case?'

They were interrupted by the arrival of Duke, Doc, and Terri who almost fell through the door to get into the warm.

Terri wrenched the gloves from her hands and threw them onto the chair. 'Oh great, toast.'

'Too late. I've eaten it all.'

'You'd better not.'

Grinning, Spike produced a plate of buttered toast, dipped his finger into the butter, and offered it to Gus, Meatball's giant cat, who had been quietly dozing on a chair.

Doc walked over to the computer. 'How you getting on, Meatball?'

'Reckon this ought to do it,' said Meatball. 'Did you bring the ball?'

Doc pulled the ball from a carrier bag and set it down on the table.

'Do that in a minute,' Duke said. 'I've got to tell you what Bernie said.'

They gathered around to listen.

'It was when he called for the money. He was just about to go, when he suddenly said, 'You know Mr Price at The Laurels, don't you?'

'I told him we did and then he asked if we'd seen him about at all, because Mr Price hadn't cancelled his milk and Bernie noticed it was piling up on his doorstep.'

'I knew it!' Spike gasped. 'What else did he say?'

'Not a lot, really, just that he's been asking around, and no-one's seen him.'

'Didn't I say?'

'Yeah, I know, Spike, but I didn't want to say anything to Bernie, so I just said, 'Oh, perhaps he's gone away on one of those trips of his, and he's forgotten to cancel the milk,' and Bernie said, 'Yeah, maybe he's getting a bit absent-minded.''

'Absent-minded? That'll be the day,' said Meatball. 'Mr Price has got a mind like a steel trap.'

'I know, but I didn't know what else to say.'

'I knew something wasn't right,' Spike said. 'I just knew it.'

'I'm sure he's all right,' Terri said, reassuringly. 'He'll probably turn up in a day or two.'

Doc nodded. 'Yeah, he's probably ok. No point worrying about it till we know for sure.'

I know already, Spike thought. Something's happened to Mr Price and I'm going to find out what.

'Well, whatever's going on,' Meatball said. 'You can bet Gullivan's in it somewhere.'

'Which brings us back to this thing,' said Doc, placing the ball on the desk. 'And this.'

The headband gleamed in the light as she sat it beside the ball. 'I mean, these are not normal, are they? A ball that flies in the air?'

'So that's got to be next,' said Duke, firmly. 'Open the ball and record it. Terri? You ready?'

Terri hesitated. 'I still don't see …'

'Oh, come on Terri, we've all had a go, we can't do it. You must be the only one. You've obviously got the gift.'

Terri gave Doc a look. 'Nice try,' she said.

'You're the only one who can open it,' said Duke. 'But look, if you don't want to, that's fine, we get it.'

Terri sighed. 'Go on, then.'

'Hang on a minute,' Spike said. 'I've thought of something. If we play it again, and it is high frequency, what about Ed? Remember before? With Leo?'

'Not a problem,' Meatball said. 'We're totally soundproofed down here in the basement. But thinking about

48

it, you might be right about Ed. Best put him and Gus upstairs in the kitchen.'

Terri lifted the band and held it once more above her head. 'You don't think ... it won't fry my brains, will it? I mean, what do I do?'

Doc grasped her by the shoulders. 'Just close your eyes and think purple.'

'Yeah, well, it's all right for you lot, isn't it? You don't have to stick this thing on your head.'

'Go on, Terri, you can do it. We have to know what that ball's all about. It might tell us something really vital.'

'Okay,' said Terri. 'But I'm keeping my eyes open.'

She slipped it onto her head. 'Here goes then,' she said, in a tremulous voice. 'Think purple. Right.'

They waited. Nothing happened.

'See a purple light!' Doc said. 'Picture it!'

Terri closed her eyes and screwed up her face in concentration.

In the centre of the band, the stone began to glow, and then the same shaft of purple light fell upon the ball, which rose and opened as before.

'Is it working?'

'Open your eyes and have a look,' Doc whispered.

Terri half-opened her eyes. 'Am I doing that?'

'Yep.'

Duke picked up the mike. 'You getting this, Meatball?'

'Think so. I'm getting something.'

One by one, Duke counted off the segments. 'And that,' he said, 'is the lot. Time to see what we've got.'

Doc reached across and picked up the ball. 'We'd better put this away somewhere safe.'

'And you can put this with it!' Terri snapped, pulling the band from her head. 'What about that big drawer over there. Cover it with something. Just in case.'

Doc reached for a jumper, wrapped the ball, and then sat it in the drawer of Meatball's filing cabinet. With the others, she huddled in a group around the keyboard, staring at the monitor.

'Perhaps it's a voice from beyond the grave,' Spike said.

Duke sniggered. 'Or a message from aliens.'

Meatball glared at them. 'If you don't shut it, we'll never know,' he said. 'Right, are we ready? Here goes.'

Meatball tapped the keyboard and a flickering line appeared across the monitor screen. 'That's sound all right,' he said, 'but it's way too high for us to hear. I'll bring the frequency down.'

They leaned forward, cupping their ears.

'Can't you turn it up?'

'It is up. Here, what's that whining noise?'

Spike screwed up his nose. 'Sounds like bagpipes.'

The whining changed to burbling.

Doc frowned. 'What's that? Surely that's not a language? Sounds more like something running. Perhaps that's why Leo didn't like it.'

'I'd love to know where Gullivan got this from,' Duke said.

'Same place he's getting everything else, I expect,' said Spike. 'Some big posh house.'

Meatball shook his head. 'It can't be from someone's house, can it? Look at it. It's high tech.'

Spike gripped the side of the desk. 'Here, you don't reckon Gullivan's some sort of spy?'

Terri picked up her toast and nibbled at it. 'Here we go.'

'What?' Spike looked at her. 'I was right before, wasn't I?'

Duke nodded. 'Yeah, you were, to be fair. You know, I was thinking about everything on the way over this morning. What about that light? That was odd n'all.'

'I saw it as well!' Spike cried. 'That light thing. I don't know if it was the same one, but as I was going down Thicketts Lane, I saw this weird light on the church roof.'

Doc leaned in closer. 'What sort of light?'

'It was like the lights the police have.'

'What … blue you mean?'

'No, it was more purple than that, but it flashed brilliant like theirs do. Only for a minute, then it disappeared.'

'So it could've been the same light we saw?'

Spike shrugged. 'Don't know, but it could've been, couldn't it?'

'We'd better keep a look out for it on the way,' Duke said.

'On the way to where?'

'Well, we've got to follow him, haven't we? We've got to see where he's going, where he's getting all this stuff. I think we should keep watch. See what he's up to.'

Terri turned a slice of bread. 'To see if he's burgling places you mean?'

'Well, he might be.' Duke glanced at his watch. 'Look, it's half eleven now, half hour to drop Ed back home …'

'Drop Ed home? Why?'

'I reckon we ought to, Spike,' Duke said. 'You know, in case he barks at Gullivan.'

Spike thought for a moment. He never liked leaving Ed behind, but he couldn't help thinking Duke might be right. Ed hated Gullivan as much as he did and you never knew if Gullivan had a gun or a knife on him. 'I guess,' he said.

Meatball glanced at his watch. 'So, what time are we going then?'

'Well, it's half eleven, now,' said Terri.

'Might be,' Spike muttered. 'Might be ten to twelve.'

'What d'you mean? Ten to twelve?'

Spike leaned forward to scoop up the final crumbs. Should he tell them about the time going all funny? No, he might have it wrong and then he'd look a right idiot. He offered the buttery crumbs to Ed. 'Nothing,' he said. 'Anyway, you'll never get into Gullivan's field unless you go through Solomon. Not since he's put the hedge in.'

'Who's Solomon?'

Spike exchanged glances with Terri.

'I'll show you when we get there,' he said. 'But I'll tell you something now. I reckon Gullivan's on to us. Like I was telling Meatball, he paid me a visit earlier on and he threatened Ed.'

Terri snatched at Spike's sleeve. 'You don't reckon he's found the torch?'

'Don't know,' Spike said, 'but I wouldn't be surprised. And if he has, he knows we've looked in that trunk. And he knows what's missing.'

'And if he knows all that,' said Meatball, gravely, 'we'd better watch our backs.'

CHAPTER EIGHT

Beyond Gullivan's field, down by the river, Spike watched an arc of brilliant purple light flickering in the sky.

Crouched down in the cover of frosted bushes, he, Duke, Doc and Terri watched the display of light and tried to make sense of it. What on earth was it?

Slightly ahead, Meatball sat perched on the top of a snowy bank.

'What is it?' Duke gasped.

'Dunno,' said Meatball. 'I've never seen anything like it.'

'Could it be some sort of weather thing?' Terri asked. 'You do see some funny things on the telly.'

Doc cupped her hands and blew on them. 'It's not like any weather thing I've ever seen.'

'Whatever it is, it doesn't feel right,' said Meatball. He looked about him. 'Nothing about this place feels right.'

Spike watched him. Meatball had a sixth sense about some things and if it didn't feel right to him, there was probably a good reason. 'What's up, Meatball?'

Meatball shook his head, vaguely. 'I don't know,' he said. 'It just doesn't feel safe here.'

Spike sighed. Following Gullivan had seemed such a good idea in the warmth of Meatball's basement, but when it came to doing it, it hadn't been so easy or straightforward as they thought.

Their first stop had been Solomon, the old oak tree, where Spike had showed them the connecting doors to Gullivan's land. Gullivan's house stood some way across the field and from the safety of the tree, Spike and the others had taken it in turns to keep watch, using binoculars to peer at the doors and windows in the vain hope of catching sight of him.

It was bitterly cold, and Spike's fingers and toes were aching. They were on the point of giving up, when Gullivan had finally returned, sliding and skidding into the snowy driveway in his car.

Gullivan got out, grabbed a couple of bags from the boot and rushed indoors. Twenty minutes later, he emerged from the back of the house, wearing old coat and trousers, and carrying a large bag and a shotgun, then he set off across the field in the direction of the river that skirted the edge of his land.

They waited a moment or two, then quietly left Solomon, and stepped out into the deep snow to follow him. At a safe distance, they kept low to the ground, hiding behind the hedging wherever they could, but the snow was already hardening and their footsteps seemed to be making far too much noise.

Gullivan stomped up to a large clump of snow-capped bushes, where he stopped, and turned, gazing out across the vast stretch of white.

Folding into the snow, they ducked down behind a hedge and held their breath.

Gullivan stood still, looking one way, then the other.

'He's heard us …'

'Don't think so.' Duke was peering out through a tiny gap in the hedgerow. 'No … no, I don't think he has. He seems to be making sure no one's about.'

'What's he up to?' Spike asked.

Duke shook his head. 'Don't know … he's moving again! Come on!'

Gullivan turned off down the lane that led toward the river, and they set off to follow, watching as he turned a corner and vanished from sight.

'Come on, we'll lose him!'

'Wait!' said Terri. 'What if he saw us? What if he's waiting around the corner?'

'She's right,' Doc said. 'You know what he's like, he might be waiting somewhere.'

Meatball tucked his hands under his arms to ease the pain of the cold. 'So, what do we do, then? Go back?'

'We can't!' Spike hissed. 'Not now! We've got to see where he's going.'

'Let's keep going,' Duke said. 'I can't stand here much longer, I can't feel my feet. Keep as low as possible and let's hope for the best.'

On they went, down the lane, past the old holly dotted with bright red berries, that looked like fairy lights against the snow, but still there was no sign of Gullivan.

'Where is he?'

'This is ridiculous,' Terri said. 'He can't just disappear.'

Duke looked around. 'Well he has, so now what?'

They were near the river, that gushed along in the autumn and trickled lazily mid-summer. Now, it was frozen beneath the snow, hiding its secrets until the spring. Stretching across it, the old bridge wore weird shapes of snow.

At that moment, an arc of brilliant purple radiated around the bridge, sending flickers of light into the air.

'What's that?' Terri gasped, as the strange light blazed before them like fireworks.

'I'll tell you what that is,' Spike said. 'That is the light I saw yesterday.'

'You sure, Spike? That's it?'

'Yeah, that's it, all right. Only I saw it reflected in the church roof.'

'Then it's probably the light we saw, as well,' said Duke. 'What d'you reckon, Meatball?'

Meatball didn't answer.

They glanced at him. He was completely still, staring vaguely at the bridge.

'Meatball? What's up?'

'I don't know,' he said. 'I just … get down out of sight!'

They crouched back down in a huddle.

'What?' Duke squinted between the tangled branches. 'What's up?'

Meatball shook his head, confused. 'I'm not sure,' he said. 'I might be wrong …'

But he wasn't.

The tall, wiry figure of Cornelius Gullivan appeared in front of them, as if he'd stepped through an invisible wall or burst through the skin of a bubble. One moment the bridge was empty, and then the tip of a boot appeared. It was followed by the ankle, then the leg, and the other leg.

The rest of Gullivan's body appeared from the waist up, blending smoothly into the empty space. There was nothing, and then there he was, right in front of them, his body distinctly outlined like a ghost. As they watched, the outline faded and he became a solid being.

Huddled down behind the bracken, Spike and the others almost choked in disbelief, too stunned to move or speak.

They'd just witnessed the impossible. A whole human being, appearing out of thin air. No props, no tricks … just a miracle.

On the bridge, just yards from where they crouched, Cornelius Gullivan stood for a moment looking about him as if trying to smell danger. His face was grubby, and his chin was covered with thick stubble. Slung across one shoulder was the shotgun, and hanging from his hand, the large bag, now distorted with some hidden weight. Pausing a moment longer, he took one last look and started along the bridge, heading straight towards them.

The dull thump of Gullivan's footsteps grew louder as he left the bridge and louder still as he approached, the heavy soles of his boots crunching on the frozen snow. Nestling down tight into the shrubbery, Spike watched through half-closed eyes as Gullivan stomped past within feet of them and strode off into the distance.

Spike kept him in sight for as long as he could, then cautiously lifted his head above the bracken.

'It's okay,' he whispered. 'He's gone.'

Stiffly, they got to their feet.

'It's not possible,' Duke muttered. 'What we just saw isn't possible, is it? People can't just appear, not in real life.' His voice faltered. 'I mean, not out of nowhere … they can't, can they?'

'Well, he definitely wasn't on that bridge before,' Doc said. 'One of us would've seen him.'

Spike stared at the bridge. 'Course he wasn't. We didn't see him, because he wasn't there. Until he was.'

'I knew it,' Meatball muttered. 'I knew something was coming. But I never dreamed ...'

'Let's think about this logically,' Doc said. 'We all know what happened, we saw it. There was an empty space and then Gullivan was in it.'

'So?'

'So if he stepped into that space, he must've stepped *out* of a different one, mustn't he?'

Duke gasped. 'I get what you're saying. There must be another side, something behind him. He's come *from* somewhere.'

'Exactly,' said Doc. 'He's stepped through a door of some kind. It's got to be. Gullivan's found a portal or something. A doorway to somewhere else.'

'Oh, come *on*, that's not possible,' said Terri. 'Is it? I know you see it in the films and things, but is it really possible?'

'Don't know,' Doc said, with a shrug, 'but it could be, couldn't it? Can you think of anything else?'

Spike snapped his fingers. 'You know, it could be! And I bet that's where he's getting all the stuff! He's not pinching it. He's getting it all from this other place!'

'Of course!'

'That makes sense,' Duke said. 'No one's missed anything, because no one this side of the door thing owns it.'

Spike whistled. 'And if what he's taking is valuable, he's going to make a fortune.'

'It's possible,' Duke said, frowning. 'It fits what we know, and what we've seen. I wonder what it is he's taking, what he's coming back with in that big bag?'

'There's something else as well,' said Terri. 'What else is he up to? You know, in this other place? If he is in another world, he could do anything and then come back here and no-one would ever know. He could murder someone even.' She looked around at the others. 'We've got to stop him.'

'There's only one way to do that,' Spike said. 'Follow him back.'

'Follow him back?' Terri shook her head. 'Are you mad? It's too dangerous. And what if we get to where he goes and we can't get back?'

'We could be stuck anywhere,' Duke said.

Spike threw out his hands. 'What choice have we got?

'Loads,' said Terri. 'We could stay here for a start. Or just watch for him. See if he comes back with any bloodstains or anything.'

'Really? And how long before he sees us, or we freeze to death?'

Meatball shook his head. 'Spike's right. We can't sit here forever, but I don't know about following him.'

'Gullivan always gets back all right, doesn't he?' Spike said. 'We'll just go where he goes.'

'What if we lose him, though?' Doc said. 'Through *there*. What if we come out somewhere different?'

'It's too risky,' said Terri. 'Think about it.'

'We'd all like to get him, Spike,' Duke said. 'But we can't take a chance on not getting back.'

Spike heaved a sigh. They're right, he thought, miserably. We'll never get him through there, it's hopeless. We can't risk it.

He thought about Billy and Gran. 'You're right,' he said. 'I wasn't thinking straight. Let's get home. I'm freezing.'

'What's the time?'

'Nearly five past one.'

'Five past?' Doc looked at her watch. 'It *is* five past.'

'I know,' Spike said. 'Doesn't seem right, does it? That's because it isn't. It's not really five past at all, it's later than that. But our watches say five past because of the lights. Least that's what I reckon.'

'What's it got to do with the lights?'

'Well, I saw the lights this morning, didn't I? When I was walking over to Meatballs, and somehow, I lost some time.'

'You might've made a mistake.'

'No, I never,' Spike retorted. 'According to my watch, and Meatball's clock, I must've flown, cause hardly any time passed. And we stopped a couple of times on the way.'

'And you think it's something to do with the lights?' Duke asked.

Spike shrugged. 'Don't know what else it can be.'

They gazed at one another in silence, except for Doc who threw out her arms, almost hitting Duke in the face.

'You see what this means?' she cried. 'It's a time anomaly. I've read about things like this, it's a place where time's distorted.'

Spike looked at her. He knew the signs. Her brain was sorting data.

'And?' he said, impatiently.

'And it could mean wherever Gullivan's going, it's probably to another time.'

Duke looked back at the place on the bridge where Gullivan had appeared. In a kind of daze, he said, 'Another time? You mean back? Or forward?'

'Either,' said Doc with a shrug. 'Could be hundreds of years. Could be yesterday ... or tomorrow. Who knows?'

A hush fell over them. Time travel, Spike thought? It was the sort of thing you read about, or saw in the films. It didn't happen in real life.

'Time travel?' said Terri. 'Well, that settles it, I'm definitely not following him.'

'Nor me,' said Doc.

'No way are we chancing that,' said Duke. 'We could end up anywhere.'

'Shut it a minute, someone's coming!'

They turned to look at Meatball.

'What, already?'

'Think so.' He walked a bit further down the lane, then swung around. 'I was right! Get down!'

In a mad scramble, they tumbled to the ground behind the spiky screen of bracken. Slowly, Spike edged far enough out to see around the corner. The chilling figure of Cornelius Gullivan was just visible. 'It's him.'

Gullivan's long legs carried him rapidly toward them in huge strides and in moments, he was beside them, the shotgun swinging malevolently from his shoulder as he strode by.

In the darkness behind the bracken, they watched him take a few more steps, then stop and look slowly around him. As his body turned, his coat flapped open to reveal two long knives at his hip.

He stood for a moment as before, alert and watching, then set off again, walking on toward the river. At the start of the bridge, he stopped, gave a final look around, and then, seemingly satisfied, stepped confidently onto the bridge. In the middle, he paused, checked his gun, and then, taking a step forward, walked through an archway of brilliant light … and vanished.

'Oh my God, he's *gone* …'

Spike gasped. 'He's done it again! What do we do now?'

'Nothing,' said Terri, nervously. 'We do nothing.'

Duke stared at the empty space on the bridge. 'We're not going after him, we've already said that, it's too dangerous. Especially if it's some of kind of time thingy.'

He turned to look at Meatball. 'Meatball? What d'you reckon?'

'Way too risky,' he said. 'Wish I knew what he was doing, though.'

'Me n'all,' Spike said. He wandered off across the bridge. 'There's nothing here now anyway. No light, nothing. You'd never know it was there.'

Terri and Doc followed him.

'There's no sign of anything,' said Doc. She reached out a hand and waved it about. 'Just empty space, look.'

'We'd better not wait here too long,' said Duke. 'In case he comes back.'

He looked across at Meatball, who'd joined them on the bridge. 'Nothing, Meatball?'

Meatball shook his head.

Duke sighed. 'Well, then, either we wait here in hiding till he comes back, or we go home. What we going to do?'

'Doesn't seem much point in hanging around,' said Doc. 'We know where he's going.'

Terri stared into the empty space. 'I dread to think what he's doing through there.'

Spike felt anger welling up inside him. It was hopeless. So close. Trust that scum to be out of reach. 'May as well go home,' he said. 'We can't chance going through there. It probably only works for him, anyway.'

Walking across, he picked up a twig and threw it in the air. It flumped on the soft snow. 'There you are, look. Nothing.'

He reached down to pick up the twig. 'Waste of ti ...'

Terri let out a shriek of horror, but too late to reach Spike's ears. In a flash of light, he was gone.

CHAPTER NINE

Darkness. Nothing, but suffocating darkness.

Crumpled on the hard, damp floor, Spike slowly lifted his head. Oh God … oh *God,* where was he?

Suddenly alert, he sat up and looked around, then scrambled to his feet. Ow! His knees hurt where he'd hit the stone floor. He leaned down to rub them. His trousers and coat were wet.

It stank in this place. A horrible stench, like mould. It filled his mouth and nose, seeping down into his lungs. Where was he?

He looked up. From somewhere up above, water was dripping.

Spike looked behind him. A wall of rock. Slowly, he put out a hand and touched it. Cold.

He was in a cave. A *cave*? How far *down* in a cave? He could be miles below ground … *no …*

Panic gripped his chest, squeezing until it was hard to breathe. His palms prickled with sweat. Billy, and Gran … he'd never see them again …

He took a deep breath, biting back tears. He must've come through that wall, perhaps he could go back.

Spike rushed at the wall. His hands hit it with a slap. He tried falling against it, kicking it, but it was what it looked. Solid rock.

This couldn't be happening … *it couldn't be happening*. Taking another breath, he swallowed hard. Think, he told himself, think. What could have happened? I was on the bridge with the others in the snow. I bent down to pick up the stick …

Oh hell, it was obvious. He'd gone through that doorway thing into somewhere else, hadn't he? *This* somewhere else.

Nausea washed over him, and he gagged.

Wait a minute, though! Perhaps this was the same place Gullivan went! Spike hated Gullivan with every fibre of his being, but he found himself praying it was the same place. Gullivan got back ok, didn't he? Course he did, they'd seen him. And if Gullivan got back, so could he!

He turned to look down a long stone corridor. Right at the end was a faint chink of light. Light! Maybe he wasn't deep underground. Moron! Of course there was light, it wasn't completely dark in here, was it?

Automatically, his feet started moving towards the light. If he could just find some fresh air.

'*SPIKE! SPIKE! WHERE ARE YOU?*'

Heart racing, Spike stopped in his tracks, and swung around. *Terri?*

'SPIKE! SPIKE! Where are you, mate?'

That was Duke's voice! Duke's voice!

'Spike! Please be here, for goodness sake ...'

Bursting with joy, he saw Terri rushing toward him, slipping and sliding on the wet rock.

'Spike!' she yelled, tears running down her cheek. 'Spike! You're all right! Thank *God*.' She wrapped her arms about him. 'Oh, thank God. We thought we'd lost you!'

Spike wasn't a great one for hugs and cuddles. He and Terri were close friends, but he didn't like all that mushy stuff. But at that moment, for all he cared, she could squeeze him till his eyes popped. They all squeezed him, and he was squeezing them right back.

He was so relieved, he could hardly stand up.

'You just disappeared,' Doc cried. She buried her head in his coat. 'We couldn't believe it!'

Spike wiped his eyes hurriedly on his sleeve. 'I only picked up that stick,' he said. 'I must've fallen right through to this place.'

'Thank God, you're all right,' Duke moaned.

'We thought you'd had it!' Meatball yelled with relief. 'We didn't know what to do, you just vanished!'

'And now we've vanished, as well,' said Terri, soberly. 'All of us. Where are we?'

'Wish I knew,' said Spike.

'I suppose we should've thought about it before we followed you,' Doc said.

'Thought what!' Meatball snapped. 'We were hardly going to leave him, were we!'

'No! No, course not,' Doc said, irritably. 'You know I didn't mean *that*. I just meant … oh, I don't know.'

'Yeah, well, loads of things are obvious if you've got time to think about it,' Duke said. 'But we didn't, did we?' He gave a long shudder. 'We're all terrified. All we thought about was getting you back, and we just ran towards it.' He stared down at the floor. 'Now I s'pose we've all had it, have we?'

'Will you shut up saying that!' Terri looked at the stone walls. 'Where are we?'

'Don't ask me,' Spike said. 'I was just going to have a look down there when you got here. There's light, see?'

'Never mind the stupid light thing!' said Doc. 'Have you tried going the other way?'

'Duh … *no* …. course I have!' Spike snapped. 'I'm not a complete idiot, what d'you think I've been doing? Stupid thing only goes one way, doesn't it!'

They looked at him.

Spike pinched the top of his nose, to stop tears. 'We're in a cave of some sort,' he muttered. 'That's all I know.'

'The same cave Gullivan came through?'

Spike shrugged. 'I don't know! You tell me!'

'All right, all right. Keep your hair on!'

Spike put a hand up to his hair. It was gelled hard in stiff spikes.

'Nothing's moving that,' said Meatball.

Doc sniggered. Beside her, Terri started to laugh, but stopped as tears threatened.

'Sorry,' Spike murmured. 'I thought I was on my own, you know …'

'Well, you're not, all right?'

'Forget it,' Duke said. 'God, it stinks in here. What are we going to do?'

'You're the one with the royal blood,' said Meatball. 'You tell us.'

Despite his fear, Spike grinned. Duke was always saying he had royal blood, even though his mum and dad said he hadn't.

'You can laugh,' Duke said. 'But I'll prove it one day. I've got it, all right.'

'That'll be what the smell is, then,' said Terri.

They laughed until the tears rolled down their faces and they dissolved into sobs.

'What if we never get out?' sniffed Doc. 'What if ...?'

Terri wiped her eyes and blew her nose. 'We will,' she said, defiantly. 'We've got to.'

Taking a deep shuddering breath, Spike looked across at Meatball, who was smearing snot across the sleeve of his coat. He'd been crying, too, with the rest of them. Meatball usually had gut feelings about stuff, yet he was worried, too, and that wasn't good.

'Is this it, then? The cave in your dream?'

Meatball sniffed. 'Maybe,' he said. 'I don't know. That's what worries me.'

Spike thought for a moment. 'Let's try the wall again. If we can't go through, we'll have to go forward.'

They tried the wall, pushing it, even throwing themselves against it.

'It's no good,' said Duke. 'We're stuck here.'

'Then we'll have to try down there,' said Spike. He pointed down the stone corridor, where a faint smear of light was clearly visible.

'Least there's a bit of light,' said Terri.

'D'you reckon this is the same cave Gullivan's using?' Doc asked. 'There's no sign of him.'

'Just as well,' Duke said. 'Last thing we need is to bump into him.'

'And he's got his gun with him,' said Meatball. 'He'd have nothing to lose if he shot us here, who'd know?'

With Spike in the lead, they started to work their way down the corridor. The damp rock felt slippery to the touch, but faintly warm. Water seemed to be dripping constantly, tapping on the floor like a stick, the air thick, muggy and hard to breathe.

The faint speck grew nearer and brighter, slowly diffusing the passageway with soft light. As they walked along, the tapping of water quietened, to be replaced by another sound, a deep drumming sound that grew louder as they approached.

They slowed a little. The light was much brighter, bouncing off the walls.

'There's an opening,' Spike hissed. 'The air smells fresher.'

Duke edged forward and peered outward in the direction of Spike's pointing finger. Ahead, there was a strong beam of light and the edge of what appeared to be an entrance.

'It's daylight,' he said, 'Spike's right. There's an opening.'

'Can you see anything else?'

'Not yet.'

They continued along by the wall, keeping their backs pressed close to the rock as the cave slowly widened in front of them. As they grew closer to the light, the tapping faded altogether, and the drumming grew louder and more persistent.

It was only as they crept around the very edge of the wall that they saw their first sign of Gullivan's presence. A heavy, battered old jacket, slung carelessly aside in a heap on the ground. So, he *was* here. Spike didn't know whether to feel relieved or terrified.

Edging slowly forward, he leaned out while Duke held onto him. The mouth of the cave was wide and yawning. Through the opening, Spike saw the source of the constant drumming sound. Rain. Not just a shower, but torrential stair-rods, battering the ground, barring the exit like a curtain.

Framed like a silhouette in the space, Cornelius Gullivan leaned against the wall, shrouded in smoke, staring out at the downpour.

Spike leaned back into the cave. His face told them all they needed to know. They couldn't move until Gullivan moved and that was clearly not happening until the rain stopped. At a signal from Duke, they slid back behind a rock, and waited.

Minutes crawled by. The drumming eased.

Peering around the corner, Spike saw that the rain was stopping. He glanced across. Gullivan was getting ready.

A few more moments, then with a jerk of his arm, Gullivan pulled the cigarette from between his lips and flicked it to the ground. He bent down, picked up his shotgun, slung the bag over his shoulder, and walked out of the mouth of the cave into what was now brilliant sunshine.

Spike waited, then took a few steps around the edge, and crept across to the far wall. Heart in his throat, he moved steadily towards the entrance, and peered out.

Gullivan was still visible. Just a few feet away, he stopped and broke his gun to check it was loaded. Nodding to himself, he snapped it shut again, and then walked off, the gun firmly in his grasp.

Spike signalled to the others who joined him at the entrance.

'Looks like he's gone,' he whispered, 'but you never know with him, so keep a look out.'

Shuffling tightly together, they stepped through the cave entrance and out into the sunshine.

The blinding sunlight dazzled them. As their eyes slowly adjusted, they squinted up into a sky of brilliant blue, a few straggly wisps of cloud being all that remained of the torrent of rain that had obscured the entrance.

Shuffling cautiously forward, they glanced around. They seemed to be on a wide plateau; an area of soil and scrub, dotted with grass and large leafy shrubs.

'Where on earth are we?'

Duke took a deep breath of the warm air. The strong smell of a rainstorm still lingered. 'It's some sort of hilltop by the look of it. It stretches right out, look.'

'We're definitely high up,' Spike said. 'Look at that lot over there.'

He pointed into the distance. Somewhere ahead of them, the plateau finished, dipping down into lush tropical forest.

Doc stared around her. 'It's like the view from the canopy up here,' she said. 'You know, like when they go over the rain forest.'

Feeling the warmth on his face, Spike felt another wave of fear. It has to be okay, he told himself, Gullivan's here, and he came back.

'Gullivan's here,' he said, aloud. 'Let's find him.' His voice squeaked. 'Then we follow him back.'

Duke took a few steps forward and gazed around. 'Where did he go, though? We know he went off over there, but he's vanished. He could be anywhere.'

They looked out over the valley. The plateau seemed like an island, surrounded by trees and tropical undergrowth, steaming in the sunshine. The only relief from the oppressive heat was a faint breeze, which lifted huge fronds and leaves dripping with water and rocked them gently. They seemed almost to be waving, beckoning them onward.

Doc wandered a little further, and looked into the distance.

'That isn't tropical rain forest,' she said. 'I mean, it is, but somehow it doesn't seem the same. Those things down there look just like cycads.'

'Cycads? Isn't that…'

Doc turned, and nodded. 'Tree ferns,' she said. 'And see those there? Waving about, look!' They followed the direction of her finger. 'I could be wrong, but I'm almost sure they're horsetails.'

Spike looked at them. Doc's right, he thought, they are horsetails, I've seen them in books. But look at the size of them! What is this place?

'We must be in some part of the world where they've been undisturbed,' said Terri. 'And they've just kept growing.'

Spike nodded. Anything was possible, he thought. They'd just fallen through a doorway into a cave.

'We need to find Gullivan,' Duke said. 'Quicker we find him, the quicker we can get home.'

Terri took a shuddering breath. 'How? He's gone. Vanished into thin air.'

'Well, we'll just have to wait around here until he comes back then, won't we? We've got no choice.'

'We could hide in there,' Doc said, pointing to a group of tall shrubs.

Terri peered at the heavy trunks and sopping wet leaves. 'What if something else is hiding in there? And what if Gullivan sees us?'

'He won't be looking, will he? He doesn't even know we're here.'

'We don't know that, Doc. You know what he's like, he could be hiding somewhere, watching.'

Spike shook his head. 'No, not Gullivan. If he'd seen us, we'd know about it by now. And anyway ...'

Terri turned to him. 'Anyway, what?'

Spike felt sick at the thought, but knew he had to say it. 'This might not be the way he goes back. Just because this is the way we got here, doesn't mean it's the way back. That might be somewhere else, which is why we couldn't get through the wall. If we want to get back, we've got to find Gullivan.'

Terri shuddered. 'Don't say that.'

'Well, it's true, isn't it?'

'He's right,' said Duke. 'We need to find him. Let's split up and have a look around, see if we can spot him before he spots us.'

Wandering across the plateau, Spike stood before the cave entrance, gazing up at it. 'If you look at it from here,' he said, 'this cave looks a bit like a pyramid. I reckon we'd be able to find it again.'

'What'll be the point, if it's not the way back?'

Spike shrugged. 'I don't know, do I?' he said. 'Just got to hope.'

'I still reckon we should hide in those bushes,' Doc said. 'We don't want to start wandering off.'

'You do what you like, Doc,' Spike said, 'but I think we ought to have a look around, as long as we keep in sight of the cave.'

He looked across at Duke.

'We've got to find him,' Duke said, nodding. 'At the moment, he's our only hope. Let's split up, cover more ground. Spike, you, Doc and Terri have a look round there. Meatball and I will see what's round the other side of the cave. All right, Meatball?'

Meatball nodded.

'Keep an eye out for him,' Duke said. 'Meet back here in five minutes, yeah?'

'Okay.' Spike turned to Doc and Terri. 'Come on,' he said. 'Let's see what's over here.'

Together, they wandered over to the edge of the plateau, and gazed vaguely down the gently sloping hillside.

'Doc, come and look at this, quick.'

Doc walked across to where Terri stood and found herself gazing down into an enormous valley that swept from the edge of the plateau away into the distance as far as they could see.

'Those things there,' said Terri. 'They're not what I think they are, are they?'

She pointed over into the distance. 'Look … there … see?'

In the middle of a clearing, lumbering slowly across the terrain, huge creatures were clearly visible.

Doc's mouth dropped open. 'That's *impossible*,' she gasped. 'They can't be … they *are* … they're *dinosaurs*.'

'Dinosaurs …?'

'Hadrosaurs.' Doc's eyes were wide with wonder. 'They're hadrosaurs. I'm sure they are.'

Terri stared hard at the creatures. 'That's what I thought, but they can't be, surely, can they? That's stupid.'

'What is?'

Terri gripped Spike's arm. 'Those things over there, Spike.' She pointed. 'What would you say they are?'

Spike stared intently at the undulating shapes in the distance. 'Holy cow.' His voice dropped to a whisper. 'They look like ...'

'Dinosaurs.' Terri nodded. 'Doc says they're hadrosaurs.'

Spike gazed at the huge creatures, stunned. They did look like the pictures in the books. Well, almost like them, but then who really knew what dinosaurs looked like anyway? Maybe we do, he thought.

'They are,' Doc said, with certainty. 'I'm telling you they are. They're hadrosaurs.'

'But if they're dinosaurs,' Terri asked, 'then what is this place? Some sort of theme park?'

'They're not real,' Doc said, scornfully. 'That's only in the films.'

'And this place isn't real, then?'

Doc was silent for a moment. 'Guess you're right,' she said, at last. 'Where are we?'

'I have absolutely no idea,' said Spike. 'But I'll be glad when we're home. Let's get back to the cave.'

Meatball and Duke were back already, desperately watching out for them.

'Five minutes, I said!' Duke snapped. 'We wondered where you were.'

'We were looking at stuff,' said Spike.

Meatball held out his hand. In his palm, lay a watch.

'We found this,' he said. 'Round there, behind those rocks. Could be Gullivan's.'

Spike held his breath. Something about that watch was familiar. Taking it carefully from Meatball's hand, he turned it over and squeezed the sides. A compartment flipped open. Spike's heart sank. This watch belonged to Mr Price.

Anguish and fear gripped Spike's throat like a steel band. Mr Price? He'd been here, in this strange place? Why? How? And where was he now?

Terri watched him. 'What's up?'

'This,' said Spike, a lump in his throat. 'This watch. It's Mr Price's.'

'What? You sure, Spike?'

Spike nodded.

'How can it be?' asked Meatball. 'We found it here.'

Spike shook his head, vaguely. 'I know,' he said. 'It doesn't make sense, but it's definitely his.'

Doc stared down at the watch. 'So Mr Price has been here as well?'

'Must've been.'

'So where is he now?'

'Don't know,' said Spike. 'That's what's worrying me.'

Duke stared first at the watch, then at Spike. 'You don't think …'

'What?'

'You don't think maybe it wasn't Mr Price who dropped it,' said Duke. 'Maybe it was Gullivan.'

Spike's heart pounded as he realised what that could mean. Gullivan had Mr Price's watch? His mind raced. Mr Price would never part with that watch, not willingly. If Gullivan had it, he must have taken it off him.

Gullivan had threatened Mr Price, more than once, and now he was missing. Meatball's words rang in Spike's head. 'Gullivan could kill someone here and no one would ever know.'

Terri gasped. 'Oh, Spike …'

Slowly, Spike lifted his head to look at them, his eyes brimming with tears. 'He's killed him,' he said.

CHAPTER TEN

It was almost two hours later when Gullivan returned to the cave. He was grubby, and battered. Blood trickled from a fresh wound on his face. On his shoulder, he carried the bag and shotgun.

Tucked down in the cover of the undergrowth, they watched him. The first drops of another tropical storm trickled down their necks, as they peered through the leaves.

At the entrance to the cave, Gullivan dragged the bag from his shoulder and let it slip to the ground, where it hit the hard earth with a thud.

'He's going back,' Duke whispered. 'Get ready.'

Over by the cave entrance, Gullivan glanced around, picked up the bag, heaved it across his back, and disappeared inside.

Pushing aside the whorls of sopping branches, Spike stepped out into the rain. 'Come on, he's off.'

They moved quickly and quietly across the plateau to the outside wall, where they flattened themselves against the rock and listened. Hearing no sound, they filtered through the entrance and into the gloom. The cave was empty: the only noise the distant dripping of water.

Spike walked across to the corridor, and peered around the edge. 'No sign of him,' he mouthed. 'Come on.'

They walked on down the stone passageway, stopping at every turn to check for Gullivan, until they reached the bleak stone wall where they had come in. There was still no sign of him.

'He's gone already,' Terri squeaked. 'He's gone.'

'Then he must've gone back through the wall, the same way we came in,' said Meatball. 'There's no other explanation. He must've done, we never passed him.'

Duke stared at the wall. 'We've got to try it,' he croaked. 'Either that or we stay here.'

Wrapping his coat tightly around him, Spike yanked the zip up to his neck and flipped up his hood. 'That's got to be the way we get out,' he said. 'It's got to be. Come on!'

Trembling, they ran at the wall … and disappeared.

Spike stumbled forward, his eyes tightly closed. A moment passed, then he felt the welcoming blast of freezing air on his skin.

He opened his eyes. The snowy lane stretched out in front of him. 'We made it,' he whispered. 'We made it.'

Shaking, Terri opened one eye. 'Is it? Are we?'

Spike nodded. His hands shook.

'Home,' he said, nodding. He looked around at the others. 'We're home.'

Duke stared straight ahead, rigid with shock. Beside him, Meatball fell to his knees and pressed his face into the snow.

'Thank goodness,' sobbed Doc. '*Oh …*'

Terri stumbled to her and they hugged. One by one, the others joined them, and for a few moments, they stood in the bitter cold, overwhelmed with relief.

No one knew how or why, but by some miracle, they were still alive.

A freezing wind gnawed their faces as they stumbled home through the barren landscape, through air that smelled strongly of new snow.

Trudging along, the world they knew and loved seemed suddenly more precious. The stark outlines of the trees and the blood red of holly berries, a cawing line of black crows stringing like a bootlace across the grey sky. Familiar sights that welcomed them home.

They turned the corner into the long main road, hurrying towards the cheery lights of the village. Past the grocer, up past the butcher and the post office and on down the lane towards the little Anglo-Saxon church: the church where that morning Spike had seen the strange purple arc of light.

The distinctive red brick of Meatball's home was just visible ahead, curls of smoke drifting from its chimneys, floating up to mingle with the pale clouds.

Once inside the basement, they closed the door against the weather, and huddled round the stove. For a while, no one spoke. Flames licked the logs and they sat staring into it. Rising to her feet, Terri wandered off toward the doorway.

'I just...I just need to use your loo, Meatball.'

Meatball nodded, vaguely. 'Wonder if Mum's got any biscuits,' he said. 'I need to eat something.'

'How can you eat?'

With effort, Meatball got to his feet. 'It's either that, or throw up.'

A few minutes later, Terri reappeared in the doorway, pale and shaking. As she walked in, Duke shot to his feet and pushed past her down the hallway to the bathroom.

Doc sat in the armchair, wringing her hands, staring at the floor. 'Still,' she said. 'At least we're all right.'

Then she burst into tears. Terri rested a hand on her arm and squeezed, her own silent tears running down her face.

Duke walked back into the basement. 'I've never been so scared in all my life,' he said.

Doc held her legs still to stop them shaking. 'Me too,' she croaked. 'I thought we were going to die.'

Meatball stepped back down the stairs at that moment, carrying milk, and biscuits and a tin of chocolate. 'Stick the kettle on,' he said, ramming another biscuit into his mouth.

Leaning across, Terri took them from him. 'I'll do it,' she said. 'It'll stop me thinking.'

She looked across at Spike, who was now staring into the flames, hands clenched tightly into fists.

'Biscuit, Spike?' she asked, hopefully.

Spike didn't move.

Meatball rammed more biscuits into his mouth and crunched. 'I nearly peed myself,' he said.

Duke swallowed the last bit of his chocolate and reached out to find the packet empty. 'You scoffed the lot?'

'My need is greater than yours,' said Meatball. 'I'll get some more later.'

Terri dipped in her pocket and pulled out a pound. 'Put this to it,' she said. 'We're always eating your biscuits.' She glanced across at Spike, who was still staring into the fire. 'For me and Spike.'

'And this,' said Doc, adding a couple of coins.

Duke put in a coin of his own. 'D'you know what I don't get? If Gullivan did kill Mr Price, then why? Why kill an innocent old man?'

'Because Gullivan's *scum*!'

Suddenly jerked into life, Spike jumped to his feet and started yelling vehemently. 'Because he's a thief and a murderer and Mr Price found out about him. Because …'

He sat down again with a bump. 'Because Mr Price is old and defenceless and Gullivan's bigger than he is -'

His voice faltered. 'Because he's a thug.'

Terri reached across and squeezed his shoulders. Hunched, staring miserably down at the floor, Spike put his fingers on his eyelids to stop the threatening tears.

'One of these days Gullivan'll get what's coming to him,' Meatball growled.

Spike took a last lingering look at the watch and then slid it back into his pocket. 'I'll have him,' he muttered. 'I'll have him if it's the last thing I do.'

'Be right behind you, Spike,' Doc said.

Terri looked into his face. 'We all will.'

For a few moments, they sat quietly, just thinking about the portal, the place beyond, Mr Price, and Gullivan.

'Well one thing I do know,' Duke said. 'There is no way I am *ever* going back to that place.'

'Me neither,' growled Meatball.

'Never going near that bridge again, either,' Doc snapped.

Terri shook her head. 'Never.'

Spike listened. 'If I never see that place again, it'll be too soon,' he said. 'Who cares if Gullivan's using it. Who cares? Maybe the portal won't open next time and he'll be stuck there for ever. Good. Maybe one of those dinosaurs will eat him. Rip him to shreds. Serve him right.'

Meatball stared at him. 'Dinosaurs?'

'Yeah. Didn't you see them?'

'Dinosaurs?' Duke asked. 'What are you talking about?'

'There were dinosaurs roaming the hills. We saw them,' Terri said.

'Oh, come on.'

'There *were*.'

'Hadrosaurs,' said Doc. 'That's what they were. Least, I think so.'

'They were down in that valley place,' said Spike. 'Wandering through the trees n'that.'

Duke laughed. 'Yeah, right. Dinosaurs. Liking it.'

'We *saw* them.' Terri shook her head. 'Didn't you?'

Meatball laughed. 'You couldn't have done. They must've been something else. Couldn't have been dinosaurs, could it? Wake up, they're extinct.'

'I'm telling you they *were*,' said Doc. 'They were hadrosaurs.'

'You're *serious*.' Meatball almost fell back into his seat. 'Dinosaurs?'

'Yes, dinosaurs. Which if you think about it, fits with the trees and the plants, doesn't it?'

Duke shook his head. 'You know what this means, don't you? It means you're right, Doc. That portal or doorway, or whatever it is on the bridge must be a door to another time.'

'That's what I said.'

'So, when we went through it,' Spike said. 'We went through into prehistoric times?'

Doc nodded.

'It's not possible, is it?'

'We were there,' Doc said.

'I know,' said Terri, quietly. 'Look, can't we stop talking about it? Bad enough, it's going over and over in my mind. I feel sick just thinking about it.'

'Terri's right,' said Doc. 'Let's change the subject.'

'Fine by me,' Duke snapped.

Terri tugged at Spike's sleeve. 'I've just had a thought. What about your gran?'

'Gran? What's she got to do with anything?'

Terri looked at him, awkwardly. 'You need to tell her, Spike. She's got to know. About Mr Price, I mean.'

'Oh hell, that's a thought,' Duke said.

'You can't go doing that,' said Meatball. 'We don't know yet. Not for sure. Even the watch isn't proof.'

'Even if you do, what will you say?' Doc said. 'We found his watch through a time portal? She's hardly going to believe that, is she?'

Terri raised her eyebrows. 'No, I know, but …'

'I'm not telling her anything yet,' Spike said. 'No point in upsetting her till we know for sure.'

With a sudden yell, Meatball stood up. 'We've forgotten something. The ball!'

Jumping up, Doc ran to the filing cabinet.'It's still here.'

'No, not that. I mean the recording we did. Let's have another look at it.'

He flicked a few switches, and the monitor burst into life. They studied the screen intently, staring at strange lines that made no sense.

'What is it?'

Meatball shrugged. 'Beats me,' he said. 'I tried one or two things to make something out of it, but it might just as well be Martian.'

'Kind of thinking it's probably not Martian,' Duke said, with a grin.

'You don't think …'

Spike leaned in closer to the screen. 'The ball and the headband thing. You don't think Gullivan could have got them from that place we went?'

Meatball hooted with laughter. 'You mean the dinosaurs made 'em?'

Everyone laughed.

'That's nearly as stupid as the Martian thing,' said Doc.

Leaning across, Meatball switched off the computer. 'So, what are we going to do about this ball thing, then? We can't just forget it, it's amazing!'

'Well, we can't show it to anyone, can we?' Doc said. 'I mean, who's going to believe us?'

Spike shrugged. 'Too late now. Look, let's just hang onto it. If no one reports it or anything, we know Gullivan stole it. If they do, we'll just make out we found it.'

Somewhere in the room, something buzzed. There was a mad scramble as everyone dived for their phones.

'Mine!' Spike shouted, triumphantly. 'Oh hello, it's Billy.' He scanned the message. '*Jake's house flooded. We're paddling.* ☺. *Be home later. Gran ok?*'

Spike stared at the message. That's the second time he's asked about Gran, he thought, but why? Maybe he had noticed something.

Lifting a finger towards the keyboard, Spike stopped. His heart skipped a beat as he remembered. The time portal and the cave.

Slowly, he raised his eyes to look at the others. 'The cave and everything,' he said. 'Billy doesn't know about it. I've got to tell him ... haven't I?'

'He'll have to know at some point,' said Doc. 'He's coming home today.'

'Then again, what he doesn't know, he won't worry about,' said Meatball.

Terri shook her head. 'I think we should tell him, he'll be really annoyed if he finds out and we haven't told him. And we're bound to let something slip, aren't we?'

'Yeah, tell him,' Duke said, nodding. 'We can play him the recording, see if he can make anything out of it. He's really clued-up on stuff.'

'True,' Spike said. 'Yeah, I'll tell him. Doesn't make much difference now, anyway. I'll wait till he gets home.'

They nodded agreement.

Shortly after, they left Meatball's to make their way home.

'What an unbelievable day,' Terri sighed, flicking a fresh snowflake from her nose. 'D'you know it's really weird, that cave thing, I know it happened today, but somehow, it seems as though it was ages ago.'

'Shock,' said Doc. 'That's what that is. Dad told me. It's your body's defence system kicking in.'

'I just want to get home,' said Duke. 'And I never want to see that place again.'

'Nor me.'

Trudging along beside them, Spike's head was spinning. So much had happened since he woke up that morning, he didn't know what to worry about first. And now Billy was coming home. He knew he'd have to tell him, they shared everything, and Duke was right, he was clever.

And then there was Gran, the one worry he hadn't mentioned to the others, or Billy. Except now there were Billy's messages.

Doc and Duke went their separate ways, but Spike barely noticed.

'See you later,' Terri said, turning towards her gate.

Spike didn't answer.

'See you later,' she repeated. He looked up. 'Yeah. See you later.'

Spike walked on towards Yew Tree Cottage. Through the kitchen window, the log fire glowed with comforting light. Gran was home.

He'd barely stepped in through the door, when a large bundle of spiky grey fur lumbered down the hall towards him.

'Hello, Ed,' he said. For a moment, Spike stood, just hugging him. Finally, he felt calmer. Ed always had that effect on him. Whenever he was down, his dog cheered him up. In between Ed's snuffles and excited grunts, Spike reached down to pull off his boots.

'That you, dear?'

'Hi, Gran,' Spike called.

'Billy's coming home early,' she said. 'Jake's dad's going to drop him off soon. Did you know?'

'Yes,' Spike said. 'He sent me a text.'

Gran's smiling face appeared around the door. 'Thought I'd make you both a nice macaroni cheese,' she said. 'I know how you love it.'

'Oh, great, Gran, thanks.'

She disappeared back into the kitchen. The aroma of cooked cheese wafted down the hall.

Spike reached across to hang his scarf and hat on a hook. Beside him, on the hall stand, something trilled. It was Gran's phone.

Without thinking, Spike glanced down at it. It was glowing purple, and on the screen were four words.

'*Cassiopeia is the key*'.

CHAPTER ELEVEN

'Billy's got some news,' said Spike.

They were standing at the bus stop in the village the following morning. There was a stillness in the air, and the smell of fresh snow on the way.

'What sort of news?' Duke asked.

'About Gullivan,' said Billy. 'It was when we stopped at the garage on the way home from Jake's last night. We were standing in the queue at the desk, when a man and a woman came in. He marched up to the desk and showed them a photo of Gullivan, and started asking whether they knew him. They said he was this woman's brother and there'd been a death in the family and they were trying to find him.'

'It was definitely Gullivan they were looking for?'

Billy nodded. 'Yeah. When the man was buying some cigarettes, he put the photo down on the side, and I saw it. It was him, all right.'

'Who'd want to be his family,' Doc said.

'Probably weren't,' said Meatball. 'What did they look like, Bill?'

'They weren't from round here,' said Billy. 'Not from the country, they were city types. The man was massive, like a brick wall, with cropped hair and a tattoo on his hand. The woman was skinny and tall, with big earrings and bright red lipstick. Didn't look very nice. She seemed to be in charge, too.'

'Bet they weren't family,' said Terri. 'Not the sort of people he hangs around with. Wonder what they want with him?'

'Something horrible, I hope,' Spike said, pulling a face.

Duke looked at his watch. 'Bus is late.'

'Probably the snow,' said Doc. 'But I'd rather be here than in that cave.'

Billy bent down to stroke Ed. 'I couldn't believe it when Spike told me about it.'

'Feels like a dream, now,' Spike said. 'Like it never happened.'

'Don't talk to me about dreams,' said Meatball. 'I did nothing else all night.'

'Wish I'd been there,' Billy said, with a sigh. 'It's not fair.'

'Be glad you weren't,' said Spike. He looked down the road. 'Where's this bus?'

'Mum offered us a lift this morning,' Doc said, pulling her scarf tighter around her neck. 'She's on a late shift at the hospital, but I thought what with yesterday ... if one of us let something slip ...'

Terri stomped her boots on the icy pavement. 'It's getting in the way already, isn't it? This stupid cave thing. Wish it had never happened. Where is this bus?'

'Here it comes. Finally!'

They looked up to see an old bus coming along the road. 'That can't be it, surely. Where's the 28?'

The bus crunched its way to the kerb beside them and the centre doors flew open.

'In the middle, kids,' said the driver. 'No fares today.'

'Eh?'

'It's free today,' the driver called. 'The 28's off the road and we're late. Everyone on.'

'Brilliant,' Duke said, clambering on. 'We'll get a burger in town.'

The others followed onto the bus. It was empty and they flopped into seats at the back, Ed squeezing in at their feet.

The doors closed with a slight sigh, and the bus set off.

'Starting to snow,' Billy said, watching through the window. He twisted in his seat. 'Tell me about the cave again, Spike.'

'Not so loud, Bill!'

Spike glanced at the front of the bus, where the dark shape of the driver was just visible. 'I've told you already.'

'Yeah, but you might have missed a bit.'

'I haven't.'

Turning to look out of the window, Spike noticed Terri looking at him. As their eyes met, she raised her eyebrows. Spike sighed. She was right, he hadn't told Billy about the watch. Billy loved Mr Price every bit as much as him and he didn't want to upset him, but he had a right to know.

'Bill, look, I'm sorry, there's something else I should have told you. We found a watch,' said Spike. 'Through that other place. And it was Mr Price's.'

'*Mr Price's*?'

'We think,' said Doc, gently.

'It is,' said Spike. He pulled the watch from his pocket. 'It's got that flippy thing with the back, look.'

Billy examined it, then nodding slowly, passed it back to Spike and leaned back in his seat. 'Yeah,' he said, quietly. 'It does look like it.'

Spike watched him. Billy was one of life's thinkers, and Spike could only guess what he was thinking now. First there was all that business with Gran, and now this.

Spike had been thinking about Gran for days now, wondering whether he should mention it to Billy. Then, the night before, Billy had suddenly sat up in bed.

'You awake, Spike?'

Spike had looked across. 'Yeah, I'm awake. What?'

'Something odd's going on with Gran, Spike,' Billy hissed. 'I know it sounds stupid, but …'

Spike bit his lip. He'd told no one about the strange light beneath Gran's door, not even Terri, and he still couldn't decide whether to tell Billy. Billy was sensible, yeah, but he loved Gran so much. Spike sighed. So did he.

After a pause, he said, 'Yeah, I know.'

Billy leaped from his bed and walked across. 'You know?'

Spike took a deep breath. 'Tell me what you've seen.'

'Well, sometimes I speak to her and she seems to be in a sort of trance and doesn't answer. And then, a couple of days before I went to Jake's, I heard that old floorboard creak on the landing, so I got up to have a look. There was nothing there, but then I heard the back door shut. I looked out of the landing window and I saw Gran, going down the garden. She disappeared round that big bush at the end and then there was sort of a purple light.'

'You should've woken me up!' Spike hissed.

'I didn't think. Anyway, you never told me about the watch!'

'Well, you might have said something.'

'No, I wouldn't! I'm not stupid, I'm more sensible than you are.'

'Course you're not!'

'I am.'

Spike sighed. 'Yes, all right, you are. Sometimes. So, what happened, then?'

'I kept watching and there was another purple flash and Gran came around the corner.'

Spike frowned at him. 'What did she say?'

'She *said* she thought she heard a fox and she went down to check the chickens, but she couldn't have, could she? The chickens are over the other side of the house.'

'That's right,' said Spike. 'They are. He thought for a moment. 'You saw a purple light?'

Billy nodded.

'Then you're right, Bill, something odd is going on,' Spike said. 'And I'm wondering if it's something to do with all these purple lights.'

'You said you saw a purple light when Gullivan appeared on the bridge!'

Spike nodded. 'Yeah, and I've seen others, 'n' all.'

He told Billy about the lights beneath Gran's door.

'D'you think we should tell the others?' Billy asked.

Spike shook his head. 'No, not yet. I don't want them to know about Gran.'

Sitting on the bus beside Billy the following day, Spike thought about their conversation. Was he right not to tell the others about Gran? He wasn't sure, but things about Gran were nothing to do with anyone else, it was just between him and Billy.

A sudden whirring noise jolted him out of his thoughts. The driver had switched the wipers to a faster speed.

'It's pouring down,' said Duke, nose pressed to the window. 'I can hardly see.'

'Looks like a blizzard,' said Doc. 'Hope we can get back all right.'

'You should've brought your new sledge, Meatball,' said Terri. She glanced at him. '*Meatball?*'

Meatball was staring down the aisle to the front of the bus. Spike and the others followed his gaze.

The bus was accelerating fast, but the driver's seat was empty. Through the front window, they saw a blinding purple light.

As the light grew nearer and enveloped the bus, Ed sat up and let out a long howl.

They were back in the cave.

Terri looked slowly around. It was definitely the same place. The smell, and the constant drip of water.

Beside her, Duke wiped a trickle of water from his forehead. 'We're back in that stinking cave again!' he yelled. '*No ...*'

Meatball spun around, staring at dark, slimy walls. 'We *can't* be ... it's not possible.'

'I don't get it,' Spike cried. 'We haven't come through the wall, or anything!'

'*The wall!*'

They turned as one and threw themselves against the wall, pushing against it, kicking it, thumping it with their fists, but it was just wall. Solid, impenetrable, and firmly closed.

'It's shut!' Doc shouted, thumping her fists on the rock. 'It's shut! How can it be shut?'

Frantic for them, Ed jumped about, barking wildly.

'Ed!' Billy wrapped his arms about the dog's neck. 'Ed, quiet! We're trying to think!'

Burying his face in Ed's fur, Spike tried to control the panic he felt inside. 'It's all right, boy,' he said, squeezing him. 'It's all right. I hope.'

Terri stared at the wall. A tear ran down her cheek before she could stop it. 'I can't understand why it's closed.'

Meatball squeezed his hands into fists. 'Why should it be open?' he asked. 'We didn't come through it!'

'This is definitely it, then, Spike?' Billy reached out to touch the wall. 'This is the place you said, where you came before?'

Spike looked at him. He so wanted to say it wasn't the same place, that they were all having a terrible dream, and when they woke up, they'd be at home with Gran. But he couldn't. Billy was only two years younger, but somehow, Spike felt responsible for him. 'Yes,' he croaked. 'Yes, it is. Though what we're doing here ...'

Terri bit back tears of shock. 'I had a feeling there was something odd about that bus.'

'Then why didn't I?' Meatball yelled. 'Why didn't I know?'

'Looks like you weren't supposed to,' said Duke. 'There's something weird going on.' He turned to look down the corridor, where the same distant splash of light marked the way out. 'Doesn't look as though we've got any choice, does it?'

They made their way down the corridor, Ed's claws clacking on the stone floor.

'I've just had a thought,' said Doc, as the light drew nearer. 'What if Gullivan's here?'

They paused for a moment.

'Chance we'll have to take,' said Meatball. 'There's no other way.'

At the end of the corridor, Duke peered around the edge. Empty. A sigh of relief shuddered through his chest. 'Ok,' he said.

Together with the others, he walked out into the mouth of the cave.

Spike gave a sudden cry. 'Look! Weapons! An axe, and some knives!'

'Must be Gullivan's,' said Meatball, turning a knife in his hand. 'We'd better leave them.'

'No way!' Spike said. 'What if those dinosaurs are a bit nearer this time?'

Duke picked up the remaining knife and slid it into his pocket. 'Damn right,' he said.

The plateau was still and empty as they stepped outside, shielding their eyes in the sudden brilliance of the daylight.

'It's boiling!' said Duke. 'It wasn't this hot last time.'

'Thank goodness we've got water with us,' Doc said.

'I've got a couple of bottles,' said Spike, patting the rucksack on his back. 'I always bring it. Ed gets thirsty these days.'

'Hey!' cried Meatball, suddenly. 'Look at those! Are they what you meant?'

He pointed to the far hills of the valley where large, lumbering creatures were visible in the distance, long willowy necks among the treetops.

Doc stared. 'Nope,' she said. 'They're apatasaurus!'

High in the sky above the valley, a huge winged creature soared effortlessly through the air, casting a long black shadow across the ground.

Billy craned his neck to watch it. 'Wow! It's massive!'

Spike ducked, despite the creature being so far above him.

'I wonder where Gullivan is?' said Terri.

'If he's here,' said Meatball. 'He might not be.'

'So how are we going to follow him back if he's not here?'

'Who knows,' Duke said. 'But there's got to be a way back somewhere. Gullivan gets back somehow.'

'Perhaps we could have a look down there,' Billy said, pointing ahead to where the plateau dipped down, sloping away into the sprawling green valley. 'I mean, even if we don't find him, we could have a look. And it'll be cooler down there.'

'If we're going to do that, let's leave our coats 'n' stuff in those bushes,' said Duke. 'If Gullivan is here, he won't see them. We'll have a look, but we won't wander too far. The last thing we need is to get lost.'

Spike bent down to pat Ed's head. 'No worries. Ed'll get us back.'

Billy gave Ed a hug. 'He'll get us back all right.'

They each took a gulp of water, poured some into the bag Spike had brought for Ed, and waited while he lapped at it. Then, with a last glance back at the cave, they began to climb the mound. At the top, they stood for a moment, gazing down, watching for movement.

It was now or never. Anything could be waiting, even Gullivan himself, but there was only one way to find out.

At the front of the group, Duke swallowed hard. 'Shall we go then?'

They nodded, and together, they started the slow trudge down the valley wall.

As they made their way down into the moist humidity of the valley, the ground gradually changed from dusty soil to thick, green shrubs and vegetation. The warm breeze was gentle, caressing their skin, heavy with the intoxicating scent of tropical flowers. Insects hummed and buzzed around them.

Terri jumped as something whizzed past her ear. 'What was that?'

'It's a dragonfly,' said Doc. 'Look at it. It's *enormous.*'

They walked steadily on. The ground was soft, and thickly coated with leaves and springy plants. Horsetails pushed their long, curled heads upwards like luxurious bottlebrushes;

broad cycad fronds burst from ridged, hairy trunks, splaying outwards as they reached for the sun.

As Spike pushed his way through, huge glossy leaves sprang back like giant paddles.

Among the stout trees, small reservoirs of water, teeming with life, nestled in sections of split bark. Large, brilliantly coloured blooms hung in the crooks of the branches, dripping nectar, their long fibrous roots dangling toward the earth.

Spike watched the fleshy leaves of a clinging plant close firmly, trapping its prey within. There was something odd about this place, something not quite right, and whatever it was, it was giving him the creeps.

Plodding slowly on, they walked tightly against the incline as the valley opened out before them. The air seemed thicker here: muggy and close. A fine mist dampened their skin and hair, and despite the heat and the sweat, their clothes had the chill of feeling damp. The slight breeze that had ruffled their hair at the top of the hill lessened as they descended, and then died completely.

They were deep into the valley basin, where the leaves dripped water, and the air was alive with insects, when Ed suddenly stiffened and gave a low growl.

Spike turned. 'Ed?'

'What is it, Ed?' Billy stared at Ed's tense, aggressive, stance. 'What's wrong?'

Ed was watching a wall of dense foliage, and baring his teeth, the growl rumbling in his throat.

'Ed? What is it, boy?'

Ed didn't respond. He was quite still, his long nose fixed on the spot, sniffing hard. Spike moved slowly to his side, and then slid a hand into the bag on his back and pulled out the axe.

'What is it, boy? You smell something?'

A slight rustle in the bushes quickly became a smacking sound. Through a sudden break in the leaves, something burst out, scampered frantically past on tiny legs and disappeared into the vegetation behind them.

Whipping around, Ed lunged, his teeth crashing together with a loud snap, only centimetres away from the creature. Spike grabbed him, yanking him back by his collar.

'Did you see that thing?' cried Billy.

Duke stared hard at the bushes where the little creature had disappeared. 'What was it?'

Ed growled again, deep and menacing, the noise reverberating in his throat until it spilled over into a loud bark.

Holding the knife ahead of him, Meatball stepped backward.

'Let's get away from here,' he said. 'There's something there, in those bushes. I can sense it.'

A sudden rustle in the leaves made them start. Slowly they edged away, hearts thumping.

At that moment, suspended among the branches barely a metre above the ground, a head suddenly punched through the leaves, bobbing like a jack-in-a-box. Tiny eyes stared at them. Flaring nostrils sniffed the air, smelling, scenting. Trickles of moisture gleamed on greyish-brown skin. Jaws gaped slightly open, revealing rows of razor-sharp teeth.

In a fit of fury, Ed threw himself forward, pulling and straining against his collar. Dropping the axe, Spike gripped Ed's collar and fought with all his strength to hold him as Ed lunged toward the creature.

Billy rushed to help, and with a final effort, they managed to yank him back.

The branches moved again. Another head appeared, jostling for space.

With a hand still on Ed's collar, Spike reached slowly down for the axe, but Ed jerked forward again, almost pulling Billy with him and the axe dropped to the ground.

One of the creatures stepped a little nearer, a strange murmur rumbling in its throat. A gust of foul-smelling breath wafted toward them from its open mouth.

Meatball stumbled backwards. Duke leaped to his side, the knife clutched tightly in his hand.

'Get Ed away!' he screamed. 'Meatball! Watch the other one!'

'Take him, Bill! You'll have to hold him!' Spike yelled.

Terri tucked her scarf through Ed's collar, and then she and Doc braced themselves and pulled, while Billy held on.

Ed was now almost upright, snarling and growling, tearing at the air with his paws.

Meatball steadied himself, the long point of the knife thrust ahead of him. At his side, Duke gripped his knife and jabbed the point at the creature.

'*Look out!*'

Doc screamed a warning, as one of the creatures took a springy step forward, the second close on its heels. Stained saliva ran from its open jaws, dribbling onto the ground.

Meatball swung his arm wildly, slicing the air with the knife as he thrust it towards the creature, narrowly missing it as it dipped and swerved. Repeatedly, he struck out until the point of the knife caught the creature's neck, drawing blood, but still it came on.

Beside him, Duke swept his knife toward the other creature, slicing into the thick skin, but it barely seemed to slow them down.

Spike bent down and grabbed the axe with both hands, lifted it high into the air, and swung it with all his might.

Powerful necks extended, the heads of the creatures bobbed and weaved, dodging the strikes. Cold reptilian eyes flickered.

Then, the first of them ducked low and pushed forward.

Whistling through the air, Spike's axe whirled around in a neat arc and struck home against the creature's body, slashing a gaping wound that erupted blood. Screaming with pain, it stumbled and overbalanced. For a moment or two, it lay there, stunned, then somehow roused itself and fled after its companion, into the sopping undergrowth.

They heard the crashing of their bodies through the trees, and then silence.

Heart drumming in his ears, Meatball gasped. 'D'you ...
d'you think ...?'

Spike shook his head, staring at the blood dripping from
the blade of his axe. 'Don't know -'

Billy looked up at him. His fingers were tight with fatigue
and fright, welded around Ed's collar. 'D'you reckon they've
gone?'

'Who knows?' Duke moved the knife painfully to his
other hand. 'What do we do if they come back?'

Ed gave one last volley of defiant barks and then flopped
into a sitting position beside Spike, who bent down to pat his
head. 'Well done, boy.' His trembling fingers tightened
around the wiry fur. 'That was close.'

Terri shook, her hands numb. 'Too close,' she said. 'Let's
get out of here.'

'What if they're still in there,' said Meatball, staring hard
at the bushes. 'What if they're following us?'

Duke pushed the knife into his pocket. 'It's not if, it's
when. We need to get back to the cave.'

'But what about Gullivan?'

'We'll have to take a chance. If we stay here -'

'Ssh!' Doc held a hand in the air. 'There's something
moving.'

They listened. More sounds were coming from the bushes,
louder sounds, the sounds of undergrowth being crushed and
swept aside.

In slow, hesitant steps, they eased away. Ed pulled at
Spike's grip and began to growl.

'We're being watched, I can sense it,' said Meatball.
'Over there ...'

'No,' Billy whispered. 'Over here ...'

At that moment the small creature that had dashed past
them earlier reappeared, and careered across the open
ground, galloping wildly through them and out of sight.

The crashing somewhere in the bushes grew louder.

'It wasn't him,' said Spike. 'There's something else. From
this direction.'

With a look of horror, Meatball gripped Duke's arm. 'The blood … you don't think …'

Duke's eyes opened wide with terror. He let out a long cry. 'Run! For God's sake, *R-U-N*!'

They charged headlong into the undergrowth, running blindly, lurching and stumbling over roots and branches, Ed flying along beside them, bounding over obstacles.

Damp leaves showered them, insects flew into their faces, and branches snagged their clothing and scraped their skin, but none of that mattered.

Nothing mattered except the appalling noise behind them. Something was moving at speed: something heavy, the chilling thud of its feet pounding the ground as it blundered and smashed its way through. A terrible, frightening sound that made their stomachs churn and their hearts pound with fear.

For now, surely, there were more than one or two creatures in pursuit. This sounded like a pack, or, more terrifyingly, something much, much larger.

Running on and on, their legs shook and their chests heaved with exertion, but they barely noticed the pain. Fear drove them onwards until they burst from the forest, pouring out into the brilliant sunlight of a clearing, to see an enormous hill rise up in front of them.

Exhausted, Terri started to slow. 'I can't breathe … I can't *breathe*!'

Gasping and choking, Spike bent over, gripping his knees. 'We have to keep going, they're …'

'Listen!'

Duke stopped. 'It's getting fainter … I swear …'

The thundering of feet faded and stopped, and a different noise began: a noise that chilled them, raising goose bumps on their skin. It was the sound of screams and shrieks, resonating and petrifying. And above this, something else, deeper, echoing and ominous.

They started again, clambering up the hill.

Almost at the top, Doc glanced over her shoulder. Down at the bottom of the hill, at the very edge of the forest, she saw a huge animal lope out into the clearing on long, gangly legs, and stop. Another pushed through the trees behind it and then another. Large heads were slowly turning in their direction. Here, in full sight, was the chilling source of the noise they'd heard in the forest.

'Oh *no*.' Doc's sobs choked her. 'They've seen us!'

Near to collapse, they staggered to the top of the hill and tumbled over the ridge onto the downward slope in an uncontrollable wave. Their legs were moving automatically, so numb with the effort, they seemed to be almost floating.

Glancing back, Spike's eyes fell on the heart-stopping scene on the hill behind them.

In full sight now, the creatures were hurtling forward, pouring down the slope like a ramshackle army charging into battle: a barrage of teeth, feet, and claws, terrifying, fascinating, and getting ever nearer.

They were running for their lives.

'Hold it!' Duke's voice rang in their ears. 'Hang on!' he yelled. '*STOP!*'

They began to slow.

Meatball bent double with pain. 'We have to keep going.'

'They've stopped,' Duke gasped.

'*What?*'

Spike leaned on Ed, wheezing and gasping. 'Stopped? What d'you mean, stopped?'

Duke pushed himself upright long enough to point up the hill. 'See for yourself.'

They swung around. Their attackers had stopped halfway down the hill and now stood jostling for space.

'He's right!' yelled Billy. 'What are they doing?'

'They're getting ready,' sobbed Terri. 'That's what they're doing. They know they've got us.'

Duke gripped his side, wincing in pain. 'What the hell are we going to do,' he wailed. 'We'll never outrun them.'

'Look at that!' Spike let out a yell. '*There! Look!*'

He pointed high up on the hill, where it dipped and flowed out onto a patch of level land. A lone animal, broken away from the others, was standing there, quite still.

Ed gave a low growl.

'It's watching us,' Doc burbled. 'It's *watching* us!' Her voice was almost a scream. With a slight whimper, she said, 'Why doesn't it …?'

Above them, the animal continued to watch. Nearby, the massed bodies of his companions pushed and shoved against each other.

'This is ridiculous,' Meatball croaked. 'They're like … like soldiers waiting -'

At that moment, the lone animal started to move, and then broke into a run, charging toward them. They watched, frozen with fear, as its feet tore into the grass.

With a jerk of his head, Ed broke free from Spike's grasp and launched himself into a run toward the advancing creature.

'*ED! NO-O-O!*'

Screaming at the top of his voice, Spike tried to stumble after him, the axe flailing wildly about in his hand, but his legs buckled beneath him, and he tumbled to his knees.

Billy staggered past him. 'ED! *Ed*!'

Meatball made a grab for Billy, but missed, colliding with Duke who managed to get a hold on Billy's shirt.

'Let me go! I've got to get him!' Billy sobbed. *'I've got to!'*

Spike hobbled forward to where Billy stood with Duke and Meatball, Terri and Doc staggering along beside him, but it was no use. They had stopped, and tight with fatigue, the muscles in their legs refused to take them any further.

They screeched and shouted, pleaded with Ed to stop. In the distance, frantic for their safety, Ed hurtled on, his huge paws pounding the ground, oblivious to their calls.

Spike slid once again to his knees, and started to sob. Billy gave one last scream of pain, that robbed him of any more speech.

Halfway up the hill, Ed was running, getting nearer to the charging animal that was thundering along the ground toward him, its enormous jaws flailing with the effort. They watched helplessly, tears streaming down their faces.

'*E-E-ED!*'

Convulsed with tears, Spike gave one last frantic call as Ed careered across the ground.

The creature was almost upon Ed, poised to attack, when it happened. As if something had punched it, the creature catapulted backwards high into the air. There was nothing there, nothing to see, yet something struck the creature full on and sent it flying through the air, and now it lay helplessly on its back, writhing and kicking.

Dazed, it managed to right itself and charge again, only to find itself on its back once more. Time after time, it rushed at the invisible barrier, until finally, as if accepting it couldn't pass, it turned and lumbered away.

But Ed was still running. Now only metres away, he launched himself at the creature, hit the barrier, and hurtled backwards through the air.

'Something's stopping them,' Spike wheezed, as he and the others reached Ed and collapsed onto the grass.

'It's a force field,' Terri said, quietly.

Spike looked at her. She was staring straight ahead, the pain and terror suddenly washed from her face.

'That's what's happening,' she said. 'They're coming up against a force field.' She broke her concentration to look at them. 'I don't know how I know, I just do.'

Doc gasped. '*A force field?* But ... but where would that come from? I mean, who could've -'

A slight noise made Duke spin around.

'*Oh hell,*' he breathed.

CHAPTER TWELVE

There were six of them. Six … *what*? Creatures? People?

Spike trembled as he gazed at the group of strange, figures standing before them. What on earth were they?

They weren't human. All right, they were standing on two feet, upright like humans, but with faces like that? No way were they human.

Spike's mind churned. What else could they be, then? Dinosaurs? No, not dinosaurs. They might have funny heads, but they looked civilised and intelligent. And they were wearing clothes.

Spike stared at them, trying to breathe calmly. Their clothes were odd, not like anything he'd seen before. The two figures standing directly in front were dressed in robes of intense purple, which draped to the ground, a blaze of silver visible between the folds as they waved slightly in the breeze. Rigid, seamless boots protruded from the hem.

Frozen to the spot, Spike carefully shifted his gaze to the four at the outer edge of the group. They were taller than the others, massive, muscular things. They stood apart, forming a perfect square of protection around the two in the robes. Guards, Spike wondered? He looked at their muscles, tight beneath their uniform. It was similar in colour, but in a close fitting, heavy material. Powerfully built, and sturdy, they towered over everyone. Definitely guards. Spike tried to guess their height. Seven … eight feet maybe?

'Holy cow! What are they?' Duke whispered.

'Don't ask me,' hissed Meatball. 'Don't move …'

Spike glanced to one side where Billy stood, frowning. 'They're reptiles, Spike.'

Shaking with fear, Terri snapped. 'Shut up, Bill! They're looking at us!'

'He's right,' said Doc. 'Look at their skin.'

'Shut up!'

'All of you shut up!' Spike whispered. Just then he felt pressure on his leg. Glancing down, he saw Ed's warm, spiky body leaning against him as if he were an armchair. Ed didn't seem in the least bit bothered by anything that was going on. Why? Why wasn't he bothered? Was that good, or bad?

Spike raised his eyes. The figure in front seemed to be staring at Ed, watching him. Why wasn't Ed growling? Maybe he was being hypnotised, or controlled, or something. Spike thought about the axe in his bag. He didn't care who they were, they weren't having his dog. He'd defend him to his last breath.

Billy watched Ed. 'Spike, why isn't Ed doing anything?'

'I don't know,' Spike murmured. 'Wish I did.'

'What do we do, now?' asked Doc.

'Wait, I s'pose,' Duke said.

Spike's hands pricked with sweat. 'For what?' he said. 'To be bumped off?'

He stopped as the taller of the two robed figures stepped forward and lowered its gaze to look at him.

Spike looked up into the face, shrouded in a metallic hood. The hairs on his arms stood up. This is it, he thought, I've had it. We've all had it. Billy …

Reaching out a hand, Spike grasped Billy's arm and yanked him behind him. They'd have to get through him before they got Bill. Behind him, he heard soft shuffling as the others followed his lead and crowded round.

Tears pricked Spike's eyes as he stared defiantly back. The figure in front of him had a large, noble head with broad set eyes and short nose. The skin of its face was strangely iridescent, with an almost leathery texture, like someone who'd spent too many years in the sun.

Spike looked again at the figure's eyes. The pupils were a deep, fiery orange. As Spike watched, an eyelid swished rapidly across the eyeball and back again.

Spike's mouth went dry. He'd seen that before, but where?

The figure blinked again, lids sweeping side to side across the orange eyes so swiftly he almost missed it.

Swish-swish.

Spike's chest tightened. A crocodile. That was where he'd seen it before. On crocodiles.

Struggling to get his breath, Spike's mind whirled. It couldn't be ... *they* couldn't be. Crocodiles were reptiles and these people were standing up. What was going on? Would they now have to fight these creatures? Who were they? *What* were they? And why weren't they doing anything?

Quaking with fear, he looked back into the eyes that gazed down into his.

As he stared into them, absurdly, he felt his fear subside and a strange sense of reassurance take its place. His mind battled against it, trying to understand. How could staring into the eyes of a reptile be reassuring?

Meatball leaned forward to whisper in his ear. 'Did you see his eyes?'

Spike nodded dumbly.

'I told you they were reptiles,' Billy hissed.

'He's right,' Doc murmured.

Biting back tears, Terri pushed herself closely to the others. 'Oh, help us,' she moaned.

Still staring at the figure, Spike felt himself start to relax. He fought the feeling desperately. He mustn't relax, he had Billy to protect. If only he knew what to do next.

Stretching himself upright, he took a deep breath and stepped boldly forward. Crocodiles eat people, the voice in his head kept saying. Crocodiles eat people.

Closer to the figure, the orange eyes loomed large: the steady gaze almost piercing. Not threatening, though, Spike told himself. Not threatening.

Swish-swish. The creature's eyelids moved rapidly.

Turning its head abruptly, it began to communicate with the creatures beside it in short, sharp bursts.

Spike held his breath. Obviously, they were using some form of communication, because their mouths were moving. He watched their lips, trying to get some idea of what they might be saying, but it was hopeless. The central figure was communicating something to his companion, who in turn, gave instruction to the guards, but there was no sound.

He took comfort in the fact that Ed, who had moved with him and now sat back down beside him, also seemed relaxed, showing no signs of unease or aggression. Looking down, he noticed Ed's long wispy tail was starting to wag. Wagging his tail? What *was* going on?

A movement made him look up.

At the edge of the group, the guards were beginning to move. Lofty and ramrod straight, two of them separated from the main party and stepped slowly past to position themselves at the rear of the group.

Meatball and Duke stood together, watching, as they went by. The guards were huge, overshadowing everything else.

Huddled in the centre, Spike looked around to see Terri and Doc clutch at each other, watching as the guards took up their position behind them all.

As he turned back, Spike saw the remaining two guards filter outwards to form a larger escort of protection at the front of the group. He watched the light bouncing off their glistening skulls, their enormous shoulders and backs beneath the heavy uniform that fitted like a second skin.

'What happens if those dinosaurs turn up again, and attack us all?' Duke said. 'I s'pose they must be able to do something, mustn't they?'

'They must have some weapons on them,' Doc said, 'they've got to have, haven't they? Stands to reason.'

Staring intently at their uniforms, Spike tried to visualise where it might be possible to conceal a weapon of some kind. That long staff they carried … that could be a weapon. The base of it blazed with light, so surely it must be something. If it was anything like that force field …

The leading figure turned to speak to him. Raising its head, it reached up to touch its throat, its lips twitching convulsively as it spoke.

'We will take you to the City, where you will be safe from the night hunters. You have nothing to fear from us, I assure you, we can protect you there. In the morning, you will be free to do as you wish.'

Spike gawped, vaguely aware his mouth had dropped open in surprise like a startled goldfish.

'We do not have the vocal capabilities to communicate in your language,' the leader continued. 'However, with the aid of this translating device, it is possible for us to understand one another.'

He pointed at his throat where a vein of purple light pulsed around a slender silver band as he spoke.

The creature turned. At his signal, they moved off as a group, the two guards ahead leading the way in large strides.

Sandwiched between the two groups of guards, they travelled on slowly, a little distance behind the leader and his companion, who walked with such grace and fluidity, they seemed almost to float across the ground. To Spike's surprise, Ed trotted along between them, his huge mouth gaping open, his tongue lolling to one side, panting with the heat.

'What's going on with Ed?' Terri breathed. 'The way he's walking with them like that. He doesn't seem worried or anything.'

Spike didn't answer, but he was watching as Ed loped along quite happily between two weird looking strangers. There had to be an explanation, there had to be. The problem was, the only explanations he could think of seemed impossible.

'I wish I knew who they were,' Doc murmured.

'I can't help thinking,' Meatball said, 'I mean, if they were going to kill us, they'd have done it back there, wouldn't they? Left us as dinner for the dinosaurs. They wouldn't bother taking us all the way home.'

'Perhaps they're going to put us in a zoo,' Spike countered. 'Like *we're* the weirdos.'

'I suppose to them, we probably are,' said Doc.

'If there was any danger, Ed would let us know.' Terri said. 'It is a bit odd, isn't it, the way he seems to have taken to them.'

'What I'd like to know is where they're taking us,' Meatball said. 'I mean, it's all very well him saying we've got nothing to worry about, but how do we know?'

Duke nodded. 'He mentioned some sort of city, didn't he?'

'Why don't we ask?' said Billy. 'Spike, can't you ask him?'

Spike looked at him. 'I'd better not,' he said. 'He might not like it.'

As if he had heard every word, the leader answered without turning his head or slowing pace. 'Be assured. We will reach the city soon.'

Spike looked at the others. They moved closer together.

In silence, they continued on down the hill into the deep basin of the valley, where the air felt thick and cloying, coating their faces.

Meatball grabbed his T-shirt and used it to mop the sweat trickling down his forehead. Spike's shirt had stuck to his back and he wiped his hands desperately down the leg of his jeans to dry his palms, but it was no use.

For the first time since they'd met these strange creatures, Spike wished they could arrive, so he could get out of the heat. He looked up ahead to where Ed was still trotting by the leader's side and wished they could stop so he could give Ed a drink. He must be gasping.

At that moment, Ed turned and trotted back to walk with him, close enough to touch. Spike poured a little water into his hand as best he could as they walked.

A low mist seemed to be descending now, shrouding the whole valley in ethereal wisps of white as the sky gradually faded through hues of purple, pink and gold, casting eerie shadows across the land. The air was full of strange cries, echoing off the slopes of the hills. Over on the horizon, the sun pulsed like a giant orange, cruising steadily out of view and as the sky faded into twilight, the first twinkling stars became faintly visible.

As the sun sank below the horizon, the robes of the figures striding before them began to glow, softly at first, then steadily brighter as the surrounding light dimmed, bathing the area in soft dappled light. Mesmerised, Spike watched as the hems of the creature's long gowns flowed back and forth in shimmering waves like fibre-optic curtains.

The evening light was almost gone when the party finally slowed and drew to a halt. The inky blackness of night closed in, the sky revealing its stars in all their brilliant glory.

Shivering with nerves, Spike and the others stood in the middle of the group, waiting.

'What now?' Terri breathed.

Spike shrugged. 'Don't know.' He reached around to his bag and felt the comforting outline of the axe handle through the heavy material.

'You can't see anything past those robes,' said Doc. 'They're so bright, it's blinding.'

'They must be doing something,' said Meatball. 'Perhaps they're contacting somebody. Get them to open the door or something.'

'Door? What door? There isn't anything.'

'Maybe we're about to find out,' Spike said. 'Something's happening over there … *look*!'

It was only a flicker at first: a mere glimpse of light. And then gradually, from a point high in the air, something began to appear. The flicker spread, pouring downwards into a thin silver arc, faint glowing beads of light shimmering around the edges. The silver arc expanded, growing into a long curve, the glowing beads joining to form a gleaming doorframe of light that sent beams splaying across the ground.

Shielding their eyes, they squinted at the enormous panel standing on the ground, pulsing gently.

The pulsing stopped and the whole panel dimmed.

Breathlessly, Spike and the others waited as the leader took a step forward. From a pyramid-shaped emblem on his robe, a shaft of purple light struck the panel, which began to melt, slowly and thickly like molten wax, drawing evenly away from the centre as though someone were pulling cords from within. It moved effortlessly, rolling over itself to collect around the outer edge of the frame where it seemed to disappear, sucked inside.

A moment's pause, then the leader signalled to move ahead and they walked slowly through.

'I don't like this,' Terri said. 'Once we're in there ...'

One of the figures turned to answer her. 'You have nothing to fear. You are safe now.'

Yeah, right, thought Spike.

As they passed through the doorway, he took a closer look at the silver doorframe. Where the edges had peeled away, the metal was fluid, swirling and contorting in coloured eddies, like a soap bubble.

He peered at it for a moment, and then jumped back with a start, as the folds of silver began to seal the opening behind them, flowing in a thick paste toward the ground. As he watched it, the panel dimmed and melded over into a solid barrier.

This is it then, he thought. Here we are, trapped inside like prisoners. Maybe for good. He looked back at the door. It was like everything else they'd encountered since they left home: solid and impenetrable.

Reaching into his rucksack, Spike pulled out his bottle of water and looked at it. A few drops. Carefully, he unscrewed the lid and poured it into his cupped hand, holding it out for Ed, who lapped at it with his long tongue, sending it everywhere. Terri bent down to add the little that remained in her bottle, then topped it with the dregs of the bottles offered by the others. For a minute or two, they watched as Ed slaked his thirst, finishing every drop.

She ruffled the hair on his head and slowly straightened up. All was quiet; the whole party, even the new faces that surrounded them, seemed to be waiting for Ed to finish.

There was a moment's further silence, before the tallest of the robed figures turned to face them.

'Welcome to our City. My name is Arisius. I am the Prime Sentinel. This is Signant Opi.'

The figure beside him bowed.

'Why are we here?' Spike said. 'What's going on? What d'you want with us?'

'Why did you rescue us from the dinosaurs?' Billy asked.

'It's perfectly natural that you should have questions,' said the Sentinel. 'And that you should be anxious. Please forgive us if we have caused you distress. All questions shall be answered.'

Meatball stepped forward. 'Yeah, that all sounds great, but how do we know this place is safe?'

'How do we know *you* are?' Duke said. 'Sorry, but you know …'

'We mean you no harm,' said Opi.

Terri moved a little nearer. 'I would like to say thank you,' she said.

The others turned to look at her.

'Well, they saved us, didn't they?' she snapped. 'From those horrific dinosaurs. They didn't have to, they could have just left us there.'

'She's got a point,' Billy said.

Terri looked back at the Sentinel. 'I think they mean what they say.' She shrugged her shoulders helplessly. 'I don't know why.'

'She could be right,' said Billy. 'I mean, Ed doesn't seem bothered, does he?'

Spike glanced at Ed, who had settled down on the floor in front of them, looking completely relaxed.

Doc stared down at him. 'Why isn't he bothered?'

'A very intelligent question,' answered the Sentinel. 'One which I look forward to discussing with you at some future date, but for now you may be assured you are safe here, as our honoured guests. You have had a long and arduous journey and must be in need of rest and refreshment. If you will permit …?'

Approaching a doorway, he placed a hand onto a panel in the wall. A door whispered open and the Sentinel passed through into a corridor. 'Follow me.'

Spike looked around at the others. 'What d'you reckon?'

Meatball took a deep breath. 'Haven't got much choice, have we?'

'No,' said Duke. 'We haven't.'

Terri stepped ahead. Ed rose with her to plod alongside.

She turned to look at them. 'Think it might be ok,' she said.

Tagging on the end, Spike prayed Terri was right.

The corridor stretched out before them, long and wide, with a high arched ceiling and smooth walls of a silver metallic material. An archway of light blossomed outward along the walls to light the way ahead, moving with them as they walked along, fading behind as they passed onto the next section.

Leaning slightly backwards, Meatball studied the wall closely, following it from the shining floor, up the walls and onto the ceiling, but he was unable to find a single join. From floor to ceiling, it appeared to flow in one continuous sheet.

'That's weird,' he murmured.

Doc nodded. 'I was looking at that,' she said. 'There's no join, is there? And have you seen that light thing? It's moving with us.'

Terry put out a hand. 'Wow … how clever is this? Feel it.'

Doc ran a hand over the wall. 'It's soft,' she said. She pushed a finger gently into it. It made a small dimple in the fabric of the wall, which popped back as she removed it. 'And it's warm.'

'Warm?'

Spike put out a hand, letting his fingers run along the wall as they walked along. It was comfortably warm and soft as skin. He nodded, slowly.

From there, his gaze flickered up toward the ceiling. Running along the top of the wall, he noticed several crystals set in pattern into the fabric. Not a random pattern: the stones seemed to be set in a definite order, repeated at intervals along the corridor. Odd place to have jewels, he thought, maybe they were lights or something.

A thought entered his head. Maybe they were some kind of weapon, lasers maybe.

The procession stopped for a moment and he gazed at the stones, tilting his head slightly to look at them from a different angle. Something about them looked familiar.

That particular bit, for instance, he was sure he'd seen before. That long line of stones. Two red, three green, one blue, two eyes, one purp … wait a minute … two *eyes*?

Zipping back along the line, he went through them again. Three green, one blue … no … two white. He must have been mistaken.

A faint whispering sound pulled his attention from the crystals. In front of them, another door had opened, and the Sentinel was leading the way into a large spacious room. Once through the doorway, he waved a hand through the air. The walls glowed at once with daylight and a cool breeze wafted gently around them. As they stepped onto it, the polished floor sank beneath them like soft carpet.

The leader addressed them, the band at his throat pulsing with light.

'With your kind permission, I should like to know your names?'

Duke was the first to speak. 'I'm Duke … um … this is Meatball.'

Meatball nodded.

'I'm Doc,' Doc said.

The Sentinel addressed Spike. 'And you, I believe, are Spike?'

Spike nodded. The spikes on his head swayed in agreement. 'I'm Spike,' he said. 'This is my brother, Billy. And this here's Terri.'

'Thank you. I am honoured to make your acquaintance. Rest for a while and Opi will arrange for some refreshment.'

'That's very kind of you,' Terri said, courteously. 'Thank you.'

Smiling, the Sentinel nodded and withdrew.

'Shouldn't bother being all nice,' Spike muttered, after the door had whispered shut. 'We don't know what's going on yet.'

'Suppose it can't hurt to keep on their good side,' said Meatball.

They looked around at their new surroundings. The room was a perfect circle, with smooth walls of the same skin-like material. Stroking the wall with her hand, Terri watched her fingers leave temporary trails in the surface. 'This is warm, too. Same stuff, I s'pose.'

Doc put out a cautious hand towards one of a number of large metallic cubes, positioned around the room.

'What d'you reckon this is?'

'Don't know. Touch it,' said Spike. 'See what happens.'

'*You* touch it.'

Spike shrugged. 'All right.' Walking across to another cube, he put out his hand to touch the surface. It felt warm and yielded to the shape of his hand.

'It's really weird,' he said. 'Like warm clay, but it's not sticky.' He pushed his hand deeper into it and then pulling it free, checked it and slowly sat himself into the centre of the cube. Immediately, it moulded itself to his body shape and supported him. 'Here,' he said, 'check this out!'

They slid carefully onto the remaining cubes. The cubes did nothing untoward, but simply supported their weight. Fascinated, they leaned from to one side to the other. Each time, the cubes moved with them.

For a few moments they sat still, looking around, then Duke pushed himself up and out of his cube and walked across the room to stare through a small panel in the door.

'D'you know, it's odd,' he said. 'But I keep feeling as though we're being watched.'

'I'm not getting any bad feelings,' said Meatball. 'That's got to be good, hasn't it?'

Spike leaped up from his cube and checked his bag for the axe.

'What you doing?' Billy asked.

'Just checking,' Spike said.

'You know, that is odd about Ed,' said Doc. 'He can't be worried, can he? He didn't even growl or anything.'

'He spent half the journey walking next to them,' Billy said. 'That's not like Ed.'

Meatball frowned. 'How did they know we were coming, anyway? I mean, they must've known, mustn't they? They were there to meet us.'

'Perhaps they've got cameras, or something. Perhaps they've been watching us all the time,' Spike said. He looked around. 'Perhaps they're watching us in here.'

'Would they have cameras?'

'They must have. They're bound to have cameras. They probably don't call it that, but you can't tell me they can have something like that panel thing and this lot, and not cameras.'

'That would explain how they knew we'd arrived,' said Duke. 'Perhaps they've got cameras everywhere. They're probably watching us right now.'

He glanced up at the ceiling, looking for any sign of a lens.

'And I bet you wouldn't be able to see them,' he said. 'Anything could be a camera.'

'Or maybe ...'

They stopped abruptly. Opi had entered the room and was now standing, watching them. His mouth moved in jerks as the purple vein pulsed across his throat and almost simultaneously translated, 'I trust you have all rested? I have arranged that some food and drink be brought to you shortly. And then the Sentinel will take you to the Elder. He will have many questions to ask you.'

Spike stepped forward. 'What sort of questions?'

'We don't know anything,' said Meatball. 'We don't even know why we're here.'

Opi smiled reassuringly. 'There is no cause for anxiety. Our Elder merely wishes to ask you some questions. We Ishmecs are a peaceful race.'

Yeah, that's easy for you to say, Spike thought, but what if Duke's right, what if there are cameras and we're being watched? With a jolt, he remembered the strange eyes in the line of crystals in the corridor. What if they weren't eyeballs at all? This lot had funny eyes, what if the ones out there were cameras? He took a long breath, his heart thudding. Should he mention it? What if they didn't like him asking?

He decided to chance it. 'Really,' he said. 'And you're not watching us?'

'Watching?'

'You mean we're not being monitored?' Duke said. 'There are no cameras in here?'

Opi looked blank.

'None whatsoever, why should -'

'I'm not talking about in here,' Spike said. 'I'm talking about out there, in the corridor.'

Opi stared. 'Out there?'

'On the wall,' said Spike. 'And don't tell me there was nothing in those holes.'

'Holes?' Billy turned to look at Spike. 'What holes?'

Opi stood silently for a moment, as if thinking. Over on his seat, Ed looked up, and his tail started to wag. A moment later, the door opened, and Arisius entered. He looked at Opi and then at their guests.

'Is there a problem?' he asked.

'Sentinel, one of our guests insists ...'

'I know what I saw,' Spike interrupted. 'And two of those holes were *eyes*.'

111

CHAPTER THIRTEEN

The Sentinel's gaze focused steadily on Spike.

'Holes?'

Spike nodded. 'Where the crystals were,' he said. 'On the wall out there. I saw them. Two of them weren't crystals, they were eyes, or something. Camera lenses, maybe.'

The Sentinel's forehead creased into a frown. 'Camera lenses?'

'Yes, camera lenses,' Spike said, again. 'Or eyes. In those holes.'

There was silence, as the Sentinel stared at him. The deep orange eyes regarded Spike for a moment longer and then he spoke.

'With your kind permission.' He turned to Opi. 'Your opinion, if you will, Signant Opi.'

They moved away and conversed for a few moments in their own tongue. Spike watched the Sentinel draw a very deep breath, then turn toward them.

'It would appear,' said the Sentinel, pressing his throat, 'that the eyes that you saw were those of my son.'

Spike and the others glanced at each other. 'Your son?'

The Sentinel nodded. 'Yes. My son. His name is Jophan. He has obviously been apprised of your arrival and I'm afraid he is inclined to be rather inquisitive. He means no harm.'

Addressing Opi, he added, 'I thank you for your time, Opi. You may return to your other duties.'

Crossing both hands in a respectful gesture, Opi bowed to them all and left the room.

'Then it was your son who was watching us?' Duke asked.

The Sentinel looked stern. 'It would appear so. They were overheard in discussion. I can only apologise for their discourtesy.'

'They?'

'My son, Jophan, and my daughter, Neeza. I regret any distress they may have caused you, but these are difficult times for them.' His expression changed. 'I must leave you now. There are urgent matters that require my attention. I shall return to escort you once you have eaten.'

He strode imperially out of the room, his noble head held high, his long robes swirling about his feet.

'Jophan and Neeza,' Meatball repeated thoughtfully, as the door swished shut. 'He's got kids, then. Wonder what they're like?'

'Like little ones of them, I s'pose,' said Spike.

'No, not what they look like, what they're like. You know, what they're *like*.'

Billy sat back down on one of the cubes. 'Well, they're not going to be like us in any way, are they? Stands to reason.'

Terri nodded. 'They're bound to be a bit odd-looking.' She lowered her voice to a whisper. 'I mean, come on, they are a bit odd-looking, aren't they?'

'You can say that again,' said Doc.

'Odd isn't the word.'

Terri put a hand onto one of the cubes, pressed it, and then cautiously sat down. 'I think we're going to be all right.'

Meatball sat down beside her. 'I don't ... well ...'

He looked at them, his head shaking vaguely. 'I'm not getting any kind of feeling about them ... or this place.'

Doc looked around her, warily. 'Is that good or bad, though?'

'It's got to be good, hasn't it?' Billy asked. 'Meatball always gets feelings about stuff.'

'S'pose,' said Spike.

'And then there's Ed,' Duke pointed out. They looked across to where Ed lay, dozing peacefully. 'There's no way Ed would be at ease like that if you were in danger, Spike.'

'If any of us were,' Terri said. She frowned. 'Though there's something odd about that, too.'

113

'It's reassuring, though,' Doc said, a little too hastily. 'I mean, the fact that he's not bothered. Isn't it?'

They fell silent, immersed in their own thoughts.

'I wonder if we'll get to meet them,' Duke said. 'Those two others … what did he say their names were?'

'Jophan,' said Meatball. 'And Neeza. Don't know. Suppose they must be about somewhere.'

'Perhaps they keep them locked up during the day,' Spike said, still unconvinced. 'Just let them out at night.'

Terri gave him a look. 'Don't be stupid.'

'You never know.'

'Shouldn't think so. Not their kids. Not if they're peaceful like they say.' Duke lowered his voice. 'Not if they're normal.' He held his head. 'My head's going round,' he said. 'I keep trying not to panic, but my heart's going mad.'

'You and me both,' said Doc.

'The kids may be all right,' Billy said. 'They could be just like us. Well, not exactly like us, obviously. They'll have those funny eyes 'n' that.'

'And lizard heads,' Spike said.

'We are normal.'

The voice came out of nowhere. A new voice, pitched higher than the other creatures. A younger voice.

With a start, they swung around but saw no one there. Twisting in their seats, they studied the walls, searched the ceiling, but there was nothing.

'Did you hear that?'

'Where did it come from?'

'I don't like this,' Doc murmured. 'There's no one there.'

Duke took a deep breath. 'Hello?'

There was no reply.

They huddled closer together, fearful, trying to watch everywhere at once.

Duke tried again. 'Hello …'

A slight noise.

'There! The wall! *There*!' Billy pointed to the wall opposite. 'It moved! I'm telling you, it moved!'

They squeezed closer together. Crouching a little, Spike stretched out for his rucksack, grabbing the handle of the axe through the material.

Across the room, Ed rose to his feet, stretched, and padded across to the wall, where he stood, sniffing.

'There's something there,' Spike growled. 'Ed can smell it.'

Deftly, he unzipped the bag, reached in, and pulled out the axe. With a set expression, he walked over to the wall. The others followed.

'I don't know where you are,' he said. 'But you better come out.'

The wall stilled, but there was no response.

Terri looked down at Ed. His tail was wagging. 'You can come in,' she said. 'Where are you?'

'Here, present,' said a voice.

Suddenly, there it was, poking through the wall, as if mounted on display. A smaller, shimmering reptilian head, the edges of the wall fitting close round its neck like a collar. Two reddish-brown eyes were looking at them with interest. As they watched, eyelids swished across.

'Wow!'

The head stared at them. 'It is permitted that I enter?'

Duke looked at the others. 'Er .... yeah,' he said, vaguely. 'Yeah, I suppose so.'

The creature, dressed simply in a basic version of the guard uniform, eased itself through the surface of the wall and stepped neatly into the room. Behind it, the wall blended immediately, leaving no evidence of its entrance.

Billy gazed at the wall. 'That's unbelievable,' he said. 'How did you do that?'

The creature blinked, then answered simply, 'I think about it.'

'Who are you?' Doc asked.

Spike answered for him. 'Jophan, that's who he is.'

Laying down the axe, he took a step closer, studying the reptilian creature, which turned its head to look at him.

'That's who you are, isn't it?'

'I am he,' the creature confirmed.

Meatball, too, moved a little closer. 'Your father told us he had a son called Jophan.'

'Did he not mention me?' said another voice. They swung around to see a second creature, similarly dressed, with a smaller and slightly rounder head, pierce the surface of the wall. Further down, a foot appeared, followed by the rest of the body. Once again, the wall blended behind it without trace.

'Of course he mentioned you,' Jophan said, glancing over his shoulder, 'but only after he'd mentioned me.'

'You must be Neeza?' Terri asked.

'I am Neeza,' she said. She stared hard at them, and then turning to Jophan, she added, 'I told you they would be of strange form.'

'It is discourteous to mention their appearance,' he hissed. 'Father says one must be tolerant of difference.'

The slender band at Neeza's throat pulsed with light. 'They were discourteous.'

Jophan waved a hand to dismiss her comment. 'One must make allowance for creatures of lesser intellect.'

Spike looked at him. This one could be trouble. 'Yeah,' he muttered. 'One must.'

Neeza moved across to Terri and stretched her hand slowly out to touch Terri's cheek.

'Your skin,' she murmured. 'It has an … unusual texture.'

'It's called smooth where we come from,' Terri said.

Neeza's gaze moved on to her hair. 'And there,' she said, pointing at Terri's springy curls. 'What is that? That substance that sprouts randomly from your head. What purpose does it serve?'

'It's called hair. It keeps my head warm.'

Neeza nodded slowly. 'I can see that could be useful.'

116

Sitting down on one of the cubes, Jophan sat bolt upright, adopting the same air of authority as his father.

'How are you known?' he demanded.

Meatball and Duke introduced themselves. 'And this,' said Duke, 'is Doc. She's the brains of the team.'

'And I'm Spike,' Spike cut in. 'This is my brother, Billy, and over there, that's Terri.'

'And what is this?'

Ed had wandered over and now sat by Jophan, sniffing his leg. Lifting his huge head, he put out his long slobbery tongue and licked Jophan's face.

Startled, Jophan threw himself backwards. 'What is it?'

'He's our dog,' Spike said. 'Our friend. He won't hurt you. That means he likes you.'

Lifting his hand, Jophan gently wiped his face, and then hesitantly he reached out and rested it on Ed's broad, spiky head, sliding his fingers through the dog's silky coat.

'I like him, too,' he breathed.

Cautiously, Neeza moved a little nearer. Ed lifted his head and licked her fingers. A slow smile spread across Neeza's face and she put out her hand and softly stroked Ed's back.

'We have a rock-crawler,' she said. 'We call it Ly. Jophan keeps it in the agripen, but Father does not know, it is not permitted.'

Jophan leaped to his feet. 'Mention nothing more, someone is coming!'

Billy glanced behind him at the door, still firmly closed. 'How d'you know?'

Jophan grabbed Neeza's hand and in an instant, they had bounded toward the wall, fallen against it and been swallowed. It had barely healed behind them, when the door breathed open and Opi stepped into the room. He was carrying a large platter, set with a meal, which he placed on the cube before them. Around the edges, the cube formed a small ridge that crept over the platter to grasp it.

Duke thanked him.

'You are most welcome,' said Opi. He hesitated, his attention veering towards the wall opposite.

Turning, they, too, stared at the wall, but it remained smooth and still, showing no sign of disturbance. Opi's gaze lingered on the wall for a second or two longer, and then he turned and left the room.

Moments later, a head reappeared.

'He's gone,' Spike whispered.

Jophan's head jerked in Spike's direction. 'He will have detected our presence.'

Beside him, Neeza's head broke through the wall and looked across at him. 'Perhaps it was unwise to borrow these.'

She pushed her hand through and pointed to the translator bands at their throats.

'They were necessary. How else were we to communicate?' Jophan demanded. 'Their speech is beyond our comprehension.'

'Will you be in trouble?' Billy asked.

Jophan gave a quick shake of his head and pushed back through the wall.

'It is of no consequence,' he said, brushing the thought aside. The wall bowed outward as Neeza followed him through into the room.

'That is not what Father will say.'

'How will he know?' Seeing her look, he added, 'Opi will not tell him.'

Neeza settled herself on one of the cubes. 'Opi has looked after us since we were small,' she said. 'He does not tell Father everything.'

'Father isn't strict,' Jophan put in, defensively, 'but he has many things on his mind.' He walked across and put a hand out to touch Spike's hair. 'It is very strange, this … hair. Why is yours unlike the others?'

'I put stuff on it,' Spike said. 'Makes it stick up.'

'And me,' said Billy, patting his own hair.

Jophan's head nodded slowly. 'I see ... for defence ... some of the land-walkers have similar adornments.'

Spike gave him a look.

'D'you know what this is?'

Terri was scrutinizing the small cakes of various shapes and colour on the platter.

'I was wondering that,' said Meatball. He picked up one of the cakes and sniffed it. 'Smells alright.'

'It will smell of whatever you wish,' Neeza said, brightly. 'It will taste of whatever you wish also.'

Duke's eyes lit up. 'Will it? I mean, it will?'

'Taste is selective,' Jophan said. 'One has only to decide.'

Doc and Duke picked up some of the cakes, turning them over in their fingers. They had the consistency of soft fudge. Squeezing one at the centre, Doc watched with curiosity as it changed colour, then back again.

Meatball hovered over the plate, trying to ignore the rumble of his stomach. 'What d'you reckon,' he asked, 'shall we chance it?'

They looked at one another, waiting for someone to take the first bite.

In a flash, Jophan reached across to the platter, selected one, bit off a piece, chewed slowly and swallowed. His expression was open; he seemed to be saying, 'You see? I live!'

'He's all right,' Duke whispered.

'Yeah, but he's a reptile,' Spike hissed. 'How do we know?'

'Well, Ed's all right,' Billy said. 'And he's just eaten a load.' He pressed his stomach. 'I'm starving.'

'Me 'n' all,' said Meatball. 'I'm gonna give it a go.'

With that, he scooped up a cake and popped it into his mouth.

The others watched with baited breath as he slowly chewed, then smacked his lips. 'He's only right, isn't he. This one tastes like cheeseburger.'

'Never ...'

119

'You're not serious!'

'It doesn't taste like burger,' Spike said, plucking up the courage to take a bite, 'it tastes like pizza.'

'Pizza!' Billy yelled. 'I love pizza!'

Terri stared at them both. 'You're having a laugh.'

Spike pushed one under Terri's nose. 'Try it if you don't believe me!'

Doc was savouring the delicious taste of fried chicken. 'Mmm,' she said. 'This is fantastic.'

'It is as we described?' Neeza asked.

'It's really nice,' Duke spluttered. 'I'm starving.'

Meatball rammed another cake into his mouth, then offered the platter to Jophan and Neeza. 'You want one?'

Exchanging glances, Jophan and Neeza leaned across to grab a cake each.

They finished the first selection, and were on a voyage of discovery through the second, when Jophan suddenly stiffened and sat up straight and alert.

'We must leave you now,' he said. 'Come Neeza.'

Taking her hand, he led her towards the wall, melting through to disappear.

On a long seat, Ed had finished enjoying a meal of his own and was now quietly dozing. Suddenly, he lifted his head and pricked his ears, then rose slowly to his feet and started wagging his tail.

'Funny how he does that,' Doc said. 'Have you noticed he always seems to do it just before …'

There was a slight sigh, the door opened, and Arisius stepped into the room and approached them, his words rapidly translated.

'The Elder is extremely frail, and tires easily, but he is most anxious to speak with you,' he said. 'If you will accompany me?'

Duke eased himself upright from one of the cubes. The others stood beside him, trying not to show the anxiety they felt.

'Of course,' Duke said. 'Um … where …'

'The Stateroom. If you will follow me?'

Once out of the room, Arisius led them slowly along an illuminated corridor, and through a set of ornate doors. From there, they stepped into a vast chamber, then up a shimmering curve of crystal steps and onto the galleried landing, where several others sat engrossed in their work. They looked up momentarily as Ed loped by on long, gangly legs.

At two enormous doors, the procession finally halted.

On either side of the doorway stood a guard, tall and broad, dressed in uniform of purple and silver. They were, without doubt, the biggest 'men' Spike had laid eyes on, and at the sentinel's approach, they snapped sharply to attention.

Then they were through, into the largest indoor space they had ever seen.

The Stateroom was vast, a seemingly endless expanse of floor and walls. Heavy columns dotted the room, supporting the massive ceiling that arched into a clear dome. It stretched the whole length of the room, giving a startling crystal-clear view of the night sky.

In silent awe, they gazed at the bright stars and planets, some radiant with light, others merely white pinpricks on a background of deep blue velvet.

Ahead of them, Arisius signalled to wait while he walked across to an elderly figure seated in a chair beside a desk. The figure bent so close to the desktop, they thought he was asleep, but at a gentle summons from Arisius, he lifted his head.

'Serene Elder, these are the young people of whom we spoke. This is Duke.'

Duke stepped forward. 'How do you do, sir,' he said.

The Elder smiled weakly. His skin was looser, thinner, and slower to respond. Huddled in his chair, he sat with shoulders stooped. Two deep-set caramel coloured eyes peered at them from under heavy brow bones.

'The Elder's sight is poor,' Arisius explained. He bent to assist the elderly Ishmec to straighten upright. 'These are

Duke's friends,' he said, waving a hand in their direction. 'This is Meatball … this is Doc, and Terri and here are Billy and Spike.'

The Elders face creased into a weak smile. 'A warm welcome to you all,' he said. 'So, you are Spike? Come a little closer.'

Spike obeyed.

'Ah, yes!' He reached out a wasted hand to touch Spike's hair. 'My grandson describes it perfectly. Quite fascinating!'

'You're Jophan and Neeza's grandfather?' asked Spike.

The old man nodded. 'I hold that honour.'

He gestured towards some seats. 'Come, sit with me,' he said. 'Tell me about yourselves.'

They settled themselves beside him.

Ed circled once or twice and flopped to the floor.

The Elder watched him. 'A wise and noble creature,' he said.

He turned back to the children. 'Firstly, how did you get here?'

'Through a time portal,' Spike answered, simply.

The old man expressed no surprise. 'A time portal?' He nodded. 'Yes, I know of their existence. But to venture into such a thing was very courageous and could have been extremely dangerous. What made you attempt it?'

'We didn't,' said Spike. 'That is, we didn't mean to.' He paused. 'It was my fault really. We were following someone and we saw him go through.'

'We weren't going to go through ourselves, we thought it was too dangerous,' Duke said. 'But then Spike fell through by accident, so we had to follow him.'

'And we found ourselves in this place,' said Terri. 'And no way were we ever coming back.'

'But then we got on a bus,' said Billy. 'We were only going to town, but suddenly the bus went purple and we found ourselves back here again.'

'It's all Gullivan's fault,' Spike snapped. 'The whole lot's his fault.'

122

The Sentinel frowned. 'Who is Gullivan?'

Spike looked at the others, as if to ask whether he should mention Gullivan.

'They're asking,' said Duke.

Spike took a deep breath and related the whole story. Ed's recovery of the bone, Spike and Terri's trip to Gullivan's cowshed and the strange things they found.

'And then there was this silver ball,' he said.

'A ball?' The old man's response was immediate. 'A silver ball, you say?'

'Yes.'

'Was it about this big?' asked Arisius, cupping his hands into the rough shape of a globe.

'I've got a picture of it!'

Delving into his pocket, Spike produced his mobile phone, flicking through until he came to a photo of the ball. 'Here you go, look, this is it.'

Arisius stepped forward to peer at the tiny screen. 'Yes. Yes, this is the one.'

Doc went on to explain how Terri had opened it and Meatball had managed to bring down the frequency, but the strange lines and dots were all they had seen.

'Nevertheless, you did well,' the old man said. 'That ball belongs to me. The noise you heard is a recording of my voice.'

Spike continued to flick through the pictures. 'Think I might have a picture of the bone somewhere, as well.'

'One moment -'

Arisius was staring at the screen. 'That image there ... no ... back a little ... that one.' He tapped the screen gently with a finger. 'That image. Of whom is that a likeness?'

Spike glanced down at the tiny photograph of Cornelius Gullivan leaving the cowshed.

'That's Gullivan,' he said. 'That's the man we told you about. The one we followed through the portal.'

Arisius looked back at the photograph and studied it carefully.

The Elder looked up. 'What is it?'

'This image fits the description of the man for whom we have been searching, Father.'

'A man fitting this description has been seen several times, digging in the caves in the valley,' he told them. 'We believe he may also be responsible for a cowardly attack on my father and two of our guards.' He looked again at the photograph. 'The ball … it was in this man's possession?'

'Spike found it on his property,' Duke said. 'And the golden band.'

'Then it would appear to be a strong possibility,' said the Elder. 'One of our guards saw him enter a cave and he did not reappear. This cave … it is the time portal you mention?'

Duke nodded.

The Elder put a hand on his son's arm. 'Then this man is beyond our reach.'

With some effort, he paused to take a breath. Turning to his guests, he said, 'I have a request to make of you. You may feel this a great imposition, and if it were not for the urgency of the situation, I would not ask it, but our time is limited. From our observations, it has become clear that an asteroid is on a collision course with this planet, and it is imperative that we leave.'

'An asteroid?' Doc looked at him. 'Like the one that killed the dinosaurs?'

Arisius nodded. 'Quite possibly. The approaching asteroid will cause catastrophic devastation and we can no longer remain. The ball you found contains data that is vital for the repair of our craft.'

The Elder continued, 'The capability to use a time portal is not available to us, it is not written. Clearly, you are bestowed with such ability. May I ask that you return to your own time and bring the ball back to me? We will ensure safe escort to the portal.'

There was a collective gasp, as they realised what they were being asked to do.

Spike swallowed hard, his heart banging. 'Bring it back? What, you mean back through the portal and come back here with it?'

The Elder nodded. 'We are aware of what we ask, of the enormity of this request,' he said. 'And of the danger.'

'*Come back again*?' Meatball croaked.

Terri fell back against her seat. 'What?'

'Look, sorry, but we can't,' Doc said. 'We only just made it back before. We don't even know if it's going to work a second time, we might be stuck here.'

Duke looked at her.

'Well, we *might*!' she said. 'How d'you know?'

He nodded, silently.

Meatball pushed a hand through his hair. 'What are we going to do?'

Spike had a sudden thought. If they refused, would these creatures still help them back to the cave? He thought about the dinosaurs. How else were they going to get home?

'Yes,' said Billy, suddenly.

The others turned. 'Yes, what?'

'We'll do it,' said Billy.

Spike glanced at his brother. Billy's face was shining. It was a look Spike had seen before, a look that told him that despite being the younger brother, Billy had thought of something he hadn't, and it was usually something obvious.

Billy stared steadily back at him. 'We have to, Spike, don't you see? That bus brought us here for a reason.'

CHAPTER FOURTEEN

In the attic of his cottage, Gullivan raised his shotgun to eye level and centred the sight on the head before him.

Gently, his fingers closed around the trigger. Two black eyes looked back at him, a black whiskered nose sniffing inquisitively at the end of the barrel.

After a moment, Gullivan lowered the gun, broke it and hung it over the crook of his arm.

'I guess we ain't so different,' he muttered. 'We're both scavengers. After a bit of a different prize though, eh?'

The large rat hesitated for a moment, and then scampered off into the shadows.

Gullivan turned and picked up a glass of whisky.

'Here's to scavenging,' he growled, lifting the glass high into the air.

He took a large swig and brought the glass down with a clink against his latest acquisition. 'And here's to Mother Nature,' he cried. 'God bless 'er!'

Throwing back his head he began to laugh. Things were going to be a hell of a lot different for him from now on.

These latest hauls were going to set him up for life. Rich he was going to be, rich beyond his wildest dreams, rich enough to get away from anything and anyone. For good.

He'd go somewhere no one would ever find him and even if they did, so what? With his wealth he could employ his own security force.

He hadn't really wanted to go back a third time yesterday, but that new cave had yielded the sort of rocks that left the others in the shade.

Walking across the room, he grabbed the table leg and shoved it to one side, then lifted the carpet and sank his hand into the well beneath. His fingers closed around the soft velvet bag and lifted it clear of the hole. Moving across to his desk, he opened it and tipped out its contents.

A collection of stones of various shapes and sizes tumbled onto the blotter.

'You little beauties are going to make me a good bit of pocket money. In the right places, of course.'

He hummed quietly to himself as he turned them over. He knew just the right places. Thorpe's face was going to be a picture when he showed him this lot. He'd try to hide it of course, looking all smug and superior as usual, but Gullivan knew that look.

A great sigh of satisfaction swelled in his chest. Swinging his feet up onto the desk, he leaned back in his chair and relaxed, dreaming of his new life: the life that these little babies would buy him. Somewhere warm and quiet, where a tranquil blue ocean lapped against silver sands.

Another rat leapt up and sent the stones flying. This time he didn't hesitate.

'Blast you, you stupid rodent,' he yelled, and picked up his knife. That was one less rat to trouble him. If only brats were so easy to deal with.

CHAPTER FIFTEEN

Standing once again outside the entrance to the cave, Spike dragged the back of his hand across his forehead, smearing the sweat that was threatening to run down his nose. It was early the following morning and the sun was rising, beating mercilessly down on the small plateau, where the five of them stood bidding their last farewells to Arisius, Opi and the guards.

'I pray your journey home is without incident,' Arisius said. 'You must take great care. If the danger is too great for you to return, then we will understand. You must not put your own lives at risk.'

'If it is possible, we will bring the ball to you, sir,' Duke told him.

Arisius bowed to them all. 'If you will permit, we have one further request. I was reluctant to mention this earlier, for fear of upsetting my father, but when he was attacked, his two guards were killed. We have located the body of one, our colleague, Lomo, but were unable to locate the other. From the description you have given us of the bone, it seems likely that Gullivan has killed Guloc also and perhaps dragged the body back through to your time.'

'But why would he do that?' Doc asked. 'Why not leave it in this time and let … well, you know …'

She wrung her hands, apologetically.

Arisius smiled down at her. 'Logic is nothing to be ashamed of.'

Billy frowned. 'Maybe Gullivan hit him or shot him, or something, but Guloc was only wounded, and he grabbed Gullivan as he was going back through the portal. Gullivan might've panicked and dragged him through with him. For some reason all he comes out with are bones, but now he's got to bury them somewhere, hasn't he?'

'You're right, Bill. He doesn't want anyone finding bones on our side or he might get found out,' Spike said. '*And* someone else might discover the time portal and he definitely doesn't want that.'

'A strong possibility,' Arisius agreed. 'Whatever the reason, it is important that we find our colleague's body. It is our belief that a blessing read over the remains frees the spirit. We only ask that should you locate him, you will spare a moment to say the words we give you as a blessing.'

His voice was stiff with emotion.

Duke stepped forward. 'Sir,' he said. 'It would be an honour.'

It sounded silly and proper and completely over the top, but for once they could only listen in admiration.

'We did it,' Doc whispered. 'We got back again. I don't know how, but we did.'

Sitting once more in Meatball's basement, Spike stared into the fire. He couldn't remember the walk home, or the fact that it was snowing. The only thing that mattered was that the portal had worked.

'I don't care how we did it,' said Meatball. 'I don't care about anything.'

Terri nodded her head as if she were answering a question. 'Thank goodness,' she said. 'Thank goodness we're back.'

'Course we're back,' said Billy. 'We've got to be, haven't we?'

Spike looked at him. 'What are you talking about?'

'Well, we can't take the ball back to them otherwise, can we?'

Meatball looked up. His face was grey. 'I suppose we've got no choice, now,' he said, quietly. 'We've got to go back again, whether we like it or not.'

They stared at one another, shivering, despite the warmth of the room.

'There's always a choice,' said Duke.

'Duke!'

'Well, there is, Terri.'

'We gave our word,' said Doc. 'You gave your word.'

'Well don't put it all on me!' Duke snapped. 'You did as well!'

'You're the one who said we'd find those bones.'

'I got carried away! Anyway, it wasn't just me!'

'We all did!' Spike yelled. 'It's no one's fault. Not even ours, really. Though I suppose if we hadn't followed Gullivan ...'

'We did though, didn't we?' Terri put a hand on Spike's arm. 'Meatball's right. We've got to go back. Now we know and everything.' She looked around at the others. 'We've got to, they're relying on us.'

'Well, they shouldn't be,' Duke muttered.

No one answered. After a few minutes, Duke sighed and got to his feet. 'I'm just shattered. You're right.'

'What about if we just take the ball back,' said Meatball. 'Don't hang about, just come straight back.'

'It's not a trip to the shops,' Spike muttered.

'I know that, don't I.'

'What about the dinosaurs?' said Billy.

'Thanks for reminding us.'

'He's got a point,' said Terri. 'What are we going to do about them?'

Spike thought about the dinosaurs. How were they expected to get past them?

'I can't help thinking,' said Billy. 'If we're meant to deliver that ball, then there must be a way.'

'There is,' said Duke. 'They eat us on the way back.'

Doc got to her feet. 'Oh, do shut up!'

'Just leave it!' Meatball yelled. 'Never mind how we're going to do it, let's just do it. Where's that ball thing?'

'Should still be in that drawer,' Spike said.

Walking across, he pulled open the cabinet. There was the ball, still innocently shimmering, cleverly camouflaging everything it contained. With some relief, he stooped to pick it up. After the last twenty-four hours, it wouldn't have surprised him to find that the ball had floated away.

He held it for a moment. What was so wonderful about this thing? Why couldn't they manage without it? Even as he thought about it, he knew. They had to do it. Everyone's fate depended on it. Jophan and Neeza, Arisius and Opi, their families and friends. So many people about to be wiped out by a monumental lump of space rock, unless they could finish the ship in time and leave Earth for a new home.

They couldn't let that happen, could they?

Somehow or other, they had to help the Ishmecs leave Earth, even if it was prehistoric Earth. His grip tightened as he placed the ball carefully into a rucksack, sliding the zip shut.

'We can't let them all die, can we?' he said.

'No,' said Terri, quietly. 'No, we can't.'

Doc heaved a sigh. 'So, what time are we going back then?'

'Well, the way I see it, it doesn't really matter much,' Billy said. 'Leastways, not here. It might matter back there I suppose, especially after what they told us.'

Duke frowned at him. 'What do you mean it doesn't matter much here?'

'Surely one of you noticed?' Billy tapped his watch. 'About the time?'

He paused expectantly, waiting for an answer that didn't come. 'We're hardly losing any.'

'We aren't?' Doc looked at her watch. 'He's right!'

'I've been keeping a check on it,' Billy said, 'and we came out today only a short time after we went in.'

Terri put her watch to her ear. 'Which means what?'

'Well I don't know,' said Billy, 'but it makes you think, doesn't it? It could mean the portal's changing or something.'

'You mean it could be on the blink? If we go back, we could be stuck there?'

'Don't know, but I can't help wondering if that's why Gullivan's back and forth like a headless chicken. Perhaps he knows something we don't.'

'He can't do. He wouldn't be stupid enough to keep going backwards and forwards.'

Duke looked up. 'He's not stupid enough to take that sort of risk.'

'He's not stupid, he's ruthless,' said Doc.

Spike's fingers closed into a fist. 'He's *evil*,' he said.

'We have to go back, whatever's happening to the portal,' Terri said. 'And we don't even know anything is. Perhaps we've made a mistake on the times. The Elder needs that ball and we said we'd take it back. We don't want him thinking we're all like Gullivan.'

They were interrupted by a knock on the door of the basement.

'Is that you, dear?'

Meatball got up and opened the door. 'Oh, hello, Mum!'

'Thought I heard you,' said his mum. She peered in through the door. 'Hello, everyone!' she called cheerfully. 'Brought you down some cake, I've just made it.'

'Thank you!' they called.

'Brilliant, mum, thanks,' said Meatball. 'I've just ordered some pizza as well.'

His mum smiled. 'Hollow legs, you lot have got,' she said.

The bell rang on Meatball's front door.

'That'll be your pizza,' she said. 'See you all later.'

'Oh, great!' Spike said. 'I'm starving.'

Meatball pushed several steaming boxes onto the table.

Opening a box, he tore a piece from a pizza, rolled it around several wedges, and took a large bite. 'Won't take me a minute to finish this lot.'

'I'd better finish this one off,' Duke said, grabbing three pieces. 'They look lonely.'

Doc stared at them. 'Any chance you pigs are going to leave any for the rest of us?'

'Sorry.' Meatball laughed. 'We can't help it if you're too slow. Survival of the fittest.' He swallowed more pizza. 'Here, I've just had a thought. What if we meet Gullivan coming back?'

Spike punched his hand with his fist. 'Then he'll get a face full of *this*.'

'You wish,' said Terri.

Spike bit into his pizza. 'Yeah, I know, but I'm going to have him one of these days.'

'Perhaps someone else will get him for us,' Meatball said.

Duke looked down at the pizza box on the floor and stamped on it, twisting his heel into the cardboard. 'Hope so,' he said. 'I wish I knew what he was after in those caves. Whatever it is, he has to be stashing it back at his place somewhere. We know it wasn't with all the other stuff in the trunk, so he must be keeping it indoors.'

'That's got to be our first job anyway,' said Billy. 'We promised Arisius we'd look for the remains of that other guard.'

'And I bet,' Spike said. 'If we go to Gullivan's place now with Ed and the bone, he'll be able to find him.' He leaned down to pat Ed on the head, knowing he could rely on him.

Doc gasped. 'Yes, the bone. We're going to need that. We'll have to nip home and get it. Won't take a minute.'

Duke nodded. 'Right, that's what we do then. You lot take Ed to find the bones. While you're doing that, Meatball and I will search Gullivan's place for any signs of the loot he's been bringing back.'

They zipped the precious ball safely into Duke's rucksack, tucked it out of sight beneath Meatball's desk, and then they wrapped themselves warmly and left.

'D'you know, whatever Gullivan's getting, it's got to be small,' Terri said, as they stomped across the snowy field on their way to Solomon, the mighty oak. 'What's small and very valuable? It must be worth a lot or Gullivan wouldn't be risking his neck.'

'I reckon it's gold,' Meatball murmured. 'Got to be. Stands to reason.'

'Not necessarily.' Doc paused to empty her boot. 'Loads of things are in caves.'

'Don't remind me,' said Terri, with a shudder.

'Here it is!'

The huge dark silhouette of Solomon loomed up ahead of them. Quickly, they opened the trunk and stepped inside.

'Doesn't look as though he's about,' Meatball murmured. Carefully, he scanned the field. 'No sign of him. I reckon it's safe.'

Terri flicked a cobweb from her face. 'Perhaps he's gone back through the portal.'

'Well, we've got to find that Guloc guy,' Duke said. 'I promised the Sentinel I'd say these words over him.'

He pulled the paper from his pocket, re-read it, then slipped it back.

Grabbing the panel, Spike moved it completely aside. 'Ed'll let us know if there's any danger,' he said. 'He can smell *him* a mile off.'

The old dog put his head toward the gap and raised his nose to sniff the air, then trotted out and spent the next few minutes watering the ground.

'Looks like it's clear,' said Billy. 'Come on.'

He stepped warily through the door to make the first soft treads on a spotless field of snow. The others followed.

The countryside was totally still, as though Nature had heard about their search for Guloc's bones and was keeping a respectful silence.

'It's getting dark early,' Duke said. Breath billowed from his mouth in a thick haze. 'And I didn't think to bring a torch.'

'It's okay, I did.' Meatball pulled a tiny silver torch from his pocket. 'But it might not be safe to put it on yet. Let's wait till we get to Gullivan's place.'

They approached Gullivan's house by the side, along by the frozen stream, past the scullery and around to the sitting room.

Cautiously they peered in, trying to see between the grimy streaks, lacy cobwebs, and the piles of dead woodlice. There was no light and only the barest of furniture, a battered armchair, and a table, with the congealed remains of something on a plate.

Meatball stepped back a pace and craned his long neck to glance at the upstairs window. 'It doesn't look as though he's in,' he said. 'Can't see any lights or anything.'

'No lights down here, either,' said Doc, peering in the scullery window. 'But how are we going to get in?'

'I've been thinking about that,' said Billy. 'We might be able to use the coal cellar.'

'Course, yeah, the coal cellar. All these old places have got them,' Spike said. 'I bet this place has ... there you are, what did I tell you?'

He led them around the corner of the wall. A small black door peeped out from the undergrowth. 'Doesn't look as though Gullivan uses it much.'

'You're going to get mucky 'n' all,' said Billy. 'It'll be pitch black.'

'I'm not bothered about that,' said Meatball. 'Where's it come out?'

'In the cellar. Should do.'

'Right, let's get on with it. Give us a hand with this, Duke.'

The outside door of the coal cellar was old and rusted, and it took three of them to prise it open wide enough for Meatball and Duke to squeeze through and crawl inside.

'Right,' Duke called. 'Meatball's got the cellar door open. See you later.'

'See you guys later,' Spike said. 'Watch out for Gullivan.'

Ed tried to squeeze past to follow Duke and Meatball into the coal cellar, but Spike grabbed his collar.

'No, Ed, we need you.' He spoke over his shoulder. 'Doc, give us that bone.'

With some difficulty, Doc pulled the bone from the long bag she carried and passed it to him.

Spike held it out for Ed to sniff. 'Find it, boy. Go fetch … *fetch*!'

Ed sniffed the bone, and then put his nose to the ground.

'He isn't going to pee is he, Spike?'

'No. He's getting the scent. Give him a minute.'

They gave him a minute. Then several minutes more. Ed walked round and round, sniffing.

'He is going to pee …'

'No, he *isn't*. Give him a minute.'

Ed walked round for a while longer, then stopped and squelched his huge blackberry of a nose flat on the ground.

'He's got it!' Spike exclaimed. 'Where is it, boy? Show us!'

With a sudden burst of speed, Ed set off towards the cowshed.

'The cowshed? But that's where we found all the loot,' said Terri. 'There was nothing in there, Spike, he couldn't have …'

Racing on, Ed kept his nose firmly to the ground. Just when they thought he would collide with the door, he veered off at a tangent and slid to a halt in the hay barn, his long claws skidding on the hard, bare earth. He sniffed for a moment and probed a mound with his nose, and then, satisfied, he sat down and waited.

Billy bent down to examine the mound. 'This earth's soft, look. Everything's rock hard, but this little place here's soft.'

'Soft enough to dig, d'you reckon?'

'Don't know,' Spike muttered. 'He'd probably have needed a pickaxe to shift the stuff underneath.'

At that moment, as if he knew their every word, Ed started to dig. His paws pounded the ground, sending it flying in all directions.

'You wouldn't need much of a hole for a few bones,' Terri said, watching.

'You would for a whole body,' Doc pointed out. 'What about the skull? And the torso?'

Terri shuddered. 'I didn't think of that. I don't think I want to watch.'

'Look! There!'

As Ed scraped away the earth, a creamy-greyish object was coming into view. It was round and dry and ominously smooth. One of his claws struck the surface and it clacked like a domino on a tabletop.

'Hold it, Spike.' Doc put a hand to her mouth. 'That looks like ...'

Billy bent down and gently brushed away some of the soil. 'It is,' he said. 'It's a skull.'

Terri stared at it. 'Oh no ...'

'I bet it's the rest of him,' Spike whispered. 'The rest of the body that goes with that leg bone. Ed knew the smell. It's got to be, hasn't it?'

'It must be the missing guard,' said Doc.

Terri nodded. 'I feel sick.'

'Unless Gullivan's murdered somebody else,' said Billy.

'Billy!'

'Well, he's right,' Spike said. 'He could've done.'

'Oh, let's just leave it,' said Terri. 'Just leave it. It's horrible. We can't move it, it's not right.'

'Terri's right,' said Doc. 'We can't go digging around. Not now we know.'

'But we don't, do we?' Spike said. 'Could be anything. We'll have to check.'

'And we did promise Arisius,' Billy put in. 'We won't know if it's the right one to read the words over.'

Terri nodded. 'I guess. Let's just see if we can find the other leg bone. We'll know for sure, then, won't we?'

Billy and Doc crouched down and carefully moved the soil. Several more bones became visible, among them a long, thin bone that almost matched the one in Spike's grasp.

Spike stared down at the remains. 'It's him all right. Got to be.'

'Well,' said Terri, with a sigh. 'Looks like we've found Guloc. I suppose now we'd better find Duke and Meatball. Wonder how they're getting on?'

It was some time before Duke and Meatball returned.

In the fading light of the hay barn, Spike, Terri, Doc and Billy huddled together with Ed, trying to keep warm by the makeshift grave.

As Meatball and Duke approached, Doc walked across to meet them. 'You've found something, haven't you?' she asked. 'What is it?'

'It took us ages,' said Meatball. 'We searched everywhere.'

'Then suddenly we spotted the loft,' Duke said. 'It had these brass handles on it and they were all shiny. It's being used.'

'There was a pole on the wall, had a hook in the top,' said Meatball. 'So we went up to have a look. You'll never guess the first thing we found up there. Talk about disgusting!'

'What was it?'

Duke pulled a face. 'There was this terrible smell and when we got up there, we found a dead rat. He'd pinned it to the table with a knife. It was all blown up and there was stuff crawling on it.'

Terri closed her eyes. 'Ugh!'

'He's revolting,' said Doc.

'What else did you find?' Billy asked. 'Was there a safe or anything?'

Meatball shook his head. 'No, not a safe. Duke found a sort of box, but there weren't any numbers on it.' He grinned, suddenly. 'But we found something better than that,' he said. 'We found *diamonds*! Least, that's what we think they are. There was a load of them in a bag under the floorboards. It was beneath the table, covered by a bit of carpet.'

'And you reckon they're diamonds?' Doc asked.

'Don't know for certain, but they really good fakes if they're not.'

'I bet they are real,' Spike said. 'He wouldn't bother with anything else.'

'That's it!' said Billy, suddenly. 'I bet that's it! Diamonds! That's what he's getting through the portal.'

'Of course!' Doc gasped. 'They said he'd been seen in caves. I bet that's where he's getting them!'

'And he doesn't care what he does to get them, either,' said Terri. She nodded towards the hole in the ground. 'We've found him.'

'Guloc?'

'Afraid so,' she said. 'You'd better come and see for yourselves.'

Quietly they gathered around the grave that Ed had unearthed.

'Poor guy,' said Duke. 'Let's cover him up.'

Carefully, Meatball and Spike replaced the soil, and then with a heavy heart, Duke reached into his pocket, pulled out the paper and read the few simple words, Terri adding a short prayer of her own.

With Ed beside them, they stood quietly for a few moments, shivering. Finally, Duke said, 'We've done our best, let's get going.'

Leaving the hay barn, they stepped out into the bleak winter light. Keeping as low as they could, they scrambled along the hedge that skirted Gullivan's land, dodging in fits and starts between drifts of snow thrown high against the bushes. In the distance, they could see Solomon's black outline etched like charcoal against the grey sky.

They were almost halfway when fresh snow started to fall in large flakes, coating their faces, making it difficult to see, and instinct told them it was only the beginning of another complete white-out. It was quiet and steady now, but if the wind increased, things could quickly become difficult, even dangerous.

'Oh, great,' Doc said. 'Let's get home, quick.'

Beside Spike, Ed gave a low growl.

'What is it, boy?'

Billy glanced down at Ed. 'He can smell something.'

At the end of a line pressed tightly against the hedge, Meatball leaned outward. 'I don't believe it! It's Gullivan! He's coming over here with his shotgun!'

'Back! Quick!'

Scrambling around, they bolted back along the hedge.

'The haybarn!' Spike hissed. 'Make for the haybarn!'

With a sudden dash, they reached the haybarn and crouched inside.

A few minutes passed. Meatball shuffled across. He could just make out Gullivan's dark, menacing figure moving steadily along the hedgerow, shotgun poised as he paused now and then to search the undergrowth.

He watched for a moment, and then dodged back down. 'He's right there,' he whispered, 'working his way around.'

Tucked down as tightly as they could, they listened to the approaching crunch of Gullivan's boots, the cursing beneath his breath, the occasional crack of branches.

In the middle of the haybarn, Spike wrapped his arms around Ed's neck and prayed. Beneath his hold, Ed was restless. He could smell Gullivan, and Spike could almost feel the anger within him. No, he thought. Please Ed, no. One growl, one whimper and it would all be over.

Terri leaned close to Ed's ear. 'Not a sound, Ed, or we're in trouble.'

Sliding his hands down Ed's wiry coat, Spike crouched down beside Billy. We can't do this for long, he thought. It's getting too cold. People die in winters like this.

Outside, the snowfall was increasing. A bitter wind was gathering, pulling heavy flakes out of the cloud and blowing them in through the opening. Spike shivered, tried to ignore the intense pain in his fingers, and listened.

Gullivan's footsteps snapped and shattered the icy ground, as he grew nearer.

Pressed against Ed's wiry, warm body, Spike felt the old dog's heart beating, and the tension in his limbs, and prayed he didn't bark or growl.

He reached out and around Billy with his other arm, and felt him shivering.

At the door, Gullivan stopped. For what seemed like hours, he stared in, his head moving occasionally to one side, as though he were listening.

Then he straightened up. 'I'll have you!' he growled, as though he was making an announcement. His voice rang through the icy air. 'Damned mutt!' he yelled. 'I'll have you! D'you hear me?'

In the tomb-like blackness of the haybarn, Spike and Billy squeezed Ed tightly between them, as they felt him stiffen.

For a long moment, Gullivan stood, just blinking his eyes in the snowflakes, then they heard his boots twist on the icy ground as he set off back across the yard.

Huddled together, they waited until the sound of his heavy boots began to fade. The echo of his footsteps grew fainter but still they waited.

When the only sound was the whistle of the increasing wind, they finally moved.

Spike relaxed his hold on Ed and Billy and then turned to the others, to see Terri wipe hot tears from her cheeks.

Meatball walked as softly as he could towards the entrance, just in time to see a sudden flash of light spread across the snow, to vanish moments later. 'I think he's gone in. A door just opened, I saw the light.'

Duke peered out into the swirling snow. 'We'll have to take a chance,' he said. 'We can't stay here much longer, we'll freeze.'

Stiffly, they picked themselves up and left the barn.

'Good boy!' Spike whispered, as Ed got unsteadily to his feet to lead the way.

Trudging back through the snow, they were only vaguely aware of having finally stepped into Solomon and out the other side.

141

'What do we do now?' Doc said. 'I don't fancy going back: not with Gullivan on the prowl.'

Meatball's broad shoulders drooped forward with exhaustion. 'Me, neither.'

'I can't anyway.' Terri looked down at her watch. 'It's getting late. Mum'll start worrying.'

'It's too dangerous to go back tonight,' Duke said firmly. 'And that's that. We'll have to chance leaving everything till tomorrow. Anyway, I need some sleep. I'm shattered.'

'I think we all do,' said Doc. 'I can't go back now. I can't.'

Spike bent down to ruffle Ed's fur. 'You've done well today, boy, but you need a break and some grub'.

Meatball yawned. 'So do I.'

'Right.' Duke looked at his watch. 'We meet at Meatball's house tomorrow,' he said. 'Nine o'clock.'

CHAPTER SIXTEEN

The following morning, Spike and Billy stood on Terri's doorstep and pressed the bell, listening as the chimes resounded down the hallway. Shortly after, a baby cried out.

The window above swung open and Terri's face appeared. 'Won't be long,' she said. 'Had to help Mum.'

Spike heaved a sigh and began tapping the iron-hard soil with his boot. It had all seemed such a good idea yesterday, but this morning he wasn't so sure.

'What if we're too late?' Billy asked. 'What if time's moved on there, and the asteroid's already hit?'

Spike shrugged. 'It is what it is,' he said.

As they waited, Spike thought about Ed. All night long he'd been dead to the world, and then he was up, ready to go anywhere and do anything that was asked of him. It was a tough decision to leave him behind this trip, but Ed wasn't that young anymore. He'd been stiff in his joints that morning and slower than usual. To be expected, Gran had said, at his age, he needed a bit of a rest.

'Hope we didn't upset Ed, leaving him behind,' said Billy.

'No, he'll be fine. Gran says he needs a rest today. Anyway, I feel better if he's there with Gran at the moment. You know.'

Billy looked at him and nodded.

All in all, it was probably for the best, Spike thought. He pictured Ed stretched before the fire. Good old Ed, he didn't do badly for an old dog. He'd found those bones yesterday, no problem.

Standing in the cold snow of the twenty-first century, Spike wondered how Guloc might have felt had he known his burial would be millions of years after he was born.

He felt rage build up inside him. Somehow, Gullivan would pay.

The front door opened and Terri stepped out, wrapped in a heavy coat and woollen scarf and hat.

'Sorry,' she said. 'Zac was screaming half the night.'

She glanced back at her mum, standing in the doorway.

'Morning, Mrs Arnold,' Billy called.

'Morning,' said Mrs Arnold. 'Morning Spike. Terri, dear, are you warm enough?'

'Yes thanks, Mum. See you later. Bye!'

'Little does she know we're going to the tropical rainforest,' said Spike, as they walked away.

'Yeah. I couldn't sleep last night for thinking about it.'

'Nor me,' said Billy.

Nor me, thought Spike. First Mr Price, then Gran and now this lot. Surely, somewhere, there's got to be a connection.

'There they are!'

He looked up to see Duke, Doc and Meatball approaching. They looked as drained as he felt.

'All right?' Duke asked.

Spike nodded. 'You ready?'

'Guess,' said Meatball.

'What about the ball?' asked Billy. 'Who's got that?'

Duke patted the bag on his back. 'S'all right. I've got it.'

The weather seemed to be taking a turn for the worse as they arrived once more at the top of the lane. The chill of the early morning had lessened slightly and the snowflakes danced daintily in the gentle breeze. Silently, they stepped onto the bridge. The snowflakes increased.

Maybe all to the good, Spike thought, as a flake landed on his eyelash, snow would cover their tracks. Just in case Gullivan was about.

Duke led the way forward, and in a few steps, they returned to the land and world of the Ishmecs. To everyone's relief, the cave was empty, and they walked once more out of the mouth of the cave and into the tropical humidity.

'My Lord Sentinel!'

The sound of Opi's voice was welcoming in this strange land so far from home. They looked up to see Arisius and Opi striding swiftly toward them, their faces creased with concern.

'What is it? Is there a problem? Is there something else you need?'

'The portal,' said Opi. 'Is it the portal? Is it now closed to you?'

The Sentinel's expression was grave. 'If this is due to our interference ... if we have prevented you from travelling back to your own time ...'

Duke smiled at them both. 'It's ok,' he said. 'We've been home, and now we're back.'

The Sentinel stared. 'Back? But we've just watched you walk into the cave.'

He looked them all up and down, scrutinising their clothes. 'Yet what you say must be true ... your garments -'

'It's been hours on our side,' said Terri. 'This is a new day for us.'

Arisius nodded slowly. 'We should not be surprised.'

'We've brought the ball, Sir,' Duke said. 'As you requested. And we have news for you about Gullivan.'

'Excellent!' Arisius smiled on them. 'All shall be told to the Elder. He will be surprised to see your return so soon.'

If the Elder was surprised, he didn't show it.

'Ah! Welcome again, my friends!'

He was sitting where they had last seen him, in the comfort of a huge chair, in the middle of his grandchildren, who were perched on the arms, their legs hanging loosely over the sides.

At their approach, Jophan leaped down from the chair, the translator band still around his throat. 'Welcome. It is good to see you.'

'Yes, welcome!' said Neeza, jumping down. 'You have returned from your own time?'

'What is it like to go through the time portal?' Jophan asked. 'Tell us all. What happened?'

'Questions will have to wait,' Arisius said. 'Grandfather wishes to talk to our guests. Wait in your rooms for now.'

'But, Father …'

'There will be other opportunities,' said Arisius, gently.

Jophan hesitated, and then with a sigh, they turned and left the room.

As the door whispered shut behind them, the Elder leaned forward in his chair and said, 'I am pleased to see you all again so soon.'

'You don't seem surprised, Sir,' Duke replied.

'I am not,' he said. 'Time portals are strange and wonderful things.'

'It's tomorrow where we come from,' Spike said.

'And it will remain so until your return?'

'We're not sure, but hopefully we'll come out more or less when we left,' said Billy.

'But of course, we don't know,' said Doc.

The Elder nodded. 'You are wise not to take anything for granted,' he said. 'Life is much too precious to waste a single moment. We have reason to know.'

Reaching into the bag, Terri pulled out the ball.

The old man gasped. 'My journal! My people and I are grateful to you. It contains an enormous amount of data vital to the scientists and technicians working on the drive for our ship.'

Leaning carefully across, Duke took the ball and placed it into the old man's gnarled hands. Almost immediately, the Elder shut his eyes and after some moments, the ball began to open. It soon became clear that the data they had managed to record was only a tiny portion of what it contained.

'It is undamaged,' the Elder sighed. 'We cannot thank you enough. It is as well, I think, that you rescued it from Gullivan?'

The Sentinel sat beside them. 'Ah yes, Gullivan. You mentioned you have some information that may be of use to us?'

Duke cleared his throat. 'Well, Sir, we have discovered -' He glanced across at the Elder.

'Pray, continue,' Arisius said. 'All has been mentioned to my Father.'

'Well, we discovered the whereabouts of your guard, Guloc, that is to say, his … um … remains. As you asked, I read the words at his graveside.'

The Sentinel nodded his head. 'Not an easy task,' he said. 'You have our gratitude.'

'We found the remains on Gullivan's land, buried in a rough grave beside the house,' Duke said, sounding more like a detective with every word. 'And whilst we were there, we conducted a thorough search of the house itself.'

'That was very courageous of you all. Your search was fruitful?'

'Well, we think we know what he's after in those caves,' Doc piped up, her eyes shining. '*Diamonds*!'

The Sentinel seemed puzzled. 'Diamonds? These things, they are valuable in your world?'

'You bet,' Spike answered. 'Bag full of them and you're made.'

Arisius looked at them. 'These diamonds. What are they like, exactly?'

'They're like them,' said Meatball, pointing at a dazzling display of coloured crystals on the wall, 'but they're white.'

'You mean clear,' Doc said. 'And some are coloured. They're extremely hard and as well as jewellery, they are also used for cutting and things.'

'Cutting?' The Sentinel looked interested. 'And they are clear, you say?' He rose from his chair and opened a drawer in the desk. 'Do you by any chance describe these?'

Dipping in a hand, he held it out for them to see. A small fortune in beautiful, sparkling diamonds blinked back at them.

'Wow!' gasped Spike. 'Look at those!'

Meatball stared at them. 'Are these yours?'

'They are plentiful in the caves around here,' said Arisius, with a smile.

'They were, you mean,' Meatball said. 'Gullivan's probably had half of them.'

A frown crinkled the shimmering skin of Arisius' face. 'And that, I assume, will make him a person of great power in your time.'

'Only because he can buy whatever he wants,' said Billy.

'The thought that something from here may help such a man is not pleasing to us,' the Elder sighed. 'One can only hope that justice will exact its own revenge.'

Arisius nodded agreement. 'You will appreciate we have more pressing matters to attend to at present. The data from the ball must be put to use immediately.'

As if by command, the doors opened and Opi appeared. He was pushing a large, comfortable chair that hovered slightly above the floor as if floating on a cushion of air.

The Elder rose and Arisius bent to support his arm and guide him into it.

'Since the cowardly attack by Gullivan, my father has great difficulty in walking,' Arisius said, 'but he is very proud and refuses to use the traveller other than for journeys of distance.'

'I bid you farewell, my friends,' said the Elder. 'Just for the present. But I look forward to future conversations with you.'

'Me too,' said Billy.

They watched as Opi guided the chair through the doorway and out into the corridor.

'Gullivan's got a lot to answer for,' Meatball muttered.

'He has indeed,' Arisius agreed. 'But he is not at present our first priority. Time is limited.'

A deep anxiety seemed to be welling up inside him.

'Then it's definite?' Doc asked quietly. 'The asteroid I mean? It's definite?'

With a sigh, Arisius nodded. 'Our scientists have been plotting its path and there is no doubt it is on a collision course with this planet. The ramifications of such a collision cannot be overstressed.'

He paused. 'We remain hopeful of finishing the drive for the ship in time. We believe we can do it.' He looked down at them all. 'We have to do it,' he said. 'We have to.'

'Father says we can escort you around the City!'

Neeza jostled Jophan to get in through the door.

Jophan corrected her loudly. '*I* am to escort them. Father asked me.'

'No, me! Father said I am to escort them!'

Jophan stared her in the face. '*I* am eldest,' he said, grandly. 'Therefore ...'

'You are eldest by ten minutes only!' snapped Neeza.

'Why don't you both do it?' said Terri, mildly. She shrugged her shoulders. 'Seems like a good idea to me.'

Jophan and Neeza stared at each other for a few moments. 'It is agreed,' said Jophan. 'Both of us shall do it.'

'Yes.' Neeza looked across at Terri. 'Yes. Both of us.'

'Hoo-ray,' Spike muttered. 'P'raps now we can get on with it.'

Jophan inclined his head. 'My apologies.'

'So,' asked Duke, as they stood looking down a long avenue of metallic walls, 'where's this lead to?'

'The City is vast,' Jophan explained. 'And it is linked by a network of corridors. One only has to stand on one of these transportation discs.'

He pointed to a faint circle outlined on the floor.

'It will be automatically replaced by another,' he said, as they climbed on and the disc rose above the ground.

Jophan closed his eyes. Moments later, the disc started to move.

'Whoa!' yelled Spike. 'What's happening?'

'We're travelling by the power of thought,' Neeza answered. 'It's how we get about here. This is the swiftest way to travel. As long as you remain on one of these discs, you can travel wherever you wish.'

'Can anyone do it?' Terri asked, staring alternately at the disc below her feet and at the walls as they slipped by. 'Us, I mean? Could we do it?'

'Probably,' said Neeza. 'If you practised. We're taught to focus our minds when we're very young.'

'Wow!' laughed Billy. 'This is brilliant! Where are we going?'

'We shall start with the Control Room,' Jophan answered. 'It is of such enormity …'

A loud rumbling noise interrupted him.

'What's that?'

Jophan dismissed it with a wave of his hand. 'It is nothing,' he said. 'Merely a storm approaching. It happens with some regularity here: it is the tropical climate. It will last for no more than an hour.'

They continued along the corridor at increasing speed, the disc skimming around bends, and nipping neatly around columns.

Above their heads, the rumbling intensified, louder and insistent.

'It sounds quite near,' Doc said.

Jophan listened. 'It is yet still far away. You will be aware when it is immediately overhead.'

Another deafening crash resounded through the ceiling.

They all looked up.

'It sounds as though it's right above our heads now,' Duke said, staring anxiously at the ceiling for signs of vibration.

'We have some spectacular storms,' Neeza explained. 'The lightning bolts are extraordinary.'

The disc slowed and stopped.

'We can show them!' Jophan cried. 'We can show them the storm!' He turned to them. 'Neeza and I often go up to the Stateroom and open the roof. It is the most incredible sight you will ever see.'

'We cannot do that, Jo,' Neeza said, reluctantly. 'You know it is forbidden. If Father should discover ...'

'He is *busy*,' said Jophan, in a hushed tone. 'He will not know.'

Neeza looked thoughtful for a moment, then her eyes sparkled. 'That is true.'

'We should take them now,' he urged. 'We will not delay. We can be back in the Control Room before we are missed.'

'Don't get into trouble on our account,' Meatball said. 'We've seen storms before.'

'Not like ours,' Neeza breathed. 'Yes. We will take you. But we will have to hurry.'

With a jolt, the disc began to accelerate in the opposite direction with such speed they struggled to keep upright.

'Our apologies,' Neeza said, hurriedly. 'I forget you are unfamiliar with this method of travel.'

From the base of the disc several narrow columns appeared, sprouting upwards to waist height and then fanning outwards to form a circular rail.

'You may find it easier to use this for support,' said Jophan. 'We must hurry.'

The disc increased in speed, negotiating corners and doorways with ease. Some minutes later, they found themselves once more nearing the doors of the Stateroom.

'We cannot enter through the main doors,' Jophan said, as the disc halted halfway along the corridor. 'During a storm, the guards will refuse us entry to the Stateroom, but Neeza and I know of a way.'

'Can't you just walk through the wall like you did last time?'

Jophan shook his head. 'Not into the Stateroom,' he said. 'It has a protective shield.'

They veered off down a narrow passageway, coming to a halt before a small door on the left.

'What's this?' Terri asked, as the disc settled onto the floor and they stepped off.

'It is a private entrance, for the use of The Assembly only,' said Neeza.

Jophan walked up to the head of the passageway and glanced around. Satisfied no one had seen them, he walked toward the door, and then, reaching into the jacket of his tunic, he pulled out a golden band that he slipped onto his head. A beam of purple light hit the door and it slid silently open.

'You must make sure you return Mother's key, Jo. If the loss is discovered -'

'I shall do it tonight,' he said and then, with a last glance around, he ushered them in through the doorway.

'Up here!'

They followed him up a sweeping staircase to the balcony.

Above them, the thunder boomed and echoed.

'Not sure I like this,' Meatball muttered. 'Something doesn't feel right.'

Climbing the stairs, they craned their necks to look up at a dome of metal shimmering above them, solid and undisturbed despite the muffled echoes of thunder that filled the space.

'It's like those films you see about the war,' Spike said. 'With all the bombing 'n' that.'

'The shield for the Viewing Hemisphere is closed at the approach of a storm,' Neeza explained, raising her voice above the increasing din. 'Jo will have to open it for us.'

Duke grabbed onto the rail. 'I suppose this is a good idea, is it?'

'I shall show you,' Jophan said. 'It is spectacular. But first I must open the shield. Remain here.'

He walked across to the opposite wall, stood before a large silver plate, and closed his eyes. A purple light shone onto the plate and, with a slight movement of his head, he tilted the beam until it passed across a small opening in the centre.

Almost at once, the surface of the shield became a swirl of molten metal. From the centre, it began to peel, the edges rippling over. Fold by fold, the shield receded into the outer edges of the dome and disappeared from sight.

Now, through the clear crystal of the Viewing Hemisphere, they could see the full might of the storm. An impenetrable arc of black menacing cloud, it was strewn with bolts of blinding light that seared through it like electrical impulses through a brain.

Terri's mouth hung open. 'Oh wow!' she yelled. 'It's like being in the middle of it!'

'We *are*,' breathed Spike.

'It's amazing!' Doc sighed.

Billy's hand reached upward. 'You can almost touch it!'

'It's incredible!' Duke stared up at the clouds, swirling and igniting above his head, covering his ears with his hands as another ear-splitting bellow of thunder shuddered around the balcony.

Beside them, Meatball stared at the spectacle above him, shielding his eyes from the brilliance. 'It's no good,' he said. 'I still don't like it. The feel of it. It doesn't feel right. I can't explain it, but it doesn't.'

Jophan threw his arms wide. 'Did we not say it was spectacular?'

'I'm telling you, it's not right,' said Meatball. 'This isn't just any storm. There's something else.'

Jophan watched the clouds churn and twist above his head. 'It is ... *darker* than previously,' he said, vaguely. 'But that is all.'

'Meatball is right,' Neeza said. 'Something is different ... I feel it too.'

They stared upward. In the heart of the cloud directly above their heads, something seemed to be developing, a glowing force, expanding as they watched.

'Do you see,' Neeza went on, 'there ... that strange glowing ... it seems ...'

Thunder exploded once more in their ears, leaving a painful ringing.

'Something's coming,' Meatball announced solemnly, 'that's what it is. There's something coming.'

'What d'you mean?'

'I can *feel* it,' he snapped irritably. 'The air's disturbed, like -'

He looked around at them all. 'Like when you're standing on a station and you can't see the express train, but you know it's coming in.'

'We should listen to him,' Spike warned. 'He can tell about things. Remember that ghost in old Woolley's place? Meatball knew it was there long before we did.'

'A ghost?' Jophan stared at him. 'What is a ghost?'

'*JOPHAN*! *NEEZA*! What do you think you are *doing*? Have you completely forgotten your teaching?'

The voice assailed them from the bottom of the stairs. Startled, they looked down to see Opi's tall, lean figure staring up at them, his eyes large with concern.

'Were you not told it is dangerous to be there in a storm, Jophan?' His voice echoed up the staircase. 'And you have opened the Viewing Hemisphere? How often must I say this?'

Jophan looked back at him. 'I was only showing ...'

Opi stepped onto the staircase. 'You will all come down here immediately,' he said. 'At *once*.'

'But, Opi ...'

'Do not question my instruction, Jophan,' Opi snapped. 'Descend the staircase at once, all of you.'

His voice reverberated in the eerie silence that seemed suddenly to have enveloped the Stateroom. Above their heads, a dull glow tinged the clouds.

'Come! *Immediately*!'

Scaling the staircase in huge bounds, Opi ushered them toward the stairs, but not before Jophan had broken free from the group. Turning, he ran across to the plate to try to close the ceiling.

Opi whirled around. 'No, Jophan, there is no time!' he roared. '*JO*!'

At that moment, a burst of blinding light blazed across the balcony like floodlights at a stadium. The sky seemed to explode with a thunderclap so loud it rocked the Stateroom.

Halfway down the staircase, the whole structure began to shake, catapulting them forward one over the other, legs and arms flailing in all directions. In vain, they reached out to clutch at the banister rail and at each other, but too late to stop them tumbling down the stairs to sprawl in a heap onto the Stateroom floor.

High above the balcony, the magnificent Viewing Hemisphere of the Stateroom showed the first signs of weakening. Fine fractures appeared in the crystal, rapidly becoming hairline cracks that raced across the dome. From these, splinters of weakness sped across the crystal to the centre, where they collided, rupturing the dome like a smashed eggshell.

Running, Opi leapt, flung himself across Jophan, and the pair of them fell as one, landing with a sickening thud.

Finally succumbing to the pressure, the dome groaned and then shattered into thousands of fragments, sending a shower of razor-sharp crystal javelins raining down onto the balcony.

In the suffocating cloud of inky blackness, Spike heard a gut-wrenching cry of pain ... and then silence.

CHAPTER SEVENTEEN

Lying in a crumpled heap, Spike lifted his head and slowly opened his eyes to stare down at the Stateroom floor. What was he doing down here? He felt the floor with his hand, and it yielded slightly beneath his touch.

Spike heaved himself upward to look around. Chaos ... it was chaos. Those alien creatures rushing everywhere. What had happened? What were they doing?

With some effort, he struggled sideways and then leaned on one hand to gaze blearily around him. His neck felt stiff and sore, as though it had been karate-chopped.

As he looked around, a sudden weight seemed to drop to the pit of his stomach. *Billy.* Billy and the others ...

In a panic, he jolted upright. 'Bill! Bill!'

'Here!'

Spike swung around. Billy was sitting up, rubbing his head. Beside him in a crumpled heap, lay Terri.

'Terri!' Billy wailed. 'Terri! Wake up!'

'Wait!' Spike yelled. 'Wait, Bill! Don't move her!'

He stretched out a hand toward Terri, just as her eyes opened.

'Spike?' She put a hand to her head. 'What happened?'

Spike took her hand and supporting her back, eased her gently into a sitting position.

'I don't know,' he said. 'I'm not sure. I think there might've been an explosion, or something.'

His words trailed off as he felt himself lifted, whisked from the ground by willing hands, and scooped high into the air. Terri's hand slipped from his as she, too, was carried away. They came to rest side by side with Billy on soft supports.

'You're ... you're bleeding,' she whispered.

Spike put a finger to his head, then wiped the blood with his sleeve, smearing it across his forehead.

'What about the others,' said Billy. 'The others, Spike. Where are they?'

Terri pushed herself unsteadily up on one elbow to look around.

Meatball appeared suddenly beside them. There were some cuts on his forehead, but he seemed otherwise unhurt.

He looked down at them with concern. 'You all right?'

They nodded. 'Yeah. You?'

'Bit shaken up,' said Meatball.

'Thank God you're ok,' said Terri. 'The others, Meatball, d'you know if they're all right?

Meatball ran a hand through his hair. 'Duke's not too bad.' He glanced around him over a crowd. 'He'll probably be here in a minute. Doc's not too good, though, cut up n'that, you know, but they reckon she's going to be all right.'

'What about Jophan and Neeza?' asked Billy.

Meatball sighed. 'Yes, and no,' he said. 'Neeza's ok, but I've just seen Jophan, and he's in a right state. They had to pull him out.'

'Pull him out?'

'Yeah. He was under Opi. When it happened, Opi must've thrown himself over Jophan to protect him, and ...'

He shook his head jerkily in disbelief. 'Something fell ... from the ceiling. It must've hit him.'

Terri gasped. 'You mean ...'

Meatball nodded. 'Opi's *dead*.'

'Oh, God, no. 'Terri's hand flew to her mouth. '*No* ...'

'I know,' he croaked. 'It's awful.'

Spike closed his eyes. His head dropped forward. 'Poor Opi.'

'Poor Jophan,' Billy whispered.

They looked up to see the tall, blond figure of Duke walking toward them. He looked anxious and drawn.

'You all right?' he asked, quietly.

They nodded.

'Doc's okay,' he reported. 'I've just spoken to her. One or two cuts from the crystal: they looked pretty deep, but apparently they're not too bad.' He glanced at Meatball. 'D'you tell them?'

Meatball nodded.

'I feel so damned guilty,' Duke said. 'If we hadn't come back …'

'What else could we do,' said Meatball. 'They needed the ball.'

'I know,' Duke snapped. 'But if we hadn't got on that stupid bus, none of this would've happened.'

'But we weren't to know it'd bring us back here, were we?'

'And we had no choice,' said Billy. 'The bus brought us here, which means we were meant to come back, doesn't it, Spike?'

Spike shrugged. 'I don't know,' he said. 'I don't know anything anymore.' He threw up his hands. 'I mean, what's all this stuff about? It's a nightmare. First Mr Price, then Gran, and now this lot.'

The others stared at him. 'What about your Gran?'

Spike glanced at Billy. 'Tell you another time.'

He looked up. Doc was walking toward them. 'It's Doc! Doc … you ok?'

Doc nodded, and tried her best to smile with a face showing signs of several cuts. Over each one, there was now a thin film of a clear, glossy substance.

Terri put a finger toward it and touched it lightly. It felt dry and soft.

'Does it hurt much?'

'Not really,' Doc said. 'Not now they've put this gel stuff on it. Stops any pain and heals it within an hour or so. Doesn't leave a scar either, so they said.'

'We were just talking about poor Opi,' Duke said.

Doc nodded. Her eyes were moist. 'I know,' she said. 'It's just terrible. I still can't believe it.'

It was a simple service. Simple and dignified. Opi was laid to rest with all the honours due to someone of such courage and devotion.

Side by side, they stood with his people in a large hall festooned with tropical plants and flowers. With some difficulty, Arisius read the now familiar farewell.

Outside, it was raining, heavy and unrelenting in the continuous sheets of a monsoon. The torrent of raindrops hammered the walls and roof, the noise almost drowning out his voice.

In the corner, Jophan sat in a chair, steeped in misery. Neeza sat beside him, staring dejectedly at the floor. It had been an accident, a tragic accident, but it would be some time before they could accept that.

Spike stood with the others, watching sadly as the mourners filed slowly out of the room past Opi's cradle. No one spoke: no words seemed adequate.

After the final mourner had left the room, Arisius and the Elder stood beside Opi's body to pay their last respects, Arisius lingering after his father had moved away, staring down at his friend. After a while, he stretched himself up, tall and erect and walked across the room to stand before them.

'We shall have to leave very soon,' he said. 'It is imperative that you delay no longer. I thank you for your patience.'

They left within the hour, well equipped for the journey back, Arisius walking among them and the same four guards keeping a silent vigil of protection. Their hearts were heavy as they trod the route Opi had so recently travelled with them.

Finally back at the cave, they turned and, giving their friends a last wave, stepped into the entrance and passed cleanly through the wall.

A moment later, they burst through into their own snow-clad world.

'It's weird,' said Terri, pulling her coat tightly around her as the icy cold made its presence felt. 'Here we are, not long after we left and yet so much has happened in the past.'

'It is odd,' Doc said. 'I suppose even though time has passed, back here it hasn't … or has it?'

'Don't say that,' said Terri.

'I've just had a terrible thought,' said Meatball. 'What if we're fifty years too late?'

Duke stared at the lane stretching out in front of them. 'We should have come back at the same time,' he said. 'Although this lane probably looked the same a hundred years ago.'

A mobile phone burst unexpectedly into life.

Meatball bent over with relief. 'Never thought I'd be so glad to hear a mobile.'

'Thank God,' said Terri.

Doc squeezed her hands into fists. 'We're back! We're back.'

Reaching into his coat pocket, Spike gripped his phone with shaking hands, somehow hiding a sigh of relief. They were home, in the right place and the right time and they'd never have to go through that stinking cave again.

Beside him, Billy watched him swipe the screen and put it to his ear. 'Who is it, Spike?'

Spike gave him a look. 'Hello, Gran. All right? Yes, yeah, we're fine, just on our way back.' He glanced at the others. 'Eh? Is he all right? Oh, ok, then. Yeah, course we can. We're heading home now. Ok, see you later.'

He rang off.

'Everything all right, Spike?'

Spike nodded. 'Yes, it's ok, Bill. Gran's had to go out, that's all. She didn't take Ed with her because she said he seems a bit tired. She was asking if we can go and check on him.'

'We'll do it now,' said Duke. 'Good old Ed.'

Terri smiled. 'Yes. Good old Ed.'

'Come on,' said Meatball. 'Let's go home. I'm fed up.'

As they walked along, Doc said suddenly, 'I hope they'll be all right. The Ishmecs. Hope they make it ok.'

Terri gave a long sigh. 'They were nice, weren't they?'

'Yeah.' Spike nodded. 'They were all right. Bit weird, but all right.'

'They probably thought we were the weird ones,' said Billy.

They set off along the frozen lane, crunching steadily through a fresh fall of snow.

Nearly there, Spike thought, nearly home again. He thought of the warmth and the cosy log fires, and their dear old Ed. How he'd missed his company.

All through the village and up the lane that led to Yew Tree Cottage, he thought of him, so much so that when they first heard Ed's booming bark, Spike wondered if he'd imagined it.

'That sounds like Ed,' said Terri.

Billy listened. 'It *is* Ed. What's he doing out?'

Spike quickened his pace. 'Ed? Ed! Here, boy!'

Ed gave a joyful leap into the air and galloped down the road to meet them all. Taking an enormous bound, he leapt up at Spike, and then at Billy, almost knocking him from his feet.

'Hello, boy,' Spike said, ruffling the dog's head, 'what are you doing out?'

Duke and Meatball were walking on ahead, looking at each other with increasing concern.

Terri pointed at the door. 'Spike! The door's open!'

Pushing Ed down to his feet, Spike broke into a run and he and the others rushed through the front door, bursting into the wide, neatly furnished hallway. All was quiet, save for the ticking of the grandfather clock, but on the thick pile of the hall rug, there were large, wet footprints.

'Who's in here?' Spike yelled.

'Spike?'

With the others, Spike charged into the living room, just as a face peered around the wing of the large fireside chair. 'I am glad to see you.'

Doc gasped. 'Oh!'

Terri's mouth dropped open in amazement.

Billy cried out in delight, and rushed towards the figure in the chair. 'Mr *Price*! Mr Price! You're back!'

'Mr Price!' Spike looked anxiously down at him. 'Mr Price, are you ok? We've been worried.'

They stared at the large lump on Joseph's head, and the scratches that criss-crossed his face. His wrists and arms bore evidence of a rope used to restrain him. 'What happened to you, Mr Price? Did you have a fall or something?'

Joseph stared back at them. 'No, no, nothing like that, Spike. Something a little more unpleasant, I'm afraid.'

Duke stepped forward. 'What d'you mean?'

'Never mind that now,' Doc said. 'We'd better call an ambulance.'

'No.' Mr Price raised a hand. 'No. No ambulance. It's kind of you, but that won't be necessary.'

Terri felt the old man's icy hands. 'Well, at the very least, you need a hot drink,' she said. 'And something to eat. Spike, you and Billy stay with Mr Price. Duke and I will see to it. Come on, Duke.'

'Right.'

They walked off toward the kitchen.

'I'll come with you,' Doc said. 'Get a cloth and some water to bathe those wounds.'

'While you're doing that, I'll nip out and chop some more wood for the fire,' said Meatball. 'You look after Mr Price.'

It was only a little later, when they were all sitting around the fire, that Joseph Price felt sufficiently recovered to continue with his story.

'I've been held prisoner for the last few days,' he said. 'Well, no, longer than that, I think. To tell you the truth, I lost track.'

Spike banged his fist on the arm of his chair. 'I knew it! Didn't I say? I told them something had happened to you.'

'Well, you were right, lad.' Joseph paused to take another sip of tea and swallowed slowly. 'But what made you think something had happened to me?'

Spike hesitated, turning to look at the others. His face was asking if he should mention the watch they'd discovered on their first trip.

'It's not that we thought that exactly,' Duke said hurriedly, 'it just seemed a possibility. You know.'

Joseph Price nodded. 'I understand.'

'So, who were they, then?' Terri asked. 'The people who held you prisoner. Was it a gang or something?'

Joseph shook his head. 'Oh no, nothing like that. No, the villain who took me prisoner was Cornelius Gullivan.'

'Gullivan!' Spike spat out the word as though it tasted disgusting. 'I knew he had something to do with it. *He's* the one who mur -'

He stopped, biting his tongue. Mr Price was an old man. Perhaps it wouldn't do to let him know how close he'd come to death.

'Who what, Spike?'

'Nothing,' said Terri, to the rescue.

Joseph Price sat for a moment, looking long and hard at each of their faces, and then he adjusted his battered body into a forward position, and crossed his hands.

'Some time ago I was crossing Gullivan's land and I had the misfortune to meet him coming the other way. I don't know if your gran's mentioned it, Spike, but Mr Gullivan and I don't see eye to eye over the right of way across his land.'

'We heard he'd threatened you,' Spike said.

'He did indeed,' Joseph continued, 'but this time things went a bit too far and he dealt me a hefty blow with the stock of his shotgun, knocking me unconscious. The next thing I remember was waking up gagged and bound. I have no idea how long I was unconscious, but when I came round, I was in

Gullivan's house. What his intentions were, I don't know, but fortunately I managed to escape.'

'How?'

'When Gullivan went out, he dragged me upstairs and locked me in a priest hole. After a while, I managed to free my hands and I was able to find something to cut through the bonds on my legs. It took me a while, because I'd been bound a long time and I was very stiff and sore, but finally they gave way and I was able to move about.'

'It must've been awful,' Doc said.

'Well, I'm old and creaky these days as it is,' he laughed. 'Still, that wasn't the main problem.'

'The priest hole,' Duke said, nodding.

'Exactly,' said Joseph. 'Fortunately for me, the lock was very old, and with several applications of my shoulder against the door, the frame splintered and gave way. But of course, even then, I was worried. I'd heard Gullivan go out some time before and I hadn't heard him come back, but I couldn't be sure. I'd made a bit of noise getting out and any minute he could have come running up the stairs, so I grabbed the first heavy thing I could lay my hands on, stood behind the door, and waited.'

'And he didn't appear?'

'No, thank goodness. I'm not sure I'd have been able to defeat someone of Gullivan's build. And the mood he seemed to be in, well … that would probably have been my lot.'

'He's evil,' Terri said.

'Well, fortunately for me he wasn't about, so I managed to slip out of the house and make my way across his field, which was just as worrying because I stuck out like a sore thumb against the snow. From there, I managed to make my way back here.'

'Thank God you did,' said Billy. 'It's freezing out.'

'I'm amazed you managed it,' said Meatball. 'At your age.'

Joseph smiled, then easing his aching frame a little further forward, he said, quietly, 'I think the time may have come to let you into my confidence. You can be relied upon to keep whatever I reveal to you between ourselves?'

They nodded, as if hypnotised.

'Very well then. To begin. Certain things are not quite what they seem to be. Always remember that. You shouldn't always believe what your eyes are telling you. I, for instance, am not what I appear to be. I can't tell you too much at present, but I think it's as well for you to know that Joseph Price is not my real name.'

Billy gasped. 'It's not?'

'It is not. Your gran's name is not her real name, either and I know that must seem very odd, particularly to you boys, but for the time being I must ask you to have faith in us both.'

Spike and Billy looked at each other. Gran?

Joseph turned back to the fire and warmed his hands. 'The other thing I must tell you all is, I know about the time portal.'

It was Spike's turn to gasp. 'You do?'

'You know about the time portal, Mr Price?'

'Yes, Duke, I do. And I also know about the Ishmecs. Arisius and I are old friends. You've met Arisius?'

They nodded, their mouths gaping in amazement.

'And how is my old friend, Zephulon?' Seeing the puzzled look on their faces, he added, 'You may know him as the Elder.'

'He's fine,' said Meatball. 'Or at least he was till Gullivan attacked him.'

Joseph Price sat up in his chair. His face was grave. 'Gullivan? Cornelius Gullivan can cross the time portal?'

He sat for a moment, then began to nod his head. 'Yes, yes, of course, I should've guessed. You must understand time portals only exist for those who are destined to use them, and they are not visible, or accessible, to any other, so we must presume there is a reason. There'll be something in it for him, that's a certainty. What is it that rattlesnake's after, d'you know? Something he finds in the valley, perhaps?'

Billy nodded. 'He's after diamonds, Mr Price. He's got loads of them. They're everywhere.'

Joseph Price gave a deep sigh. 'I see … and you say he attacked Zephulon?'

'Yes. And two of his guards. He killed the guards,' Spike added.

Joseph shook his head. 'We can only hope that man will get what he deserves.'

'Mr Price?'

Joseph turned to look at Doc.

'Mr Price, how do you know about the time portals?'

Joseph smiled at her. 'It's only natural you should have questions,' he said. 'And in time they will all be answered.'

Spike dipped a hand into his pocket. 'Would you like this back, Mr Price?'

'Like what back?'

Spike pulled out the watch.

'We found it,' said Duke. 'On the other side of the time portal.'

'That's why we were so worried,' Terri said, earnestly. 'We thought … well …'

'We thought something had happened to you,' said Meatball.

Joseph took the watch in his hand and examined it. 'It isn't mine,' he said. He pulled a watch from his pocket. 'Luckily Gullivan never found it. I didn't want him getting his hands on it. That's not *his* real name either, by the way.'

'That doesn't surprise me,' said Meatball. 'But if that watch we found isn't yours, then whose is it?'

Joseph Price considered for a moment. 'I suspect it may be Zephulon's,' he said. 'Gullivan probably dropped it when he was killing the guard.'

'He brought the other guard back here,' said Terri. 'We found the bones on Gullivan's land. Arisius asked us to read some words over him.'

Joseph beamed at them. 'That was a very brave and charitable thing to do,' he said. 'Your grandmother was right. But then she always is.'

'Gran?'

'Yes, your gran. She told me on my last visit to you that you and your friends were very kind and thoughtful. But now, we must talk business. I have a very important task for you all. I need you to find something, something I believe … I hope … may still be somewhere in Gullivan's house. Tell me, when you were at Gullivan's, did you have a look around his house at all?'

'Duke and Meatball did.'

'Excellent. That, unfortunately, was the one thing I could not do.'

'So what d'you want us to do?'

Joseph took a last sip of his tea and swallowed. 'As I said, I want you to retrieve something for me. It's something I was carrying when I was attacked by Gullivan.'

'How did he know about it?'

'He didn't. It was just unfortunate that I had it with me when I encountered him. The item I want you to retrieve is a crystal.'

'A crystal?'

Joseph nodded. 'Yes, Billy. The crystal itself is in a case and if Gullivan has been trying to open it, he'll be wasting his time. Only the person who has the ability can open it. The case is impenetrable to anyone else. But it is vitally important and it must be retrieved at all costs.'

'Why?'

'That's a very good question, Billy,' said Joseph. 'And the answer is, so you can complete the second task I need you to perform for me.'

He leaned back in his chair, resting his head against the cushion. 'I need you to take the crystal to the Ishmecs. They will shortly become aware that the crystal they have is no longer viable.'

Spike's heart began to pound. No, not again. Not back there, through that awful cave.

He glanced at Duke and Meatball. Their faces told the same story.

'You mean back through the portal?' Spike asked.

'Yes, Spike. I'm afraid it means travelling back through the portal. Can I rely on you?'

Every fibre of Spike's being wanted to say yes. He and Billy adored Mr Price, loved him like a grandfather. They'd do anything for him, but …

'You can rely on us, Mr Price,' said Billy.

Spike looked at him. Billy's eyes were shining. 'We've got to, haven't we?' he said. 'We took that ball back so they could escape and now they can't, so we have to do it. That bus took us through for a reason, Spike.'

Spike stared at him for a moment, then looked around at the others. Nodding, he said, 'Of course, Mr Price. You can rely on us.'

'And us,' said Duke and Meatball together.

'Where one goes, we all go,' said Terri.

Doc nodded.

'Very well then,' said Joseph. 'It is only fair to warn you it will be dangerous. Retrieving the crystal from Gullivan's house will be risky. That man is ruthless and now he has access to the past, he will think he has the ideal opportunity to do whatever he wants, so you must take great care. Check and check again. Now, as to the crystal. It's in a case, as I told you, but it may now be anywhere in his house.'

He leaned a little closer. 'The case itself is square. It has a pad on the top.'

'We saw that!' Meatball nudged Duke. 'That box you saw in the attic, Duke. It had a pad of some sort on it, didn't it?'

'Yes!'

Joseph smiled. 'Excellent! Under no circumstances, should you try to open the inner box. The Ishmecs will know how to open it. It must be delivered to Zephulon personally and that is where the real danger lies: crossing the time portal.'

He turned his head to look at Terri. 'Your particular ability may be of crucial importance, my dear.'

'*My* ability?'

He nodded. 'Remember, Arisius will not be expecting you. And you will need to make your own way to the city.'

Spike's eyes opened wide. 'The dinosaurs …'

'It is imperative that the crystal is delivered to the Ishmecs as soon as possible. They do not have much time.'

'You mean the asteroid,' Doc said.

'Yes, my dear, the asteroid. Time is of the essence.' With a sigh, Joseph leaned wearily back in his chair. 'Remember the crystal.'

Beads of perspiration appeared on his brow. 'Forgive me, I am tired.'

His eyes slowly closed, his lips murmuring indistinctly.

'He's exhausted,' said Terri. 'Who wouldn't be after what he's been through?'

'He may even be suffering from mild concussion,' Doc remarked. 'That's some bump on his head.'

Spike leaned across and put a hand on Joseph's shoulder. 'Don't worry,' he said. 'We'll do everything we can.'

Joseph responded with a strained nod.

Meatball fetched a cushion and slipped it behind his head, while Terri pulled a large tartan blanket from the sofa and draped it around his legs.

'Right,' said Duke. 'You heard what he said. Let's go.'

'I don't understand it,' said Terri, as she helped Spike close up the fire. 'I mean, when we go back, it'll be the same time we left, won't it?'

Spike shrugged. 'Who knows,' he said. 'I've given up trying to work it out. Come on, we've got to search.'

'Spike, d'you think …'

He turned to look at her. 'What?'

'Opi … d'you think we should have told Mr Price about Opi? I mean, from what he says, he might know him.'

She looked at the others. 'Don't you think we should have told him?'

Duke chewed his lip. 'I did wonder that myself.'

'Well, it's too late now. We'd better get a move on,' Spike said. 'We've got to search.'

'What for?'

Spike looked at Doc. 'Weapons, of course. You've seen the size of those dinosaurs.'

'He's right,' Duke said. 'Come on, Meatball, let's look around, see if there's anything we can use.'

Doc screwed the top back on a water bottle and pushed it into her bag. 'Nothing we take is going to make much difference against them, though, is it? Even the smaller ones. What can we take?'

'Perhaps we won't meet any,' Terry said in a quiet voice. 'It's a big place.'

'Yes, and it's a long trip to the city,' Spike said. 'And they don't know we're coming.'

Duke stepped in through the back door. 'I've just had a look in your gran's shed. There's another axe.'

'That's about it,' Meatball said, following him in. 'Everything else is too big to take.'

'That'll have to do, then,' Spike said. 'We can't waste any more time. We'd better get going.'

He bent down to Ed, who was stretched before the fire. 'Look after Mr Price, Ed. Just till Gran gets back.'

Ed lifted his head, and snuffled, then licked Spike's nose. Billy crouched down to cuddle him, hiding his face in his fur.

Leaning down, Spike squeezed Billy's shoulder. 'If you'd rather not go, Bill,' he said. 'It's all right.'

Billy wiped his nose and stood up. 'Course I'm going,' he said.

They looked back at Joseph Price, who was now fast asleep in the chair.

'Come on,' said Spike. 'Let's go.'

Halfway down the path, Spike stopped. He couldn't explain it, but something, some little thought, was niggling at him. Would Mr Price be ok while they were gone? Perhaps, after all, they should've called the doctor. And yet ...

He glanced back over his shoulder at Yew Tree Cottage.

'Hold on!' he called. 'I've just got to check something! Catch you up!'

'I'll come with you.'

'No, no, Bill, you wait here. Won't take a sec.'

At the front door, Spike reached out for the handle and then stopped, and moved across to the window of the sitting room. Joseph Price was up and out of his chair, standing before the fire, looking into the mirror that hung over the fireplace.

Watching through the window, Spike held his breath as the wounds on Joseph's face and wrists melted away and then disappeared altogether.

CHAPTER EIGHTEEN

In the back seat of a warm taxi whisking him home from the station, Gullivan thought about his day.

He grinned as he remembered the look on Eric Thorpe's face when he'd showed him the diamonds. Disbelief, suspicion, and pure greed. Gullivan had watched the look of greed in Thorpe's eyes overtake everything else as he'd worked his way through the stones.

Nothing unusual in that, of course. Thorpe was an oily, back-stabbing tick who would sell his best friend if there were profit in it for him, so the look of greed had come as no surprise.

But this time, something was different. This time there had been something else in Thorpe's face, and Gullivan had been trying to pin it down all the way home. Thorpe had seemed jittery and nervous, as though he was anxious to be rid of him.

Travelling home on the train later that day, Gullivan remembered Thorpe's odd behaviour and it troubled him. Something wasn't right, and as the taxi turned into the top of his road, Gullivan suddenly realised what that something was.

Fear. That's what he'd seen in Thorpe's greasy face. Fear. Something had spooked him. Or maybe someone?

'Eight pound fifty, guv.'

The voice hovered on the outside of Gullivan's thoughts. 'Eh?'

The taxi driver looked at him over the seat. 'Eight pound fifty.'

Reaching into his pocket, Gullivan pulled out his wallet and thrust a ten-pound note into the waiting hand.

'Keep the change,' he muttered.

He strode in through the front door, slammed it shut and leaned against it. Why was he worrying? The McKendricks didn't know where he was, did they? Thorpe didn't know where he was, and he couldn't tell them what he didn't know.

Gullivan began to calm down. He was safe here, in the back of beyond: safe, and miles away from anywhere. No one in this godforsaken little village knew who he really was. Even if they found this place, the McKendricks would be looking for Jan Van Der Groet, not Cornelius Gullivan.

He looked down at the bag on the floor. Stop worrying, he told himself, there's more than enough in there to get me wherever I need to be. The McKendricks will never find me.

He broke into a whistle as he climbed the stairs. It was time for Cornelius Gullivan to disappear, just as Jan Van Der Groet had done. Few things to tidy up and that was that.

He thought about the few things. The old guy, for a start. Couldn't have him croaking, not yet. Getting rid of some reptile from the other side was one thing; no one in this time would miss him, but Joseph Price? Gullivan shook his head. That was a different kettle of fish. He was a well-known face in the village and sooner or later someone was going to notice.

Still smiling, he walked along the landing and into the room at the end. He'd left him some drink that morning, so he should be okay.

Gullivan stopped in his tracks. Across the room, the door stood open. In a panic, he raced across and up the steps to take a closer look. The priest's hole contained the drink, and nothing else.

Joseph Price had gone.

Damn! Curse that old fool: he should've killed him when he had the chance. He glanced through the window. Across the smooth blanket of snow, a line of erratic footprints was clearly visible, leading away across the field.

Running from the room, he sprinted down the stairs in fits and spurts, landing with a crash in the hallway.

No, he told himself, think. The old man could've been gone for hours, no point in chasing the footprints. He sat down on the stair. Where would he go? Well, home of course. Home, where he felt safe. Where else would an old man go? But Price wasn't your typical old man, was he?

Gullivan stood up. His reflection stared back at him in the hall mirror. 'No, he wouldn't go home,' he said. 'He'd go to the police.'

But if he had, wouldn't they by here by now?

And even if he had, it was only Price's word against his, wasn't it? Price, a stupid, muddle-headed old man, always disappearing on little jaunts. He could hardly tell them he popped to the past; they'd lock him away. If he hadn't followed Price that day and seen him disappear, *he'd* never have believed it.

A grin creased Gullivan's face. He shook his head, slowly. No. Price wouldn't go to the police. He had one or two secrets of his own, didn't he, and they might just ask a few awkward questions.

With sudden certainty, he knew Joseph Price had gone home.

Maybe it was time for a little visit. He wouldn't rush over there, he'd take his time, and wait until it was an appropriate moment to pay a house call. Of course, if the old man was on his own … well …

The sound of a car echoed in the driveway outside. Instinctively, Gullivan snapped off the light, threw himself against a wall, and peered through the curtain.

It wasn't the police, not unless a sleek black jag was their car of choice these days.

Straining his eyes, he looked out, but it was hard to see who was sitting inside the car through tinted windows. One shadow … or was it two?

The obvious hit him like a hammer.

The taxi driver. The McKendricks had got to him.

Gullivan turned, and ran.

174

CHAPTER NINETEEN

'Watch where you're sticking your foot, will you?'

Spike glanced back at Terri. 'I can't help it,' he snapped. 'I can't see anything.'

'Will you two shut it?' Doc scrambled along the floor of the coal cellar in Gullivan's house, desperately trying to forget that she'd just put her hand in something squishy. 'Someone'll hear us.'

'Like who? There's no one else here.'

'We don't know that,' said Billy. 'Gullivan could be anywhere.'

Climbing to the top of the steps, Duke put his fingers to the latch on the cellar door and lifted. A sliver of light shone onto his hand through the tiny gap.

'The light's on!'

Then, as if someone had heard his words, the light went out.

It was bitterly cold in the coal cellar, but the prospect of the whole sorry crowd of them coming face to face with the terrifying end of a shotgun made Spike's palms erupt with sweat.

It remained agonisingly hushed and black. Gently, Duke took the latch between finger and thumb and lifted. It made a slight scraping sound. Hearts thumping, they waited. Still quiet.

Taking a firmer grip on the latch, Duke applied a little force to the door, then watched with horror as it slipped away from the dampness of his palm and flew open, striking the wall behind it with a crash.

In the gloom of the cellar, they prayed. There was no sound, but that didn't mean Gullivan wasn't sitting behind the door, waiting his moment.

Duke looked back at Meatball. There was only one way to know for sure. Gulping in the cold air, Duke stepped out through the door, and into an empty hallway. No sign of Gullivan. He felt weak with relief.

'It's all right!' he whispered, glancing back at the others, who were creeping out behind him. 'There's no-one here. It must've been Gullivan, but he's gone.'

In the half-light, they stared at one another, breathing deeply.

'I've got a feeling we're not going to see Gullivan for a while,' said Spike, who had clambered onto the stairs and now stood leaning on the ledge, looking out of the window. 'He's going like a bat out of hell across the back field.'

Meatball joined him at the window. 'To the portal d'you reckon?'

'Who knows? But something's spooked him by the look of things.'

'Something … or some*one*,' said Doc. She was by the front door, peering through the glass. 'I hate to say it, guys, but it looks like we've got company.'

Spike whizzed down the banister, landing on the floorboards with scarcely a sound and ducked beneath the window.

Squinting through a gap in the curtain, he saw a large and expensive car.

Duke looked. 'That's some car. Who are they?'

Standing beside the car, were two strangers. The first, a man, was tall, broad, and greying with the kind of face Spike had often seen in newspapers. A large fur collar hid his neck.

A woman stood next to him, balancing precariously on heels you could spear sausages with. She looked younger than the man, but was obviously in charge. Her hair was cut incredibly short and her ears drooped with the weight of two heavy gold earrings.

As Spike watched, her pillar-box red lips moved rapidly. The man shrugged and reached into his jacket to pull out a notebook.

'Yes,' he seemed to be saying. 'This is the place.'

'It's them!' Billy crouched down beside Spike. 'It's the two I told you about, the two we saw at the garage!'

Terri peered carefully beneath the edge of the curtain. 'They don't look very nice. I wonder what they want?'

She watched the woman's glossy red nails as she reached into her bag. The glossy red nails reappeared a moment later, curled around a small shimmering object. 'She's got a gun. Maybe they're the police.'

'Don't look like police to me,' Duke said. 'We need to get out of here.'

'But we can't go without the crystal,' Spike said. 'We promised Mr Price we'd get it.'

'They're going to come in and search the place,' Doc said. 'They're not just going to knock and leave, are they?'

'They might,' said Spike, staring at the woman, who was speaking rapidly on a mobile phone, 'they might just -'

'The guy's going,' Duke hissed. 'He's disappeared.' His eyes opened wide with alarm. 'He must be going round the back. Down the cellar! Quick!'

In a sudden rush, they crammed through the cellar door, squeezing inside in the darkness, pulling the door shut behind them.

It had scarcely closed when they heard another door and the sound of heavy boots walking through the kitchen. In the gloom of the cellar, a ray of light filtered through the tiniest of cracks, and through it Spike watched the long, black-trousered legs as they crossed the hallway, walking swiftly across to the front door. It opened wide, and the pair of heels strode in, clacking on the parquet flooring.

'Well?' the woman demanded.

'No sign,' the man said. 'And the back door was open. He's made a run for it.'

She rounded on him. 'You idiot. That's exactly what he wants us to think. And all the while he's stashed away nice and cosy upstairs somewhere. You have searched upstairs, I suppose?'

177

'Just about to.'

'Well, get on with it!'

Behind the cellar door, Spike watched the man pull a gun from his pocket and scale the staircase two or three treads at a time. In the hallway, the woman paced up and down.

Moments later, the man reappeared at the top of the stairs.

'Nothin',' he called.

'Did you try the attic?'

The man shook his head.

'Why *NOT*!'

Her voice had increased to a scream.

The man swung around and ran back along the landing. Shortly after, they heard the faint sound of the ladder.

'He's up in the loft.' Behind the cellar door, Spike mouthed the words over his shoulder to the others, and then returned to squint through the gap.

'*WELL*?' the woman shrieked, as the man appeared once more on the staircase.

'Nothin'. Just a dead rat.'

The woman's hands clenched and unclenched with rage. 'Yeah, and the next one's gonna be De Groet. That double-crossing skunk's been here, I can *smell him*!'

'Well, he ain't upstairs.'

'Well, don't just stand there, you useless lump, search down here.' She pointed a long bony finger at the cellar door. 'What about that, where's that go?'

The man shrugged. 'Dunno.'

The woman gave a cry of exasperation. 'Well, go and bloody look! Do I have to do everything myself?'

Through the tiny gap in the cellar door, Spike saw the man hesitate, then start across the hallway towards them.

'Get out!' he hissed. 'Quick!'

They whirled around and began to scramble back down into the cellar, but there was no time to make for the door. They just managed to throw themselves against the walls in the darkness, when the cellar door opened, and a bright shaft of light flooded the steps.

Then, as the man's foot hovered over the first step, everything changed.

Outside, in the cold stillness of the drive, a car horn burst into life and kept on shrieking, the deafening hoot blotting out everything else.

'He's trying to get away!' the woman shrieked. 'After him!'

Releasing his hold on the handle, the man ran to the front door, threw it open and leapt outside, closely followed by the woman, skidding and sliding on the wooden floor.

At the cellar door, Spike leaned out. 'They've gone outside! They think Gullivan's out there, trying to nick their car!'

'Can't be him, he's gone.'

Billy's face appeared out of the gloom, like a cuckoo in a clock. He was grinning.

'It was me,' he said. 'I nipped out and set off the alarm.'

Spike beamed at him. 'Brilliant.'

'Good thinking,' Duke said. 'That'll give us time to get upstairs. Hopefully, even if they come back in the house, they won't go up there. They've looked already.'

Bursting from the cellar, they poured up the stairs onto the landing and into one of the rooms at the front of the house, where they crouched down behind the ledge to watch through the window. Outside, the deafening blare of the car horn abruptly stopped.

The woman's voice screamed out.

'That scum's here somewhere. Search that lot!'

Duke lifted the corner of a tatty curtain and looked out to see the woman wave an arm in the general direction of the ramshackle outbuildings that littered Gullivan's land.

He watched as the man pulled a torch from his pocket and marched off towards the cowshed.

'We're all right for a bit, they're searching around outside,' he said.

Stepping across to the ladder, Meatball scaled it, Spike close on his heels.

'Hang on there, I'll pass it down.'

He dragged the box out, lifted it to the loft opening, and passed it down into Spike's hands.

'D'you reckon this is it?' Billy asked. 'The box with the crystal in it?'

'It's got to be,' said Spike. 'Let's get it outside quick, before those two come back. All clear, Duke?'

Duke nodded.

Carrying the box, they hurried down the stairs into the hall and out of the back door, not stopping until they were clear of the house and well across the field.

'Solomon?'

Meatball puffed the suggestion out into the freezing air. Spike nodded.

'It'll buy us a bit of time,' said Duke, 'and we'll be out of sight once we're inside. Might be an idea to check it as well. We don't know for sure if it's the right box, do we?'

'If it isn't the right one, we'll just have to keep going back till we find it,' Spike puffed. 'Look, there's Solomon!'

The magnificent old oak tree stood before them, dressed in a white cloak of snow, holding out its branches like huge, welcoming arms, as though it was waiting for their arrival.

Terri and Doc stomped on ahead to open the panel. Following behind, Meatball ducked through the shallow opening, squeezed inside, and then took the box as Duke, Spike and Billy followed. The girls stepped in last, closing the panel securely behind them.

'We made it!'

Terri's words wafted out in swirls into the icy air.

Reaching into his pocket, Meatball pulled out his torch and flicked it on and together they crouched around to inspect the box.

'If only we could get this open,' he said, 'we could make sure the crystal's inside.'

Duke ran his hand over the seamless surface of the box. 'There doesn't seem to be any opening,' he said. 'That's a bit odd, isn't it?'

'There must be an opening,' Billy said. 'There's got to be. Have a look underneath.'

Carefully, they tilted the box on one edge and peered beneath.

'Nope.'

'Look at that keypad. What sort of keypad is that?' Doc asked. 'It's just a purple circle. Where d'you tap in the numbers?'

'Perhaps you don't,' Meatball answered. 'Perhaps it's one of those palm-print things.'

He placed a hand on the pad. Then he pushed it, but nothing happened.

'You try, Doc.'

Doc tried tapping the pad. Still nothing happened.

Spike looked at Terri. 'You try,' he said. 'You opened the ball, didn't you?'

Terri put out a hand to the circle. Nothing. She lowered her palm until it was actually touching the plate. Still nothing.

'Try thinking about it,' Billy said. 'You know, like you did with the ball.'

'D'you reckon?' Terri shrugged. 'Ok.'

Closing her eyes, she began to concentrate. Almost at once, the pad started to glow.

'It's working!'

'You've got it, keep going!' Doc cried.

In the centre of the circular pad, the purple was changing to a brilliant shade of gold. It filled the entire pad, glowing like the sun in the darkness of the tree trunk.

The gold then began to melt away from the centre, until all that remained was a crystal disc. As they watched, a beam of light burst from the centre of the disc and ballooned out into a large holographic image.

'Look at *that* ...'

Terri opened her eyes to look at it. 'It's beautiful!'

Floating in mid-air, high above the panel, was a hollow sphere of the deepest midnight blue, peppered with silver stars, pulsing with light.

Meatball watched it slowly rotate. 'What is it?'

'It's like fairy lights,' said Billy.

Doc studied the sphere intently. 'I can tell you exactly what that is,' she said. 'It's a map of the heavens. Or at least part of it. And if I'm not mistaken, that constellation there is Cassiopeia.'

'Amazing!'

'Don't see how that helps us, though,' Duke said. 'We're no nearer to opening the box.'

'Wait a minute,' Terri said. 'Didn't Mr Price say not to open the box?'

'No, he said not to try opening the box the crystal's in,' Doc said. 'He never said anything about the outer box. If we can get it out of this thing, it'll be easier to carry.'

Spike grabbed Doc's sleeve. 'What did you say?'

'I said if we can get it out of this, it'll be …'

'Not that. Before,' Spike said. 'When you said about the map.' He tugged at her sleeve. 'What did you say that constellation was called?'

'Cassiopeia,' Doc said. 'I'm almost certain.'

Spike stared at the sphere, watching the constellation drift back towards him.

'What is it, Spike?'

Spike glanced at his brother. 'Cassiopeia,' he said. 'That's what I saw on Gran's phone.'

Duke frowned. 'On her phone? When?'

'Few days back. When I got in. I was standing in the hallway and Gran's phone glowed purple.'

'*Purple* …'

'Why didn't you tell me?'

'I've only just remembered, Bill. Her phone suddenly buzzed and glowed purple, and when I looked at the screen, it just said, '*Cassiopeia is the key.*'

'That's got to be more than coincidence.'

'Does your gran's phone always glow purple?' Terri asked.

Spike shook his head.

'Then that is weird,' said Duke.

Yes, thought Spike, it is. And it can join the list. He was glad he and Billy hadn't told them about any of the other things. He thought suddenly of Mr Price and what he'd seen through the window of Yew Tree Cottage. Not even Billy knew about that.

Terri gazed at the sphere. 'Which one did you say was Cassiopeia, Doc?'

'It's just coming round. There, look. That one there.'

Mesmerised, Terri put out a finger and touched a single bright star at its heart.

The sphere halted at once. For a split second, Cassiopeia seemed to burst with light and then as dramatically as it had appeared, the hologram vanished, sucked back into the crystal disc.

'Well I dunno what you did, Terri, but -'

Doc let out a squeal. 'It's going!'

The heavy outer casing began to flow away, starting at the circular pad and creeping, treacle-like, across the surface and oozing down the sides, where it seeped beneath the box and vanished.

'Now *that*,' breathed Meatball, 'is what I call a security system.'

'It's gone,' Billy gasped.

Spike stared at it in amazement. 'There's nothing left,' he said. 'Except this.'

They looked at the object: the only thing remaining of the box they'd carried into Solomon. It was a pyramid of deepest purple, translucent enough to reveal the precious cargo trapped inside.

'That must be it,' Duke said. 'The crystal Mr Price was talking about. That must be what we have to take back to the Ishmecs.'

'Somehow I thought it'd be bigger than that,' Doc said, measuring it against her hand. 'But then I suppose tiny things can be powerful.'

Spike pulled his rucksack open, placed the crystal carefully inside, and zipped it up. 'Tiny or not, it's really important.'

'All the more reason to get a move on,' said Meatball. Reaching out, he pulled aside the panel and stepped out into the snow up to his knees. 'We've wasted too much time already. Come on.'

But things were not to be that easy. It was impossible to rush. The snow was falling once more, thick dollops that grew deeper and heavier as they walked, holding every tread in a tenacious grip. The journey across the field took far longer than they hoped and it was twenty minutes later when they finally clambered over the stile into Thicketts Lane.

'Should make better speed here,' Duke puffed. 'Walk in the car tracks. There won't be any traffic this time of day.'

'You had to say it, didn't you?'

Spike was looking over his shoulder at a large car further down the lane, crunching and wobbling its way along the deep-frozen ridges.

'Oh hell,' said Meatball, 'it's them. It's the car from the house.'

'Don't panic,' said Duke. 'Just keep walking.'

Behind them, the car crawled nearer and nearer, slipping and jolting until it slowed beside them. They heard muffled words exchanged inside, and then the window purred open and a large square head leaned out.

'Oi! You kids! Seen this man?'

The driver flicked a photograph toward them.

Adopting a look of complete innocence and bewilderment, Duke and Meatball leaned across and studied the photo.

'Mr Gullivan?' said Duke. 'Oh yes, we've seen him.'

Inside the car, the woman hurled herself across the man's chest, almost strangling him with his seatbelt.

'Where?' she demanded. 'When did you see him?'

'A while back,' said Meatball. 'Hightailing it across that field he was, as though his butt was on fire.'

With a tremendous heave, the man forced the woman back into her seat. 'Thanks, lads,' he said. 'No idea where he might be headed, I suppose?'

'Headed?' Duke did his best to look thoughtful.

'Across that field?' Meatball screwed up his eyes, as though he was thinking intently. 'I'd say probably the main road into Westonbridge. It's the next big town.'

'Yeah, Westonbridge,' Spike echoed.

'Near the airport,' Billy added.

The woman gripped the man's arm. 'Airport?' she shrieked. 'Get the hell after him!'

The man thrust his foot onto the pedal and the car jerked forward, skidding, and sliding from side to side.

'Looks like they didn't know about the airport,' Billy said, as they watched the car struggle to turn the corner.

They started to laugh.

'They do now,' said Spike.

CHAPTER TWENTY

'No good waiting here, is it?'

In the bitter cold, Spike stood with his brother and their friends. The countryside around them was deathly silent, shrouded in a blanket of fresh snow.

Meatball looked vaguely across the bridge to the other side. 'Wish I felt better,' he said.

Doc looked at him with concern. 'Aren't you feeling ok?'

'Yeah,' he said. 'But not about this.'

'The dream?' Duke asked.

Meatball nodded. 'I keep seeing bits of it,' he said. 'And none of it's good.'

'We promised we'd do it,' said Terri.

'I know.'

'Wish Ed was with us,' Billy said.

They stood for a few moments, shivering in the icy breeze that whistled down the river, then stepped onto the bridge and through the portal.

The tropical heat hit them like a steaming towel as they stepped out of the cave. Dazzling sunshine was beating down from a cloudless sky, heating the ground and rocks to blistering heat. A syrupy haze hung wispily about the rainforest below.

Standing on the dusty plateau, they gazed down into the valley. Everywhere was strangely still, as if nature was having an afternoon nap.

Meatball stared straight ahead.

'What is it?' Terri whispered.

'I can't remember,' he said. He looked at her. 'That's the problem.'

She nodded. 'I feel it, too. Something's not right.'

'It's very quiet,' said Billy. 'Wasn't this quiet last time.'

Despite the heat, Spike shivered. It was definitely the same place, but somehow, it felt different. There was a sense of uneasiness in the air, as though everything was standing still, waiting for something.

He strode across to the grassy mound and stood on the top to get a better view.

'Can't see much,' he said. 'Nothing seems to be moving down there.'

Billy climbed the mound beside him. 'It's so hot. Feels like the heat's pressing down on your head.'

Sweat was already pricking on Doc's face. She tugged at her t-shirt. 'Maybe there's going to be another storm. Or maybe …'

'What?'

'Well, it could be something to do with the asteroid. Birds and animals go quiet before a storm, don't they? Maybe it's the same thing before an asteroid hit, or a meteorite or something.'

'We need to get going,' said Meatball, gruffly.

'Yeah.' Duke gazed down into the valley. 'It'll probably be cooler down there. Let's go.'

They moved off the mound and began the steep descent down the valley wall towards the forest.

This is where it gets dangerous, Spike thought, watching up ahead for any sudden movement. Instinctively, he grabbed Billy and pulled him close. 'The Ishmecs don't know we're coming,' he said. 'and there might not be any force field this time.'

'Maybe the dinosaurs are asleep in this heat,' Terri said.

Yeah, thought Spike. And maybe they're not.

They could smell the thick, heady fragrance from the flowers long before they entered the forest. Inside, among the slippery tree trunks and saturated undergrowth, it was quiet, the silence broken only by the hum of insects. The heat was almost unbearable, the air suffocating and difficult to breathe. Leaves lay still, trickling with water.

The mere effort of walking soaked their bodies with sweat; it ran down their faces into their eyes and dripped off their noses. The heady scent of colourful blooms seemed to be pouring out into the air in a thick, sickly wave. Around their satiny petals, insects jostled for space, giddy and intoxicated.

Billy watched the bright butterflies dart past his eyes as they flitted from one flower to another, struggling to beat their wings through the syrupy air.

He looked warily about him. They had stepped through into a small clearing.

'This is it,' Terri whispered. 'This is where we met the dinosaurs.'

Spike strained his ears to hear any sound from the forest behind them. Everything was all so still. *Too* still.

They trudged on. At the front, Duke turned. 'We're nearly through. I can see the hill through the trees.'

'Thank God.' Meatball wiped his face on a T-shirt already soaked with sweat. 'At least out there, we can see what's coming.'

A few moments more and they were free of the forest, out into the light and looking up at the clear expanse of open land that led up the hill.

Steadily, they began the steep climb. Doc looked nervously behind her. This was the exact spot where they'd first seen those huge creatures.

Just before they reached the summit, they stopped to catch their breath and gulp down some water.

'You all right with that bag, Spike?' Duke said. 'I can take a turn if you want.'

Spike tightened the straps. 'No, thanks. I'm all right,' he said. 'I told Mr Price I'd do it.'

Behind them in the forest, everything was still.

'Let's not stop,' Terri said. 'Let's keep going.'

They set off again towards the top of the hill.

'I can't understand why we haven't seen any dinosaurs,' said Meatball. 'I thought we'd have seen something by now.'

'Perhaps they're waiting till we get in the valley, so they can trap us,' Billy said. 'That's what I'd do if I was a dinosaur.'

Spike glanced at him. 'Not sure we need your logic just at the moment, Bill,' he said. He heaved the bag higher onto his back. 'Come on, let's keep going.'

'I suppose the force field could be on,' said Doc. 'Maybe it's on all the time.'

With a final long stride, Meatball stood on the summit. 'It won't be if they've already left.'

'But they can't, can they? Not without the crystal.'

'Unless they don't realise they need it,' said Duke. 'Until it's too late.'

'Don't say that,' Terri said.

Meatball turned to glance down the hill. 'Oh, *no*,' he said.

They clambered up to stand beside him, and were suddenly faced with what he'd seen.

Directly before them, in the middle of the large stretch of land between them and any hope of reaching the Ishmec city, lay the body of an enormous dinosaur.

Surrounding it, ripping at its flesh in a bloodbath of vicious teeth and claws, were creatures they had seen before, the huge, bony-headed dinosaurs that had rebounded at the force field. There, directly in front of them, was the reason they hadn't seen these creatures in the forest.

The colour drained from Doc's face. 'It's them, isn't it? It's the ones from the forest. The killing machines.'

Duke swallowed hard. 'Now what do we do?'

'What *can* we do?' asked Terri. 'Go back?'

'We can't do that.' Spike shook his head. 'We can't. We can't go back.'

'Well, we sure as hell can't go forward,' snapped Meatball.

'We've got to do *something*,' Doc said. 'There must be an answer. *Think*!'

'I *am*.'

'I've got an idea,' said Billy, quietly.

Spike looked at him. His eyes were shining. Maybe, he thought, just maybe. 'Ok, Bill. What is it?'

'We go around them,' Billy said. He smiled. 'Well, we could, couldn't we?'

'Round? How are we meant to do that?'

'We can't just walk round them, Bill,' Terri said.

'Why not?' Billy pointed at the long ridge topping the hill behind them. 'We go up back there and walk along the top. It's a bit longer, but we can cross further down. They might not see us if we're high enough up.'

'D'you know what,' Duke said, glancing thoughtfully at Billy, 'that might not be such a bad idea. Billy's right, if we go along the top there, we might be able to keep out of sight until we can cross further down. Unless anyone's got a better idea.'

'I suppose it might work,' said Doc.

Terri pulled a face. 'I don't see we've got any choice.'

Spike nodded. 'You're right, Bill, it is our only choice. I say we go for it, we've got to get past them somehow. And there's no way I'm going back. What d'you reckon, Meatball?'

Meatball shrugged. 'I reckon nothing feels right in this rotten place,' he said. 'Something's wrong here and it's getting worse.'

Keeping a watchful gaze on the frenzy of feeding in the distance, they started up the side of the hill towards the ridge.

Reaching the top, they slowed for a moment to look down on the scene below. Red with blood, the dinosaurs squabbled and fought over the carcass.

At that moment, jerking upright from the horrific scene around the body, a lone creature raised its head and looked in their direction.

They froze.

In the appalling reality of the next few moments, Terri closed her eyes and prayed. She prayed and prayed until her head hurt and a sudden flood of purple light drenched her mind.

Stricken with horror, they watched, transfixed, as the creature in the distance sniffed the air and began to move towards them in gangly, tentative steps. Alerted by the movement, two others were now following its lead.

'They can smell us.'

Terri stood silently, eyes still closed.

'Your *bag*, Spike!'

Spike turned around. Doc was staring at his rucksack. 'It's glowing!' she hissed. 'Look at it! It's glowing!'

Spike threw his head back, trying to peer over his shoulder.

Wrenching his gaze from the creatures in the distance, Meatball turned to glance at it. 'She's right!' he gasped. 'What's happening to it?'

Pulling the bag from his back as though it had bitten him, Spike lowered it to the floor. He lifted the flap and stared at the crystal inside as it pulsed with light.

Then he caught sight of Terri. Swaying slightly, she stood as if in a trance.

Suddenly, a column of purple burst forth from the bag and cascaded out, forming an umbrella of light, that poured to the ground, spread like a shock wave halfway across the field, and stopped.

Slowly, Terri opened her eyes. 'It's me,' she said, faintly, 'I'm doing it. I can see it in my head.'

They stared above them at the deep purple, forming a perfect canopy over their heads.

'What is it?'

Spike was looking across the field, where three dinosaurs waited, heads raised, scenting the air.

'It must be a force field,' he said. 'And it had better work, because we're going to have visitors.'

As he spoke, one of the dinosaurs approached the perimeter of the purple canopy. A crackle of energy shot from the force field, striking the creature in the chest.

'It can't get through!' Meatball cried. 'It can't get at us!'

He turned to look at Terri. 'How are you doing that?'

Duke stepped to Terri's side. Spike and Billy were supporting her, but she was still swaying slightly with the strain, and she looked pale and drawn.

'Let's get going,' said Doc. 'Terri can't keep this up for ever.'

Breaking into a run, they careered across the field. The force field moved with them, the air crackling, as time and time again the dinosaurs plunged ahead, but were sent sprawling backwards by a bolt of energy. They were almost at the edge of the field, when, despite the others supporting her, Terri missed her footing, tripped, and went sprawling across the grass.

Spike and Billy rushed to pull her to her feet, but it was too late. As Spike straightened up, he saw the force field behind them flicker, and then completely disappear.

'It's *gone*!' Spike screamed. 'The force field's gone! *RUN FOR IT*!'

'It's all right!' Terri struggled to reply between gasps. 'It's all right, they know we're coming!'

At that moment, out of a swirling mist, a dome of shimmering silver came into view and started to melt from the centre.

'How's … how's that happening?' Spike panted. 'Who's doing it? That you, Terri?'

'Never mind *how*!' screeched Doc. '*Let's get inside*!'

Hurling themselves headlong through the melted opening, they landed with a sickening crunch on the floor. Duke hit it first, a wheezing Doc piled in on top of him, Meatball, Spike, Terri and Billy tumbling over each other onto the floor.

Behind them, the door flowed shut.

'You are unhurt?'

Clamouring for breath and aching in every limb, Spike looked up straight into the faces of Jophan and Neeza.

The purple band at Jophan's throat pulsed with light. 'You are unhurt?' he repeated.

Spike managed a nod, before collapsing again.

'It is fortunate we were watching,' Neeza said. 'Did you receive my message, Terri? I said we would open the door for you.'

Terri reached up and touched her forehead with her finger. 'I *did*.' She laughed, in wonder. 'So that's how I knew.'

'We were greatly concerned about the wild ones,' Jophan continued, as they helped them to their feet. 'There have been many attacks and for some time we have been unable to activate the force field.'

'The crystal!' Spike pulled at the backpack, wrenching it open. 'Hope it's not damaged.'

'That is extremely unlikely.'

The tall, slender figure of Arisius loomed out of the shadows.

'Welcome,' he said. 'We are relieved to see you safe. It is wonderful to see you all again.'

Spike reached into the bag and placed the pyramid into Arisius' hands.

'Once again, we are in your debt,' Arisius said. 'The crystal we have is no longer viable.'

Two robed figures appeared at his side and Arisius passed the crystal into their hands, then, turning back to face them, he added, 'Please come and speak to my father before you leave. Then, my friends, you must go. We leave this planet within hours. I shall ensure you have safe escort back to the portal.'

'A gift for you all,' Arisius said, handing them a small package. 'To serve as a reminder of your time with us.'

They were standing once more by the cave entrance, their task completed. Duke took the gift from his hands. 'Thank you,' he said. 'I'm afraid we have nothing -'

The Sentinel smiled. 'You have already given us more than we can repay.'

'Excuse me, Sentinel.' Doc looked at him, thoughtfully. 'How much time has passed here? Since our last visit. How long ago was that?'

Arisius answered promptly. 'Three months.'

'Three *months*? Then the portal's definitely on the blink.'

'Three months?' Spike looked across at Meatball, who was pressing the heel of his hand against his forehead. 'What's up, Meatball? You remembered something?'

'No ... no, I just ... there's something. If only I could remember. If only I could *see* ...'

Arisius sensed their concern. 'There is a problem?'

'No ... no, we should be okay,' said Doc. 'We might be a bit late, that's all.'

'But you will be safe?'

Duke nodded. 'Of course, sir, it's like Doc says, we'll just be a bit late.'

'*Late*?' mocked Terri, as they said their last goodbyes and slipped on their coats. 'We'll probably be reported as missing by now. Mum'll be frantic.'

'We should come out when we left,' Spike said. He hurried on, anxious to be home. Please, he thought, please let us come out when we left.

Duke stopped. 'What are we going to do if we come out a hundred years too early?'

'That won't happen.' The alarm in Terri's voice echoed in the cave. 'It won't happen ... will it? We'll come out the right time, we've got to.'

'We'll be all right,' Billy said. He glanced up at Spike. 'We will, won't we, Spike?'

They rounded the corner. Spike shook his head vaguely. 'I wish I knew,' he said.

In front of them, the cold grey rock loomed up like an enormous barrier. For a moment, they stared at it.

'Only one way to find out,' Duke said.

Together, they rushed towards the wall. And together, they rebounded as chests and arms smacked against solid rock.

Duke rushed again at the wall and groaned at the pain. 'What the -'

Pushing the others aside, Meatball hurled his full weight against the wall. 'No!' he yelled, rubbing his shoulder. 'It's closed! The portal's closed!'

'No ... *no!*' Terri threw herself against the wall, clawing frantically at it with her fingers. 'That's not possible ... it can't be ...'

'But what's happened to it?' Doc cried. 'It was all right before.'

'Maybe it's just temporary,' Billy said. 'Maybe it'll be all right in a minute.'

Spike took a shaky deep breath. 'Yeah, yeah. Course. A temporary fault. We'll try again in a minute.'

Terri whirled around. 'This isn't the telly. This is our life we're talking about!'

Duke and Spike looked at each other and then back at Terri.

'Can you think of anything else?'

Terri bit her lip. Her eyes misted. 'No,' she said. 'No, I can't.'

'It's got to be okay,' Doc burbled, staring at the wall. 'It's got to be.'

Meatball laughed: a silly unconvincing laugh. 'We'll try again in a bit.'

They gave it ten minutes. And another ten minutes. They tried all the walls, even the floor, but the portal had disappeared. Still, they waited. An hour later, they were exhausted and still the portal refused to open.

'Now what do we do?' Billy asked.

'We check it all again,' Spike said. 'And then -'

'What? And then what?'

Spike stared down at his feet. He didn't know. For the first time since the whole adventure began, he felt completely and utterly lost. This couldn't be happening. What was the point in bringing them through here if they couldn't ever get back? Tears pricked his eyes. How could Mr Price do this? What on earth were they going to do now?

'I don't know,' he said, weakly. 'I don't know. I just keep thinking … well, this can't be it, can it?'

'This *isn't* it,' Meatball declared. 'It can't be. I'd know it if it was. I don't know *how*,' he stressed, in answer to a look from Doc, 'I just know I would. There must be something we can do. We just need to think about it.'

Terri turned. 'I can't stand it in here anymore. I've got to get out.'

'Let's all get out,' said Duke, miserably. 'Maybe a bit of fresh air will help us think.'

Huddling together, they filtered out of the cave opening.

'I reckon I'd feel a whole lot better if I could remember,' Meatball murmured.

'Remember what?'

'I can't remember.'

They sat down on the mound, huddled together against a creeping chill in the air.

On the tropical horizon, the sun was beginning to set, slipping behind ribbons of cloud, throwing streaks across the sky and turning the whole landscape ethereal shades of orange and pink. In the fading light, faint stars were becoming visible, pulsing softly in the porcelain sky. The moon was out already, but only in its first quarter, a thin banana of creamy radiance.

A kind of apprehensive hush was settling on the world. Nothing moved. There were no dinosaurs roaming the land or giant winged creatures that had soared overhead, screeching and calling.

'It's getting cold,' Doc said, tugging on her coat.

'And it's so *quiet*,' Terri breathed.

They looked down at the trees with the ferns and flowers that now stood rigid, like cardboard cut-outs.

'Did you feel that?'

Spike looked at Billy. 'What?'

Slowly, Billy got to his feet. 'The ground's shaking.'

'He's right,' said Duke. 'There is something.'

Meatball jumped up. 'What *is* that?'

The ground moved again, just gently, no more than a faint ripple in the soil.

'I felt that,' Doc said. The ground rumbled again. 'What's happening now?'

'That's a regular beat,' Meatball declared, staring down at the earth.

The trembling beneath their feet increased to a dull rumble. The grassy mound on which they stood started to shake.

Then, with it, came a noise, like thunder rolling around the sky: a cavernous sound that seemed to come from deep within the earth. It grew louder and louder, until the grassy mound on which they stood split wide open and crumbled into a pile of soil.

Meatball's face went white. '*Now* I remember ...'

CHAPTER TWENTY-ONE

Slipping and sliding on what was left of the mound, they snatched crazily at each other for support, struggling to keep their balance as the mound splayed outward into a pool of shifting soil and stones.

Beneath them, the earth rocked and shuddered into rippling patterns. They staggered backward, arms waving wildly in the air, almost tripping over each other's feet.

Over the mounting din of the quaking ground, they glanced down into the valley below. In the deepest part, the lush green land was beginning to shake.

'Look at that!'

Doc pointed a trembling finger toward the valley basin. In the middle, the ground was slowly rising.

As they watched, the centre of the ground bulged upwards until an enormous split broke the surface, creating a huge gash in the earth that was snaking its way at devastating speed across the valley floor.

In the opposite direction, a second gash appeared, which was now careering across to collide with the first.

Where they finally met, partway up the valley wall, they became a deep tear in the earth that widened and stretched into a massive ravine.

Slowly, the ravine began to swallow the whole side of the valley like some monstrous harvester. Soil, shrubs, trees, even dinosaurs running from the noise began to slither helplessly into the gaping wound.

Standing precariously on the shaking plateau above, they watched the scene playing out before them, the ground yawning, the black cliffs of soil, and the living things disappearing into the gloom of the abyss.

'Those trees,' Terri gasped, her attention caught by a movement, 'those trees … they're getting bigger!'

'They're not getting bigger,' Billy said. 'They're going *up*!'

'What trees?'

'Over on the hill there. *Look*!'

Terri pointed to the enormous hills beyond the valley.

Tearing their eyes from the drama of the valley floor, they stared at a skyline that seemed to be rising into the air.

'The hillside … it's growing, look. *It's growing*!'

'No, it's not growing,' Spike croaked. 'It's moving upwards …'

The entire hillside was on the move, swelling and lifting like a baking loaf, rising into the sky. A colossal chunk of land torn from its roots, shedding enormous quantities of earth, trees and rock that rained downwards, cascading into the gaping hole.

'I don't believe it!' Meatball yelled. 'The whole hillside's moving! Look at the size of it!'

The enormous mass of earth that had once been the hillside, began to vibrate. At the same time, a high-pitched scream howled through the red and purple sky, bouncing around the echo chamber of the valley walls.

The noise was mind numbing. Falling to their knees in the dust, they covered their ears with their arms in a feeble attempt to shut it out.

Squinting through half-closed eyes, they watched the floating hillside crack apart, crumble, and fall away in enormous jagged fragments, plunging into the valley to send up billowing clouds of dust.

After some moments the screaming lessened, and then faded and died, leaving only a dull murmur that throbbed through the ground with a regular pulse.

Then, in the eerie aftermath, they caught their first glimpse of something, still vaguely shrouded in what remained of the crumbling hillside.

Spike's mouth dropped open in utter disbelief. What *was* that? Something coming up out of the earth?

'What's that?'

'Back in the *cave!*' Duke yelled.

Clutching wildly at each other, they stumbled back towards the cave and scrambled inside, just as a blinding flash lit up the plateau.

They peered out.

Hovering in the celestial blue of the early evening sky, blotting out a vast portion of the twinkling stars, was a cylindrical star ship of unbelievable proportions, the outside surface swirling in whirlpools and eddies of silver.

Mouth gaping, Spike stared up at the huge craft. It was so enormous. It could only be one thing.

'*It must be their spaceship …*'

'It's got to be,' Duke whispered. 'It's *massive …*'

Getting unsteadily to their feet, they moved as if in a trance and stepped outside onto the plateau.

Terri's eyes brimmed with tears of wonder. 'It's *breath-taking -*'

Glistening in the last remnants of the sun, the star ship hovered, hanging in the air, pulsing with brilliance.

A tear ran down Meatball's face. '*Fantastic … it's fantastic.*'

For a time, the star ship floated just above what was left of the hills, casting a shadow across the whole of the valley. They scarcely moved, captivated by the churning and rippling of the outer casing.

Then abruptly, as though someone had flicked a switch, the swirling stopped. The outer shell melded into a solid shape, which began to pulse steadily with a deep purple light.

'How beautiful,' Terri whispered.

Spellbound, they waited, watching.

As it pulsed, the ship's outer casing pixelated into symmetrical pieces. Huge chunks shunted one against the other, shuffling and rearranging, before finally contracting into a giant silver ball. Slowly, the ball began to turn, light throbbing at its centre like a beating heart. A deep drone resonated about them, growing louder as the ball increased in speed, and then, with one final ear-shattering blast, it was gone.

For a long moment, they could hear distant reverberations, a heavy, booming, drumming of thunder … and then the sky was full of an echoing emptiness.

Shell-shocked, they stood for a few moments, staring at the sky.

'Wow,' said Billy.

Spike shook his head. Goose pimples rippled down his skin. '*Brilliant*,' he said.

Meatball nodded. 'How amazing was that.'

'*Unbelievable*,' Terri whispered.

They looked at each other. 'So now what?'

Still reeling from the launch of the star ship, Spike struggled to think. The star ship had gone, which meant the Ishmecs were gone. The only people they knew in this terrifying world had left and they were on their own.

In a fit of panic, he spun around. The portal was closed and they couldn't get home. What were they going to do?

Duke took a long, tremulous breath. 'So,' he said. 'What do we do now, then?'

'We try the portal again,' said Meatball. 'What else can we do?'

Terri looked up. From out of nowhere the clouds seemed to have increased and were now being blown across the sky in an increasing wind. On her face, she felt the first faint drops of rain.

'Oh great,' she mumbled. 'That's all we need.' Suddenly, beneath her feet, the ground shook. 'The ground's still moving.'

'What? *Still*?'

'It is,' Duke said. 'I can feel it.'

They stared down at the ground. 'That's weird,' said Meatball. 'Some kind of after-shock, d'you think?'

'After-shock?' Doc said. 'You get them after an earthquake, don't you?'

Spike stared. 'An earthquake?'

'But that wasn't an earthquake,' said Meatball. 'That was the star ship taking off. We saw it.'

'Then what's *that*?' Billy yelled.

On the far side of the valley, beyond the huge chasm left by the star ship, the hillside had collapsed.

Unsupported, and succumbing to pressure from the other side, it had crumbled away and disappeared beneath a colossal tidal wave of water that had cascaded in a torrent over the ridge and was now flooding into the valley, sweeping away everything in its path.

In seconds, the water had almost filled what was left of the valley and it was still pouring relentlessly over the hillside, snatching and pulling at anything that lived, dragging it to oblivion.

'The portal!' Doc screamed. 'We've got to get to the portal!'

'No! We haven't got time!' Spike yelled. 'We'll get trapped inside!'

'We've got to get to higher ground!' snapped Meatball. 'Out of the path of the water, it's our only hope!'

In a rush, they clambered up the hill and onto the roof of the cave, where they stood for a moment, dragging in painful gasps of breath.

Above, the sky suddenly darkened.

Perched on the roof of the cave, they glanced down. The water was still climbing and was now almost level with the plateau. The surface was turgid, littered with bodies and trees. Huge clods of soil were spinning effortlessly around in the swirling mass.

'It's like a whole sea's coming in! We've got to get higher!'

'Where?!'

'There!' Spike's voice rang out. He pointed high in the air at the face of the cliffs. 'That's where we make for! Up there!'

There was a blinding flash as lightning seared across the sky, followed by a deafening bellow of thunder.

Spike blundered forward, scrambling up the incline, then reached down for Billy's hand as he followed. Terri and Meatball clambered up behind them, Doc and Duke followed, struggling to get a foothold on the slippery cliff face.

Searching desperately for crevices and handholds in the rocks, they dragged themselves slowly upwards and onto a small ledge.

Around them, the storm broke, battering the cliff face with torrential rain.

They barely had strength to stand upright before the water roared into the cave, battering the rear wall, shaking the ledge beneath them.

Grasping at Meatball's arm, Spike leaned carefully outward, and felt nausea wash over him. *'It's up to the cave already and it's still coming! We have to get higher!'*

'The top of the cliff!' Duke screamed. *'We have to get up to the top of the cliff!'*

Pushing themselves on, higher and higher, they ignored the cuts and the searing pain in their muscles, conscious only of the terrifying roar of the rising water.

Halfway up the rocky crags, Terri's hand slipped and screaming, she slid violently downwards, scraping the skin from her leg, little rivulets of rainwater pouring across her face as she groped desperately at the cliff.

Turning, Meatball lunged across, trying to hold her steady, but her foot slipped from the mossy rock and she slid further down.

'Terri!' Billy screamed.

'Terri!' Spike yelled. 'Hold on!'

Duke stretched himself as far as he could and grabbed at Terri, grasping her coat, while Doc moved across to wedge her slender shoulder against Terri's legs to stop her falling any further.

Meatball gripped with all his might at a slippery crevice in the rock, whilst he felt for a foothold from which to support himself, and then he leaned down to grip Terri's outstretched hand and pull her back up.

Exhausted and shaking, Terri leaned against the cliff for a moment.

'*You all right, Terri*?' Spike screamed.

She nodded, tears mixing with the rain running down her face.

'She's ok!' yelled Meatball. He looked down at her, and at the gushing water beneath them. The cave had now disappeared beneath the waves.

Terri looked back at him. His face was bleeding. 'Keep going!' he yelled.

Swallowing hard, she began to climb.

Further down, tears started to trickle down Doc's cheeks. Averting her gaze from the billowing water below, she lifted her face to the lashing rain to wash them away.

Duke wedged his hand into a crevice in the rock and pulled himself up, dragging Doc up to join him. Somewhere above, an enormous bolt of lightning blazed across the sky, and exploded. Thunder followed seconds later, drumming around the sky.

In the ominous silence that followed, they heard the sound of ripping timber.

Spike glanced up. High above them, on the top of the cliff, a huge tree was swaying violently in the wind.

As he watched, a lone branch broke away, and cascaded down the cliff face, showering splinters on its way down.

'Keep in!'

There was a loud crack, as the heavy trunk of the tree snapped, keeled over, and toppled sideways off the cliff. It plummeted down, sweeping down the cliff face like a giant witch's broom, until it plunged into the water beneath.

As it hit the surface, an enormous surge of water ballooned upwards and smashed against the cliff.

In that instant, the wave swept them all from the cliff face and down, down into the swirling water below.

Hitting the water with a sickening smack, Spike plunged beneath the waves. Water filled his ears, his eyes and nose. Holding desperately onto a breath of air, he struck out for the surface, battling his way up through the murky water against the dragging pull of his sodden coat.

His lungs were almost bursting as he made one final effort and broke the surface, gasping and choking, spitting out water. He dragged in painful gasps of air and looked frantically about for any sign of Billy and the others.

'*BILL! BILL!*'

Over the incessant din, he could just make out faint cries. Treading water desperately, he looked across the filthy surface as it rose and fell in enormous swells, bobbing him up and down like a cork. Huge branches spiralled among foaming lumps of earth.

'*Spike!*'

Spike craned his neck to look around. Doc was making her way towards him, splashing wildly.

'*Doc!*' He launched himself towards her, and grabbed her coat.

'*The others ...*'

'*I know!*' he screamed. '*I can't find them! I can't find Bill!*'

Doc grabbed his sleeve and tugged violently. 'The tree trunk, look! There, Spike! Let's get to it!'

They pulled through the water towards the trunk. As they reached it, Meatball's terrified face bobbed up through the branches. Beside him, Duke was lying, gripping the bark, utterly exhausted.

'Have you seen Terri!' said Meatball. 'I can't find her!'

'We can't find Bill, either,' Spike sobbed.

'They've got to be here! TERRI! BILL!'

Cupping his hands, Spike and Doc shrieked their names at the top of their voices.

A moment later, they heard a faint cry. '*Over here! Spike! We're over here!*'

Pushing off from the tree trunk, Spike and Meatball swam towards the cry.

Billy was clinging desperately to a small branch, struggling to keep Terri's head out of the water. 'She's not moving, Spike!' he wailed. 'She's not moving!'

'Oh my God! *Terri!*'

Terri choked, and vomited filthy water.

'I'll take Terri!' Meatball cried. 'You help Bill, he's shattered!'

They struck out once more towards the tree, Terri clinging tightly around Meatball's shoulders. Spike followed behind, swimming steadily with Billy, gripping his coat. At the tree trunk, Duke and Doc helped drag Terri out of the water.

'Come on, Spike!'

Willing hands stretched out towards them.

Yanking Billy forward, Spike reached out, and at that moment, the surface of the water erupted. With an enormous heave, the body of a dinosaur exploded from the deep, head and legs flailing as it gasped for air.

They clung desperately to the tree, one moment submerged beneath the churning waves, the next rocking about on the surface, as the terrified creature scrambled frenziedly in the water in its last throes of drowning.

'*WE'RE GOING DOWN!*' Duke screamed.

Lunging towards Billy, Spike grabbed his hand, and together they reached out to the tree, just as the dinosaur reared once more into the air, and crashed down, plunging the tree deep below the surface.

A wave of murky water sucked at them as they struggled, and catapulted them against the dinosaur's huge body.

No waves ... no sound ... no light ... *nothing.*

CHAPTER TWENTY-TWO

Darkness. Nothing, but suffocating darkness.

Crumpled on the hard floor, Spike slowly lifted his head. Where am I? Please, don't say I'm back in a cave.

He felt a warm body move beside him.

'Spike?' Billy sat up. 'Where are we?'

Spike hugged him. 'Billy! Thank goodness! Everyone else ok?'

To Spike's relief, they answered.

'What happened?' Terri cried. 'I don't understand.'

'You all right, Terri?'

Terri peered at Spike through the gloom. 'I'm fine,' she said.

'What just happened?' Duke asked.

'Don't know.' Meatball held his head. 'Where's … where's the water?

Doc felt her coat. 'We're dry! But …'

'We're in Solomon!' Billy cried. 'We're back in the tree!'

'We *can't* be.' Spike reached out and felt the crumbly, sooty bark. 'We *are*. It must be, mustn't it? How many other trees are like this?'

Stupified, Duke looked around. 'How did we get here?'

'Don't know.' Spike looked at them. 'How come we're all here?'

'And still alive,' Doc said.

'What *is* going on?'

'I'm getting out.' Scrambling up, Duke walked across to the panel and lifted it clear. Brilliant daylight flooded the tree.

Terri stood beside him, gazing out at the snow. 'Looks like home.'

'We don't know it's the same time, though, do we?' asked Billy.

'No.' Spike walked across to look out. 'No, we don't.'

They stepped outside, and sank into the freezing snow that had piled up against the tree.

'There's lights over there,' Doc said. 'But that doesn't mean anything.'

Meatball gave a heavy sigh. 'Oh, who cares,' he said. 'Let's go and find out.'

The icy blast took their breath away as they started down the country lane. The trees were still laden with snow, the hedgerows piled high in huge drifts. A string of crows lifted off, as they passed. In the distance, trails of smoke drifted from chimneys.

'It's very quiet,' said Duke, as they walked along.

'Maybe it's Sunday,' said Billy.

'Haven't heard any bells,' Spike muttered. 'The church bells usually ring on Sunday.'

Terri tutted. 'Well, duh, they don't ring all day.'

They started to giggle.

'Bong-bong, bong-bong,' Billy laughed.

'You can laugh,' said Doc, quietly. 'But church would be good now, we can pray we've come out the same time we left.'

They were silent for a while as they walked on.

Terri said, 'I'm not going to think about it anymore. I can't bear it.'

'Nor me,' said Duke, fighting the croak in his throat. 'It hasn't happened. That's all. It hasn't. And if it has, we'll find another way back somehow. Won't we?'

No one answered.

Spike walked between Duke and Billy, deep in his own thoughts. What if it *was* a different time? What were they going to do?

And what about Gran and Mr Price? His heart ached as he thought of them. And Ed … his wonderful, gorgeous Ed.

How he loved him. What if he never saw him again? His eyes swam with tears. Taking a deep breath, he held it for a moment. Whatever happened, he must look after Billy, Gran would expect no less. His eyes pricked. Would he ever see Gran again?

'There's a van!' said Billy. 'Over there, look, going round by the church!'

Meatball squinted into the distance. 'That's not a van, it's the bus! *It's the bus!*'

'Yes!' Duke yelled. 'We're home!'

'Come on!' cried Meatball. 'Race you!'

Stomping as fast as they could down the lane, they slipped and slid through the gate of Yew Tree Cottage. Suddenly, a loud bark shattered the silence.

'That's Ed!' Billy cried.

'It is!'

Around the corner came a large, hairy shape. Halfway across the garden, they collided.

'ED!'

Spike and Billy threw their arms about Ed's neck and buried their faces in his warm, wiry fur. Finally releasing him, they stepped back as the others hugged Ed and kissed his head.

'It's so good to see you!' Duke cried.

'Hello, boy!' Meatball sighed, joyfully.

Doc squealed with pleasure as Ed's huge head rested on her shoulder. 'Thank God you're here!' she said.

She turned to see Terri staring into Ed's gentle face, as though they were talking to one another. Ed gave a muffled groan of sheer delight.

'*Spike*? Spike! Billy! Is that you? *Joseph!*' Gran yelled at the top of her voice. '*Joseph, they're back!*'

'*GRAN*!

'Gran!' Spike yelled. 'Mr Price!'

'Welcome home! Oh, welcome home!' Gran cried, as she wrapped her arms about them. Mr Price gathered them all together, and between them, they hugged them tightly.

'Come inside and get warm,' said Joseph. 'You've had quite an adventure.'

'But I must phone Mum!' Terri cried. 'She'll be frantic!'

'And me!'

'Me, too!'

Gran smiled at them. 'By all means use the phone if you wish. But rest assured, as far as life here is concerned, only an hour has passed since you left.'

'But we've been away ages, Gran,' said Billy.

'Time's relative,' said Joseph. 'And I don't suppose that makes the slightest sense to any of you, but your Gran is correct. Only an hour has passed here. Well, fifty-seven minutes, to be exact.'

'Come in and sit by the fire,' Gran said. 'And do give your family a call if you'd like to, while I get us all something to eat.'

Terri walked down the hallway to the phone. 'Just want to hear Mum's voice,' she said.

Doc followed. 'Me, too.'

'Give us a shout when you've finished,' Duke called after them.

'And me!'

'It's probably best,' Gran said, as they sat in the sitting room later that morning, 'if you ask me any questions you have, and Joseph and I will try to answer them as best we can. Of course, there are certain circumstances over which we have limited control, so we're hoping you can fill in those details for us.'

She leaned forward in her chair. 'Spike? Would you like to start?'

Spike had been staring at the logs on the fire, but now he looked up. 'How did we get here, Gran? From the water, I mean ... how did we get here?'

'Through a time portal,' she said.

'But the portal was closed, Gran.'

'Time portals can open, or close, whenever, and wherever they wish,' said Joseph. 'Solomon sometimes opens in the old oak tree in the far field.'

'Solomon?' Billy's eyes sparkled. 'You mean Solomon is a time portal?'

'When he wants to be,' said Gran.

'So, the tree … the tree that was floating in the water?' Duke asked. '*That* was a time portal?'

'But it fell off the cliff, Gran,' Billy said. 'And it was all broken.'

'I'm sure it was,' Joseph said. 'So would you be after a fall like that.'

Doc stared. 'So, it didn't matter, then? That it was broken?'

Clasping their hands, Gran leaned closer. 'It wasn't the tree that brought you home,' she said. 'It was the dinosaur.'

Spike gaped. 'The *dinosaur?* The dinosaur was a time portal? But …'

'How is that possible?' Duke asked.

'Time portals aren't always inanimate objects,' Joseph replied. 'Anything can be a time portal, even a human being.'

Gran cut some slices of cake and passed them around. 'Enough about portals for the moment,' she said. 'You'll learn more about those in time. Tell us about your adventures.'

The room became alive with voices as they all tried to speak at once, interrupting, talking across one another, recounting everything that had happened since Ed found a bone on Gullivan's land, from the first trip to the last, when they discovered the portal had closed.

'You kept your heads,' Joseph said. 'That's the main thing.'

'Why was the portal in the cave closed, Mr Price?' Terri asked.

'Time Portals are tenuous things,' he explained. 'That is to say, they can be affected by the smallest of disturbances. In most circumstances their position remains constant, but their properties can be affected. I suspect the portal in the cave was affected by the electrical storm you mentioned.'

'I thought we were going to die,' Spike said.

'So did I,' said Doc. 'But we didn't, did we?'

'No,' said Billy. He looked at Gran. His eyes were shining. 'We didn't, did we? So, why not?'

Gran exchanged a glance with Mr Price. 'Time to explain, I think, Joseph.'

Joseph nodded. 'We are all part of a sort of universal plan,' he said. 'A predetermined and unalterable plan for the universe: a plan of which you, I, and Gran, are just a small, but vital part.'

'Gran and I are custodians, caretakers, if you like, of Time Portals. It's our job to see that they are used safely and correctly.'

'This is also to be your Destiny. The task you have just completed is the first of many Destiny has mapped out for you, but one day you will have acquired sufficient knowledge and experience to become Custodians yourselves.'

'And the Ishmecs?' asked Meatball. 'Are they part of the plan?'

'The Ishmecs are an ancient race that settled on the earth many millions of years ago, after their own planet in the Cassiopeia constellation was in danger. They have painstakingly collected the DNA profile of many of the prehistoric life forms on Earth and have stored them for possible re-creation at a later date.'

'Why could the Ishmecs not come through the portal?' Terri asked.

'Because they were not destined to do so at this time,' Gran said. 'Nothing from the past can ever come forward in time, in *living* form. Only those that Destiny has chosen can cross a time portal and survive.'

'But Gullivan crossed it,' Billy pointed out.

'Quite right, Billy. He did. And for a moment, I did wonder about that. But of course, had he not crossed, you would not have followed him that day and discovered the time portal, and the Ishmecs would not have been saved.'

'D'you think Gullivan knows something?'

Gran shook her head. A lock of hair dislodged itself from an ornate clasp and fell across her eyes. 'It's unlikely, Duke,' she said, tucking it neatly behind her ear. 'Though with that man one can never be sure.'

'One can never be sure of anything where Cornelius Gullivan is concerned,' Joseph muttered. 'As I told you, there are certain things about which even we have limited knowledge. He may well be used in the future.'

He paused to look at Spike, who was studying him intently. 'Yes, Spike? You have another question?'

Spike grinned and shook his head. 'No, it's ok. I've just found another answer, that's all.'

Terri turned to him. 'What d'you mean?'

'Gran's brooch,' said Spike. 'It's the one you always wear, isn't it, Gran?'

Gran nodded.

'I knew I'd seen them somewhere before,' Spike said.

'The crystals!' Duke said. 'The row of crystals in the City.'

Gran smiled, and patted her brooch. 'It was a gift.'

In front of the fire, Ed looked up and yawned. Billy leaned down to stroke him.

'It was odd that, wasn't it?' he said, looking up. 'About Ed, I mean. He didn't seem at all bothered by the Ishmecs.'

'I daresay Arisius spoke to him by thought,' Gran said. 'They can do that, you know, with intelligent creatures.'

'I believe they tried it with the dinosaurs in the beginning,' Joseph added, 'but they were too stupid.'

Doc shivered at the memory of the razor-sharp teeth and claws. 'They didn't look very stupid when they were chasing us,' she said, 'that one nearly had us.'

'Don't want to think about all that stuff,' murmured Terri, quietly.

'Don't think about it,' Spike said. 'It never got us, did it, so there's no point thinking about it.'

Duke nodded. 'Spike's right,' he said. 'We're all safe, aren't we? That's what matters.'

'I guess,' Meatball murmured. He stood up and walked across to the window, watching tiny particles of dust floating in the rays of the winter sun. 'But now what happens? Things aren't going to be the same, are they?'

He turned.

'No,' said Joseph. 'Things won't be the same, but for the time being, they will carry on as normal.'

Billy sighed. 'No one would believe us if we told them.'

The conversation faded, as memories flooded back, and a strange stillness overcame them.

'It all seems so weird,' Terri said, 'like it happened to someone else.'

'It will take some adjustment,' Gran said, softly.

Joseph Price bent down and placed another log on the fire. 'We'll be here to support you,' he said.

At that moment, Spike spun around in his seat. 'The package! The Ishmecs gave us a present before we left!'

Doc leaped to her feet. 'Oh *yes*, I'd forgotten all about that. What happened to it? We didn't drop it, did we?'

'It's okay, I've got it.'

Dipping into his pocket, Duke pulled out a small, pyramid-shaped box covered in seamless silver, and held it up for them all to see. He turned it a couple of times, and then shrugged, and passed it across to Terri.

'Looks like you've got to open it,' he said.

Terri took it from him and placed it down on the carpet. Gazing at the pyramid, she focused on its heart and then closed her eyes.

Almost at once, it began to open in sections like a flower. From the tip of each petal, a beam of shimmering light splayed outwards and upwards like floodlights and as the lights lifted, several holographic figures began to appear.

Meatball gave a yell. 'Arisius!'

'And the Elder!' Doc cried. 'And Jophan, look, and Neeza!'

'Our greetings to you all.'

The figure of Arisius stared straight ahead. 'By the time you view this message we will be on our way to our new home. But we could not leave without saying farewell and expressing our heartfelt gratitude for all you have done.'

'You have shown exemplary courage,' the Elder continued, 'and our people will be forever in your debt.'

'Terri!' said Neeza. 'Practise every day, you have the gift!'

'Neeza and I wish to give you something,' Jophan interrupted, leaning forward. 'You'll find it in Spike's bag.'

Arisius silenced them with a wave of his hand. 'This is not a final farewell, my friends, for we are destined to meet again, but until that time our thoughts and prayers go with you.'

'Goodbye!' called Neeza.

'Goodbye!'

The figure of Jophan darted forward as the image faded. Then it disappeared, sucked rapidly back into the pyramid, and the room was silent again, save for the heavy ticking of the clock.

Doc heaved a sigh. 'I shall miss them,' she said, quietly.

'Will we really see them again?' Duke asked.

Joseph Price nodded. 'Oh yes. That's why it was so vital to get the crystal to the Ishmecs, so they could escape before the asteroid hit the earth. They had to be protected at all costs, for it is they who, in the future, will come to our assistance.'

Terri stood, staring down at the pyramid, feeling rather satisfied. 'Neeza says I have a gift,' she murmured. 'D'you reckon I have, Spike? Spike ...?'

She twisted around. Spike's seat was empty. From somewhere out in the hallway, they heard a cry.

'Wow! Diamonds!'

'Obviously a few Gullivan didn't manage to acquire,' Joseph said, leaning back in his chair. 'But his prospecting days may soon be over.' A smile touched his face. 'I think maybe this time I may have arranged for him to meet his match.'

Gran looked at him. 'Joseph, what have you done?'

Joseph simply smiled.

EPILOGUE

Gullivan listened as a second cartridge dropped into the barrel of Old Bessie with a comforting rap.

Snapping it shut, he slid it across the front seat of the taxi, where it nestled with his gun and an assortment of knives and ammunition.

He nodded in satisfaction. Should be enough there to last a while in Dinoland.

With some effort, he heaved open the rear door and threw in a large rucksack filled with supplies, then taking one last glance at the house, he jumped back into the driver's seat.

Time was short and it wouldn't take the McKendricks long to pick up his trail.

It had been a damn near thing at the airport. If he hadn't nipped out for that cigarette, he'd never have seen that ugly great moron until it was too late.

As it was, he'd only escaped by the skin of his teeth. Thank God for taxis. That guy wouldn't leave the engine running a second time.

He wanted to laugh, especially when he thought of the look on Molly McKendrick's face as he'd sailed past her in the taxi. She was just sitting there, waiting for that brain-dead Neanderthal to figure out what was going on.

Gullivan wanted so much to laugh, but the terror that was building up in his gut was threatening to overwhelm him and he knew if he started to laugh, he'd bawl his eyes out.

In a panic, the car keys slipped from his sweating hands and fell to the floor. He bent down, cursing, fumbling for them on the carpet, grabbed them, and slid the key into the lock.

The engine spluttered and died.

'Please, *start!*'

A bead of sweat rolled down his nose and dripped onto the steering wheel.

Again, he turned the key. The starter motor screamed, the engine faltered twice and then roared into life.

Skidding on the snow-crusted driveway, Gullivan pulled out into the gloom of the country lane and accelerated away. Flat out would be good, but not on this road, the bends were too dangerous.

He flicked the headlights to full beam. The road up ahead was winding and treacherous even in the daytime and he needed all the help he could get.

Damn this weather! He didn't seem to be getting anywhere, even the trees, skeletal and laden with snow, seemed to be bending down to grasp him as he passed.

He swallowed hard and tightened his grip on the steering wheel as he swerved into another bend.

Then something in the rear-view mirror caught his eye. Imagination? No, there it was again. The outline of a large black car.

God … No! The McKendricks! And they'd spotted him. Cursing, he slammed his foot down hard on the pedal and felt the engine bolt away. If he could just get to the bridge.

Racing along, he careered wildly around the next bend, wrenching the wheel hard over, skidding on the icy road. Behind him, the large black car increased its speed, looming once more into his mirror.

Almost there. Not long now …

Frantically, Gullivan swung around the final corner and along the track. He'd have to leave the supplies, just grab his gun.

Stamping on the brakes, the tyres of the taxi slewed to a halt, sending it skidding sideways.

Gullivan leaped from the driver's seat, grabbed the shotgun, and ran full pelt towards the bridge.

Seconds behind, the large black car screeched to a halt. 'There he is! Follow him, you fool!'

The black car surged ahead, bouncing along the rocky ground.

An electric window purred downward, and a woman's arm reached out and pointed a gun at Gullivan's retreating body. An index finger closed around the trigger.

In a desperate panic, Gullivan bounded forward onto the bridge. If he could just make the portal before a bullet hit him.

Somewhere behind him, he heard the gun fire. Once … twice …

Gullivan kept running, something inside him still waiting for the searing pain.

Nothing happened. A deep-throated laugh of relief welled up inside him. Missed! She missed! She couldn't hit a barn door with a banjo. Well, he wouldn't miss *them*!

Swift as lightning, he swung back around and whipped Bessie up to his shoulder.

Then he stopped, the shotgun slipping down his shirt. *What?*

The space before him was empty. Nothing.

Gullivan's mouth dropped. How was that possible?

Inside the large black car, the silence was equally deafening as Molly McKendrick and her bodyguard stared at the empty bridge. Slowly, she pulled in the gun.

Beside her, the man looked down at Molly, who, for once, had been struck dumb.

'Where the hell did he go?'

Exhausted and totally disorientated, Gullivan gawped at the sight before him, his mouth dropping further open. What on earth was going on? Where were the cars? Where was the snow? Where were the McKendricks?

The shotgun slid from his grasp and onto the ground as terror slowly subsided into relief and then, blissfully, into uncontrollable laughter. Stupid fool! He was already through the portal.

A sharp jab in his back brought him up short.

Trembling, Gullivan turned around.

Over lethal metallic points, he saw six men. Tanned, olive complexions, dark eyes. Heads protected with helmets. Bodies shielded with armour of metal plates.

Gullivan's eyes focused on the short swords at their belts and then back along the spears that were pushed towards him, only centimetres away from his body. He'd seen uniforms like this in the museum. His heart throbbed. *Romans*.

Beads of sweat pricked his face. Over an increasingly dry throat, he struggled to swallow. What the hell had happened?

His eyes flicked quickly to the surroundings. He was in a field: a large field of long grass that stretched far into the distance. This wasn't Dinoland. This wasn't anything *like it*.

Gullivan started to shake, the knot in the pit of his stomach tightening as he realised the awful truth.

Something had gone wrong with the portal, and he'd come out somewhere different.

Something had catapulted him somewhere else. And that somewhere else was Roman Britain.

New Release for Autumn 2021

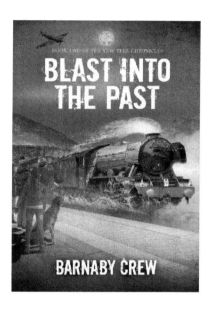

What would you do if the world you knew and loved was in danger?

Blackwater Manor hides a secret.

Warned of impending disaster, somehow Spike, Billy and their friends must find a way to prevent a world-wide catastrophe.

Things are difficult enough without bullying thug Brett Tyler getting in the way, and the sudden reappearance of Cornelius Gullivan.

Completing their mission is one thing, getting back home is quite another.

Copyright © 2021 Barnaby Crew

All Rights Reserved

Printed in Great Britain
by Amazon

74225712R00132